"Vanessa Miller hits all the right notes in her engaging book. The story sings of the high hopes and dashed dreams of not only Shar Gracey, a rising singer, but every girl who has ever longed to stand on the stage and belt her heart out before an audience. You'll feel the story's crescendo as you meet Shar's favorite gospel singers and songwriters whose names and music we all know. You'll also meet those who break her heart. From the first page, this amazingly colorful story will reel you in hook, line, and singer. Vanessa Miller has landed a huge hit!"

—Babbie Mason, award-winning gospel singer, songwriter, and author

Other Abingdon Press Books by Vanessa Miller

Long Time Coming

Blessed Assurance, Book 2 of the Gospel Series
(available May 2015)

How Sweet the Sound

Gospel Series Book 1

Vanessa Miller

Abingdon fiction
a novel approach to faith

How Sweet the Sound

Copyright © 2014 by Vanessa Miller

ISBN-13: 978-1-4267-4928-5

Published by Abingdon Press, P.O. Box 801, Nashville, TN 37202

www.abingdonpress.com

All rights reserved.

The persons and events portrayed in this work of fiction are the creations of the author, and any resemblance to persons living or dead is purely coincidental.

Published in association of the Natasha Kern Literary Agency

Library of Congress Cataloging-in-Publication Data has been requested.

Printed in the United States of America

1 2 3 4 5 6 7 8 9 10 / 19 18 17 16 15 14

To my beautiful granddaughter,
Amarrea Harris.
May the music in your life
always be sweet.

Acknowledgments

Being that this was the first historical I have ever attempted to write, this book was a challenge for me. So I'd like to thank my wonderful agent, Natasha Kern, for believing in this project and my editor at Abingdon Press, Ramona Richards, for giving me the chance to write this historical.

I would also like to thank my readers and book club members who have continued to read my books through the years. I couldn't do this without all of you. As always, my family members are big supporters of my career, and I thank them for putting up with my crazy schedule and deadlines.

I was amazed by all the information I uncovered during my research for this book. I hope you enjoy *How Sweet the Sound* as much as I enjoyed writing and researching it. Blessings and happy reading!

1

August 12, 1933
Negro Day

"You look like a beautiful bride, Shar. We should have saved this dress for your wedding rather than this pageant," Marlene Gracey said to her daughter.

Gazing at her reflection in the full length mirror, Shar found herself agreeing with her mother. The shimmering white dress did, indeed, look like a wedding dress, but she wasn't thinking about no wedding right now. "Mama, I'm only seventeen. Daddy said you ain't allowed to marry me off before I'm full grown."

"What's full grown? I was sixteen when I started courting your daddy, and we doing just fine."

"Mama, I keep telling you that marriage and babies is far from my mind. All I want to do right now is sing in this competition today." For so long, the Miss America pageant had denied colored girls entry into their pageant. But now they would have their own pageant. The prize was a hundred dollars in gold and three hundred dollars in gifts. Shar desperately wanted to win those prizes. Her family could do a lot with a hundred dollars worth of gold. So she needed to focus.

"You and your daddy got singing in your blood. Your daddy done gave up on his own singing ambitions, so now he trying to live through you. But one day you gon' have to wake up and see that singing didn't get your daddy nowhere and it's gon' be the same for you."

Shar didn't want to argue with her mother. All her life it seemed that she had only been able to please one parent at a time. If she was singing, her daddy was happy. If she was cleaning and cooking, her mama was tickled pink. Shar just hadn't been able to figure out how to make them both smile at the same time. But she knew what made her happy and that was singing. "God gave me this voice for a reason. And I intend to use it for His glory. And I'm not going to let nobody stop me."

"I don't care what you do with that voice of yours, Shar Gracey. But what you ain't gon' do is talk to me like I'm some stranger on the street. I'm your mama. And I'm going to get some respect."

Shar lowered her head. "Yes, ma'am. I surely never meant to disrespect you."

Marlene put a gentle hand on Shar's arm. "Forget what I said, hon. You just go on out there and win this pagent."

Standing at the corner of 61st and Wabash avenues, Pastor Landon Norstrom watched the Negro Day parade kick off. It was the most colorful exhibit Landon had ever seen, with floats, cars, and marching bands lining the streets for miles on end. Landon noted several white men sprinkled throughout the parade, "Friends of the Race," as the *Chicago Defender* referred to them. The first colored state senator, Adelbert H. Roberts, was on one of the floats, along with several other colored officials.

Seeing these men participate in an event such as Negro Day, which was a day of celebration for the triumphs of colored people, put Landon at ease. He had been in Chicago all of one week. He'd arrived to take over as pastor of United Worship Center, but he'd been recruited out of Alabama for another purpose as well. Landon's church was smack-dab in the middle of the Black Belt, the area where colored folks had been relegated to.

The Black Belt was overcrowded and filled with dilapidated houses. So his first order of business, outside of running his church, would be to work with Robert R. Taylor to garner decent housing for the people in his community. The pastor before him had been involved in this movement before he passed away, and Landon would continue the fight. Robert R. Taylor was the manager of the Rosenwald Apartment buildings. The apartments had been built in 1929 by Julius Rosenwald, the president of Sears, Roebuck and Company as a means of meeting the need of low-cost housing for colored people.

He would meet up with Robert Taylor at the Miss Bronze America pageant, which was being held at Soldiers Field. They would see each other later on, but for now, Landon set his mind to enjoying the parade and watching the floats go by.

"Hey, Pastor Landon!" one of his parishioners yelled at him from his seat on one of the floats.

Landon didn't remember the man's name, but he did recall meeting him during his first Sunday at United Worship Center. Landon raised his hand and waved. "See you tomorrow at church."

"No doubt!" His float drifted down the street.

The parade ended at the A Century of Progress exposition. Landon and the rest of the participants walked around the area, viewing the artwork. By the time he made it over to Soldiers Field to look for Robert Taylor, the Miss Bronze America pageant had already begun. Landon glanced up and viewed the most exquisite women he'd ever seen in his life. Most of the colored women he came in contact with worked as maids and were too tired to worry about hair and makeup after a hard day of house cleaning.

"They're beautiful, aren't they?" a man said as he approached Landon.

Landon noticed that the man had on a black jacket and black hat as Robert told him he'd be wearing, so Landon took a guess. "Robert Taylor?"

The man took off his hat and bowed gallantly. "At your service, Pastor Landon."

"How'd you know who I was?" Landon asked.

Robert put the hat back on his head. "You're the first man I've run into today in all brown who actually looks like a preacher, so it wasn't hard to figure out."

The two men shook hands. "It's nice to finally meet you," Landon said.

"Likewise. Have you gotten settled in?"

"Almost. I didn't bring much besides my clothes and shoes. The previous pastor had already furnished the house."

"That's good. Let's go have a seat so we can get down to business."

Landon and Robert sat down and began their discussion. They became so engrossed in the conversation that for almost an hour the noise from the activities around them didn't faze them. But then a beautiful young woman in a long shimmering white gown took hold of the microphone and began singing "Surely God Is Able."

Landon looked up. He recognized the song as being written by a Reverend Herbert W. Brewster. He was a Memphis preacher, and Landon had visited East Trigg Baptist Church and heard the reverend and his choir perform that song with his own ears. But the sound coming out of this bronze beauty was unlike anything he'd ever heard. Her angelic voice mesmerized him. He stood to get a better view.

"She's something else, isn't she?" Robert stood up also.

She sang. "God is able to carry you through . . ."

"Who is she?" Landon had to know the identity of the woman with the caramel skin and coal black hair who had so captured his attention that he would gladly spend a lifetime with this space in time locked in his memory bank.

"You haven't met Shar Gracey yet?" Robert asked with a lifted brow.

"If I had, I sure don't think I would have forgotten," Landon said, eyes still transfixed on her beauty.

Her song continued. "He'll be a mother to the motherless, a father to the fatherless."

"She attends United Worship Center."

"Is that right?" Landon decided to make it his mission to get to know all of his parishioners . . . and especially Shar Gracey.

"Looks like her mother is walking our way. Would you like me to make the introduction?"

Landon turned to see the short, plump woman walking toward them. He nodded.

"Mrs. Marlene, you are sure raising up that child of yours. Shar sounds like an angel." Robert hugged Marlene and then made the introductions.

"I'm not interrupting anything, am I?" Marlene looked from Landon to Robert Taylor, both men shook their heads.

"As a matter of fact," Robert began as he glanced at his watch, "we just finished our business for the day, and I'm on my way to another meeting."

As Robert Taylor walked off, Marlene turned to Pastor Landon and said, "I hope the good people of United Worship Center been treating you right."

Landond nodded. "Everyone has been wonderful. I'm just sorry that I didn't get a chance to meet you and your daughter last Sunday."

"We were there, but we had to leave directly after service so we could get the washing done for some of the ladies I do housekeeping for. But I was sure sorry that we had to leave before having a proper introduction. I wanted my Shar to meet you. Yes, indeed. So, I hope you have time to meet her today."

Landon grinned at Marlene. He had dealt with his share of match-making mothers back in Alabama. But this was one match that Landon wouldn't hide away from. "I'd love to meet your daughter, Mrs. Marlene. And don't worry, I can wait until they crown her the winner of this here pagent."

"You think she's going to win, huh?"

Landon wasn't sure why the look of despair crept into Mrs. Marlene's eyes at his suggesion that her daughter just might win the pageant. But he decided not to get into it. They were about to announce the winner so he turned toward the stage with her. Shar was among the five women still competing, and Landon believed that she had a real good shot, especially with that magestic voice of hers.

The announcer started calling off runner-up number five. He went all the way down to number three without mentioning Shar's name. Landon leaned down and whispered into Mrs. Marlene's ear, "I think she's got it."

Then the announcer said, "And runner-up number two is . . . Shar Gracey."

Landon was sure he saw a smile of relief on Mrs. Marlene's face as she clapped for her daughter.

"That girl did a fine job today. She didn't have to win no prize for me to be happy."

Landon started clapping too. When Shar came down off the stage and stood next to them, she looked as if she wanted to cry, so he told her, "You're too pretty to be frowning like that, Miss Shar. And besides we all know that you should have won that crown. I would have given it to you after the way you sang that song. Yes, ma'am, you're a winner."

"Thank you for your kind words, Pastor Landon. I'm sorry that I didn't get a chance to welcome you to the church last week. But you had a long line of folks waiting to shake your hand, and Mama and me had to get home and finish the washing."

"Don't talk the good pastor's ear off about our chores," Marlene told her daughter, then turned to Landon. "I hope we're not keeping you from anything."

"Don't worry yourself about that at all, Mrs. Marlene. I just completed my business here and was just getting ready to ask Miss Shar why in the world, with a voice like that, she wasn't singing in our choir."

"United Worship Center doesn't have a choir." Shar said this as if providing him with information he didn't know.

"We do now," Landon told her. "I'm making it my business to find the best choir director the city of Chicago has available . . . that is if you'll agree to sing at our church."

Grinning from ear to ear, Shar told him, "Why I'd be honored."

"But only if she has the time," Marlene chimed in. "We get really busy a couple Sundays a month."

"Come on, Mama." Shar's eyes implored her mother to understand. "I want to sing so bad that I dream about it all the time. Being allowed to sing in the choir would be like making my dreams come to life."

"What do you say, Mrs. Marlene?" Landon looked from mother to daughter. "I don't think you want to be responsible for crushing your beautiful daughter's dreams, now do you?"

"I tell you what, Pastor," she hooked her arm around his. "You walk me and my beautiful daughter home, and I'll give you my answer about this choir business on the way."

"Yes, ma'am," Landon quickly agreed.

The three began walking down the street, and Marlene said, "While we walk, Shar, won't you tell the good pastor about some of your other talents."

With a look of confusion on her face, Shar asked, "What other talents?"

Marlene laughed. "Stop fooling around, chile. Tell the good pastor about them good old butter beans you cooked last night."

The look of horror on Shar's face was priceless. Landon wanted to tell Shar not to fret, that he knew this was a setup and wasn't complaining one bit.

2

1935
Depression in the Black Belt

"Shar Gracey, you better get yo' little narrow behind back here."

Her mother was doing it again, and Shar was about to have a natural fit. "Please go back inside. The wind is blowing somethin' fierce out here this morning."

Shar and her mother had stayed up half the night, then had gotten up at five that morning to finish the washing and ironing for Mrs. Jansen. Her mother had been hacking and coughing the whole way through. Now she was standing on the porch with nothing but her thin housecoat on, and that thing was so raggedy that Shar could see more of her mother's flesh than she wanted to.

"Don't forget this." Marlene handed her daughter a sweet potato pie. "You give that pie to Pastor Landon, ya' hear. Let that man see just how good he'd be getting it if he takes your hand in marriage."

Protesting, Shar nevertheless took the pie. "Ma, Pastor Landon knows that I'm not the one making these pies. And this is the thirties. Colored women aren't only in the kitchen cooking up somethin' good for the menfolk. We're writers, like that Zora Neale Hurston up in Harlem, and singers, like Mahalia Jackson." Shar was more like her daddy than her mama and she knew it, for she was an unrepentant, head-in-the-clouds dreamer.

"Hush, chile, and get on from around here with that foolish talk. You just take that pie to Pastor Landon."

"Okay, I've got the pie, now can you please go back in the house?"

"And don't forget to smile real pretty for him," Marlene said, right before the hacking started up again.

As Shar watched her mama walk back into the house, she lifted her face to heaven and prayed that God would help her find a way to make some money. She needed that money yesterday but would take it any day it showed up . . . just as long as she could get her mama to a doctor.

Shar's shoulders slumped with the knowledge of just how poor and perplexed she was. She had nothing and no way to make anything better. She had dreams bigger than the stampede of Negroes who left the South for friendlier northern lands. Her daddy had promised that things would be better up north. But here they were on the South Side of Chicago, living in the Black Belt, where things didn't seem no better.

Oh, they weren't getting lynched like so many of her family members had in the South, but the white folks in Chicago acted like colored folks was trying to steal something from 'em. They put restrictions on everything, just like them Jim Crow southerners. The Restrictive Covenants in the North meant that her family was going to be living in the same old dilapidated shack that they thought they had left behind. Her daddy couldn't even find work half the time, while she and her mama took in rich white ladies' washing to help put food on the table.

If only she could have won that hundred dollars of gold from that Miss Bronze America pageant. But the judges weren't too thrilled with the song she'd picked. The winner had been a girl who sang "Amazing Grace," a song that twenty-five other contestants had chosen to sing. Shar had been down in the dumps after that contest. But Pastor Landon had come up to her after the competition and told her that she sounded like an angel singing praises to the Lord.

Pastor Landon had even said that she was the prettiest girl in the pageant and had walked her home. On the way home, Shar's mama had nudged her and whispered, "Smile, girl, show the man those deep dimples." As if that was going to cause him to ask for her hand in marriage right then and there. But nevertheless, Shar smiled like her mama told her. And she'd been smiling ever since. Because a year after they met, Landon had come to the house and asked her father if he could court her. Now she and Pastor Landon kept company at least one day a week. She loved when Landon walked her home or when he talked to her about his dreams of helping the people in their community. Her mama kept telling her that Landon would be asking for her hand soon and very soon. But then Landon would get so tied up with his work that Shar began wondering if she and her mama was just wishing in the wind.

As far as Shar was concerned, she was stuck where she was, with no change in sight. At nineteen, Shar Gracey had had her fill of living in poor and restrictive conditions. She wanted to be free. Josephine Baker was free. That woman was living the high life in France . . . with nobody telling her that she couldn't go here or step foot there. Josephine Baker was singing and dancing where she pleased . . . and getting paid a good wage for it, too. Not that Shar wanted to be like Josephine Baker. The way she heard tell of it, Josephine Baker wore hardly any clothes at all when she performed. That was way too risqué for her taste. The good Lord didn't give her the singing voice she had to prance all over Europe like a stripper. Shar wanted to use her voice to sing praises to the Lord.

After crossing over State Street, Shar ran down an alley and across another street. Along the way she passed more dilapidated houses and down-on-their-luck brothers than her eyes cared to see. *Lord, when will times get better for us?*

"Hey, sister, won't you let me have a taste of that pie?" a grungy-looking man asked as he approached her at the end of the alley.

"Can't . . . sorry." The church was across the street, so Shar picked up the pace, hoping that the man wouldn't follow her. Actually, she would have loved to give him the whole pie, but her mother would kill her if Pastor Landon didn't get his sweet potato pie. As if Landon was going to take one bite, then get down on his knee and pull out an engagement ring. Shar had done a whole bunch of daydreaming about marrying Pastor Landon. After all she'd been courting the man for a year now. But not one of her dreams ever had him on bended knee because of the taste of a sweet potato pie.

"Slow down, Sister Shar, you're on time," Pastor Landon said. He was standing outside, greeting parishioners as they made their way through the church doors.

Shar stopped in front of him. He was wearing his snowy white preacher's robe, which looked so good up against his chocolate skin. Landon was always cleanly shaven and smelling like Old Spice. Most men she knew smelled like earth and sweat. She took a step toward him as she breathed in his clean, cologne scent, then jumped back and shoved the pie in his direction, all the while reminding herself that Landon was a preacher and they were standing in front of a church, so she needed to get her mind on the things of the Lord. She had no business drooling over a preacherman on a Sunday morning. "Mama sent you another pie for your anniversary dinner."

Smiling, he took the pie out of Shar's hand. "Sister Shar, you are going to spoil me rotten."

He always called her Sister Shar when they were at the church, and she called him pastor. But when he was walking her home or they were sitting on her porch, she simply called him Landon. "Not me, Pastor. I can't cook a lick," Shar said. "Ma just likes fattening you up with her sweet potato pies."

"Well, tell Mrs. Marlene that I appreciate her kindness, even if it is adding extra pounds to me."

"I'll do that as soon as I get back home." Shar gave him a deep dimpled smile.

"Your smile just lights up the day, Sister Shar."

When he said things like that, the wedding march played in Shar's head. She prayed that the next thing out of his mouth would be something like, "Shar Gracey, I sure would like to marry you." But he never said it, so Shar had started to wonder if maybe Landon was waiting on something better to come along.

Landon put his hand on Shar's arm and leaned a bit closer. "I have a surprise for you," he told her and then bent down and picked something off the ground.

When he straigtened back up, Shar saw that he was still holding the pie in one hand, but now his other hand held a bright colorful flower. He handed the flower to her.

"I was walking through this field yesterday that had so many beautiful flowers as far as the eye could see. I told myself, 'Shar needs flowers as beautiful as these.' So, I picked a bundle of them."

Giddy over the flower in her hand and Landon's words, Shar's eyes sparkled as she said, "Thank you so much. I've never seen a flower as wonderful as this one."

"I'm glad you like it. I'll bring the rest of them to your house this evening when I come to see you."

"So are you walking me home today?"

Landon shook his head. "Not today. I have to head out right after the anniversary dinner. So, I won't be able to walk you home, but your dad is allowing me to keep company with you today. So, I'll see you at your house later."

"Oh, Landon, I wondered if you would be coming by today. Mama hinted at it, but she wouldn't come right out and fess up." She smelled her flower, eyes still sparkling. "Thanks again for my flower."

"Like I said, there's plenty more where that one came from." Landon was grinning at her as if he had something else to say but was holding it in.

"What?"

"That's for me to know and you to find out."

"When am I going to find out?"

"When I come visiting this evening," he said, then ushered her into the church before she could ask anymore questions. "Now Sister Shar, you go on and get yourself prepared to sing to God's glory today."

Shar scuttled into the sanctuary, greeting friends as she passed by them. But in her heart she wondered if today would be the day that Landon would finally ask for her hand in marriage.

3

The United Worship Center had five hundred members on the roll books, but about three hundred attended faithfully every Sunday. Before they started the choir only about a hundred attended on the regular. These men, women, and children had become Shar's surrogate family, since her mother hadn't been attending much lately because she was always feeling ill but never had a chance to sit down and rest. Her father just flat out refused to step foot inside the church. They had come to Chicago by way of Louisiana, where the rest of Shar's family still lived, so it was nice to have sisters and brothers in Christ that she could talk to from time to time.

"Hey, Shar, I heard that you've got the solo today. I can't wait to hear you," Sister Barbara Tucker said as she passed by, carrying an armload of Bibles. Sister Tucker was the head usher, and it was her job to make sure that things ran smoothly in the sanctuary during service.

"Let me help you with those, Sister Tucker," Shar said, as she took four Bibles from the stack Sister Tucker was carrying. She put the flower Pastor Landon had given her in her mouth as she passed out the Bibles.

"You're sweeter than sugar. Thanks for helping me. But you need to get on."

Shar took the flower out of her mouth and hugged Sister Tucker, then headed toward the choir stand.

"It's nice of you to join us. You're such a busy and important person that we are just plum grateful whenever you show up," Nettie Johnson said.

Every family had one member who made a sister think about doing some premeditated repenting. Like jumping across the seats and slapping the taste out of Nettie's mouth, even though Shar knew full well that she would be begging the Lord's pardon for doing so. Not wanting to do something that she knew was wrong, Shar plastered a smile on her face and hoped the Lord would forgive her for lying as she said, "Why, Nettie, I never knew that you cared so much about my comings and goings, but I'm glad to be with you all this fine Sunday morning."

"I don't care what you do, Shar Gracey," Nettie spat. "But when you keep the pastor out on the stoop when he should be in the church getting ready to deliver one of his fine messages, then it's all of our concern."

"I wasn't keeping Pastor Landon from his duties," Shar protested.

"Oh really?" Nettie pointed toward Shar's hand. "Nice flower."

Looking as if she'd been caught in the cookie jar, Shar began sputtering, "I . . . I—"

"Hush, you two. I'm not in the mood to referee," Mother Barnett chimed in. "My knees haven't given me a bit of trouble all morning. And you know what that means."

Mother Barnett always claimed that she could tell what the weather was going to be like by the way her knees ached. If her knee was feeling itchy, then it was going to rain. If her pain was terrible, then it was going to be a gloomy day. But on days when she had no pain at all, Mother Barnett said, the good Lord wasn't trying to tell her nothing about the weather that day, but about some good news coming to somebody.

"So, who is gon' get some good news today?" Shar asked, hoping that Mother Barnett would say that the relief of pain in her knees was about God showing her that Landon was going to be proposing today.

Mother Barnett rubbed her knees as if she was checking for pain, then she said, "I guess the good Lord will reveal it to us before the day is over. Who knows, maybe my Herbert is finally coming back home."

Ten years ago, Mother Barnett's husband had run off with the cigarette girl who had rented a room from them. To this day, Mother Barnett kept a light in the window for her husband and prayed that every no-knee-pain day meant that Herbert was coming home. As far as Shar was concerned, that would be a waste of a good no-knee-pain day. Good riddance to bad rubbish was the way Shar saw that one. For the life of her, she couldn't understand why women ran after all these no-account men, who wasn't thinking about them two seconds after they walked out the front door. She sure wouldn't waste a nickel on a box of tissue, crying over one of 'em.

Calvin started tuning up the piano as Marcus fiddled with his guitar. Not many churches allowed their choir to sing with musical instruments. "Okay, everyone, stand up so we can warm up those vocals," Calvin instructed.

Calvin could be temperamental at times. Shar never liked to get on his bad side on the days that she was scheduled to sing. Because if she made him mad enough, he'd just cancel her solo. And there was no way she wanted to continue living in a world where she was poor, colored, and not allowed to sing. So Shar immediately jumped out of her seat and did as she was instructed.

"Place your hand on either side of your mouth and use the tips of your fingers to hold up the weight of your cheeks," Calvin said as he looked around to ensure that everyone was following his instructions, then he continued, "Now keep your lips very loose and floppy and blow, like you would after you finish a day of washing and ironing or of standing all day on your elevator boy job."

Hot, tired breaths blew all across the choir stand.

"Now, hold that pose and make a dopey MMMMMM sound."

The choir followed suit.

When they finished warming up, Calvin smiled at the group as he told them, "I have a surprise for you all." He hesitated, then trodded on, "Thomas Dorsey will be at our church today."

"So now we know why you made sure that Shar had the only solo today." Nettie's venom was now directed at Calvin.

Shar didn't understand Nettie at all. The girl didn't live dirt-poor like the rest of them. Her father was in city politics, and he treated Nettie like a princess, giving her everything that her heart desired. But for some reason Nettie disliked her and made it seem as if Shar had everything that she wanted. When Shar knew that she didn't have much at all.

Calvin cleared his throat. "I'm not playing favorites, if that's what you think, Nettie. But when a man like Thomas Dorsey visits our church, I think Pastor Landon would want me to put our best singer up, don't you?"

Nettie was glaring at Calvin as Mother Barnett said, "Why's this Thomas Dorsey interested in us anyway?"

Calvin's chest puffed a bit as he said, "United Worship Center is one of the few churches around that believes in worshiping God in song and music. Mr. Dorsey taught himself how to play the piano and loves the sound of music. So, when I told Mr. Dorsey that I played the piano and that we had the best singer in Chicago at our church, he said to me, 'I got to come see that.'" Calvin raised a hand and added, "Now, I'm not completely sure that Mr. Dorsey will be here today. He just told me that he would try to make it. So, whether he shows up or not, we all need to do our best and sing for God's glory for the congregation, right?"

"Right," the choir members aswered back.

But Calvin's news got Shar to thinking. Maybe Mother Barnett's no-knee-pain day wasn't about Landon proposing at all. Maybe it was a sign that Mr. Dorsey would offer her a spot on his touring choir and then she would be able to earn enough money to get her mama to a doctor.

Calvin looked to Shar. "Are you ready?"

"I'm ready, but what if he doesn't show up until after I get finished singing?"

"You let me worry about that. Now let's grab hands and pray real quick because they're getting ready to start service."

✒

Sister Betty said the welcoming prayer, and then the choir sang two praise songs. Shar was mumbling the words most of the time because she couldn't concentrate. She looked to heaven and silently prayed, Lord, forgive me. I know I should have my mind stayed on you during praise and worship time, but I surely wish you would send Mr. Dorsey to service today.

As the deacons passed the collection plate, the door opened. Shar sat up with a look of expectation on her face. But her facial expression changed, and she leaned back in her seat as she watched Miss Mattie Perkins from two doors down drag her late self into the church house. When the collection plate made it to Shar, she emptied her purse of all the coins she had, hoping that her sacrifice would be noticed by God.

Calvin began playing the music for "His Eye Is on the Sparrow." The choir stood, and Shar walked down and took her place in front of the choir. She looked to heaven one more time and silently prayed, Well, Lord, he didn't come today. But I'm gon' sing this here song to You, like I should have wanted to do in the first place.

Shar opened her mouth and began:

Why should I feel discouraged?
Why should the shadows come . . .

The moment Shar belted out the first few words, people began clapping and standing up all around the sanctuary. Her voice had a soulful, blues-like feel to it that somehow became all gospel when Shar Gracey opened her mouth to sing. It was like pairing the blues with a little dose of heaven. Shar had a voice that could make angels stop and listen. The sanctuary door opened again. This time, Thomas Dorsey walked through the door, and a smile appeared on Shar's face. The devil himself wouldn't have been able to turn that smile into a frown.

I sing because I'm happy and I sing because I'm free.

Shar was no longer in the mood to just sing the song. She began walking around the church performing. Letting all the saints know that she was happy because if God's eyes was on the sparrow, then she sure 'nuf knew He was watching over little ol' Shar Gracey as well. Didn't He prove it by having Mr. Dorsey walk in the church while she was singing so good, that folks was nearly 'bout ready to break out into a shout?

4

Didn't nobody know how to light up a room like Shar Gracey. And Landon Norstrom loved to hear her sing praises to God and enjoyed it even more when the spirit moved on her like it was doing now. Shar was beautiful, with long black hair that flowed down her back and swayed from side to side when she sang praises to the Lord. The first time he'd seen Shar, her hair had been pinned up on top of her head, so he'd had no idea how gloriously long her hair was. But he had noticed how her caramel skin tone perfectly accented those sweet brown eyes of hers.

Landon hadn't wanted to leave Alabama after graduating from theology school. But, knowing that the white folks in town felt that he was uppity and a troublemaker, his parents feared that they'd one day find their son with a noose around his neck. So he packed up and left the Jim Crow laws of the South, for the stay-in-your-place covenants of Chicago. The one bit of brightness he'd found in Chicago was Shar Gracey.

He hadn't noticed Shar in church on his first Sunday as pastor. But he sure noticed her at the Negro Day celebration. Landon had been mesmerized by her. She had the voice of an angel, even if it was a bit bluesy. What he saw and heard that day caused him to want to know so much more about this woman with a voice that even the angels must envy.

And now, as she was cutting up, strutting around his church like the Holy Ghost done took her over, Landon considered himself blessed among men. For this was the day that he would be asking her daddy for her hand in marriage. Landon had been walking Shar home from church at least twice a month, since her eighteenth birthday. Her daddy even allowed him to keep company with Shar a few times a month. But Landon needed more . . . so much more where Shar was concerned. He loved her, and although he'd put off declaring his love, he couldn't wait another day.

Shar's mama had seen right through him, though. All these months that he and Shar had been keeping company, Mrs. Marlene had been plotting on ways to get him to fess up and admit his true feelings. He couldn't count the number of times that Mrs. Marlene sent cakes and pies to him by way of Shar, or the number of times Mrs. Marlene informed him that Shar was going to make some lucky man a good and responsible wife. But he hadn't needed Mrs. Marlene's nudging. He found out on his own what a wonderful woman Shar Gracey was.

He'd made it his business to seek Mr. Johnny Gracey, Shar's daddy, out last week and asked if he could come by on Saturday. Mr. Johnny told him that the women would be far too busy with the washing and ironing on Saturday, so he told him to come by on Sunday after church. That day had finally arrived.

The choir sat down, and it was time for him to get up and preach. Landon almost wanted to deliver the "Jesus wept" sermon, so he could be quick about it. He would then eat his anniversary dinner and go to Shar's house and speak with her daddy. But he couldn't do that, not when his belly was so full with the joy of the Lord. He had to get up and testify of the goodness of God.

And that's exactly what he did. Many of Landon's parishioners had migrated from the South, as he had. They left miserable conditions hoping to find better days in the North. However, they were met with hatred and mistrust, and were put in some of the same conditions that they'd left behind. His parishioners needed a revival of hope, and that's what he tried to give them every Sunday when he stood behind his pulpit. During the week, he worked with as many organizations as possible to find jobs and homes for his parishioners. Things were bound to get better. He didn't know if he would live to see those better days, but he preached about them and set his congregation on fire with hope.

"Whew! Pastor Landon, you put your foot in that message today," Nettie Johnson said as she rushed over to Landon once service had ended.

Landon was busy shaking the hands of visitors as they left the church. He turned to Nettie and said, "Why, thank you, Sister Nettie, I'm glad you enjoyed the sermon."

"Sure did. But I enjoy everything you preach."

Landon shook a few more hands. "Are you staying for the dinner today?"

"Are you kidding? I wouldn't miss celebrating your second-year anniversary for the world. I even made a peach cobbler."

Betty, the woman who gave the announcements every Sunday, walked up on them and said, "Nettie, you need to stop all that lying. Yo' mama made that cobbler and you know it."

Nettie turned cold eyes on Betty. "Well, of course she did, but I helped. So, it's the same as making it myself."

"Mmph," Betty said as she grabbed Pastor Landon's arm and guided him toward the basement. "Come on, Pastor, dinner is ready and the people are hungry enough to eat it all up and you'll be left with nothing but the crumbs."

Nettie followed behind them as they went downstairs to the eating area. But Landon hadn't even realized that Nettie was following him as he scanned the room for Shar. When he caught sight of her, he was immediately struck by a sadness in her eyes. She was sitting at a corner table in the back of the room all by herself.

Landon walked over to where Shar was sitting and asked, "Would you like some company?"

She looked up and smiled. "Of course. Have a seat, Pastor."

He sat down, and then Nettie pulled out a chair to sit also, but Landon stopped her. "Ah, Nettie, would you mind getting me a slice of that peach cobbler you told me about?"

"Sure thing, Pastor. I'll be back in a jiff." Nettie then rolled her eyes at Shar as she left the table.

"So why are you sitting over here by yourself looking so sad?" Landon asked Shar after Nettie strutted off.

Shar shifted in her seat a bit and then asked, "Do you really believe all that stuff you preach, about us going into better days?"

"Of course I do. Don't you?"

"I try to believe it. But sometimes I think that things will never change. Colored folks will keep living in shacks and toting ice or being elevator boys and washing and ironing white folks' clothes, but nothing else is ever going to come to us."

That's the other thing he loved about Shar Gracey. She didn't put on airs and act like she believed something that she didn't just to impress folks. She saw the world the way it was and then responded to it. However, it was his job to help increase her faith. "But we as a people are so much more than that even now, Shar Gracey. Look at how much Booker T. Washington accomplished in his lifetime. He was an educated man who educated others. Mr. W. E. B. Du Bois graduated from Harvard and the man helped start the NAACP. Ida B. Wells-Barnett, God rest her soul, believed that things could change, not just for colored men, but for women also."

"I guess you're right about those people doing great things, despite being colored, but I don't know them and it's hard to keep my mind full of hope when all I see every day is poor-going-nowhere-special colored folks."

Landon was bothered by Shar's assessment of the people around her because he was one of them. "I'm sorry if that's the way you see us."

Shar sat up straighter and put her hand on Landon's arm. "I didn't mean you, Landon. You're an educated man, and you do a lot of good for this community. But most of the people I know don't have no education, including me. I stopped going to school to help bring some money into the house. Now I'm stuck over at that beauty parlor, shampooing heads and sweeping the floor. But what I really want to do is find a way to earn some real money to get my family to some of them better days you preach about."

"Wow, Shar, I'm surprised at how down in the mouth you are. Especially since Thomas Dorsey showed up at the church today. I would think you'd be on cloud nine."

A bit of merriment danced in her eyes. "I was when I first saw him. I sang my heart out, I was so excited. But he didn't even ask my name or nothing after service. He just got up and walked out the door."

"Don't you know how beautifully you sing? Why do you need Thomas Dorsey telling you something that everybody in this church has already said a hundred or more times?"

Shar shrugged.

Nettie came back over to the table and handed Landon a nice helping of peach cobbler, and then she said, "You'd best go on to the head table before folks get to wondering why you're sitting back here with Sister Shar."

Landon stood up. He wanted to take Shar to the head table with him, but since he hadn't yet asked for her hand in marriage, he decided not to do such a bold thing as that. The last thing he wanted was to cause Shar's name to be run through the mud. She was a good Christian girl, and he wouldn't have anyone think differently. "I'll talk to you later, Sister Shar. I have been summoned to the head table."

"Don't forget to take a bite of my cobbler," Nettie reminded Landon.

Landon took a bite of his cobbler. He felt like humming as the cobbler juice and bread floated down his throat. "Mmph, mmph, mmph, this is some good cobbler."

"I'm glad you like it, Pastor. I can bring you your very own batch next Sunday. And you can take it home with you and not have to share with anybody," Nettie said.

"Don't put yourself to all that trouble. What I have now is enough to comfort me for a month of Sundays." Shar giggled, and Landon's heart leaped. He loved the sound of Shar's laughter almost as much as he loved to hear her sing. He handed Nettie the cobbler and said, "Would you mind taking this to my table?"

Nettie took the plate from him and walked away without saying another word.

Landon leaned down and asked Shar, "Are you okay? Because I can't rightly enjoy myself if you're over here looking all sad face."

She smiled at him. "Your talk did me some good. I feel better already." Shar nodded toward the head table. "You go on. I'll be all right."

Landon kept his eyes on her for longer than was proper, but he didn't want to turn away. One day soon he wouldn't have to, and Landon thanked God for that. It made it a little easier to walk away. "I'll see you at your house this evening."

Betty set a plate of collard greens, yams, cornbread, and fried chicken in front of Landon as he sat down. Landon ate as much as he could. He laughed and joked with his parishioners and generally enjoyed himself, but his eyes kept drifting back to Shar. Although she tried to put on a brave face, he could tell that something was weighing heavy on her mind. Landon wanted to spend the rest of his life putting a smile on Shar's face and easing her mind from worry. All he had to do now was get Shar's father to allow him to ask Shar for her hand in marriage. Landon said a silent prayer as he wiped his mouth and put the napkin on his plate.

After dinner Landon grabbed the rest of the flowers he'd picked for Shar and left the church in the hands of the women so they could clean up. Shar stayed behind to help clean the dishes and sweep up. Shar was always so helpful. She wasn't like most young girls, willing to work as long as someone was there to see and be impressed by their labor. No, Shar would have helped the women with kitchen duty even if Landon hadn't been there to hear her offer; that was just the way she was. They would make a good team.

As Landon walked down the street toward Shar's house, he kept reminding himself that he had made the right decision and that it was well past time for him to settle down. He wasn't getting any younger. At twenty-seven, he was ready to start a family.

His stomach fluttered as he approached Shar's house. But men didn't get nervous stomachs over things like this, so Landon chocked the fluttering in his stomach up to indigestion. Those collards must have been cooked with too much fatback. He knocked on the door and waited.

The door opened, and Marlene Gracey greeted him. "Pastor Landon, it is so nice to see you. Johnny told me that you was finally coming to speak with us."

He caught the "finally" and smiled. "Yes, I thought it was high time that I talked to you and your husband."

"Well, come on in." She opened the door wider and stepped back to let him walk through.

Landon took off his straw hat and entered the Gracey's small but neat home. The furniture in the parlor room was dated and had been duct-taped in certain spots where it was ripped. But Mrs. Marlene kept the house in such a clean and organized manner that one barely noticed the duct tape. What Landon did notice was that Thomas Dorsey was seated on that sofa.

Johnny stood up as Landon entered the room and said, "Well, Reverend, looks like you're a day late and a dollar short."

What was this man talking about? Surely he hadn't given Shar's hand in marriage to Thomas Dorsey. Thomas had lost his wife and newborn baby after a rough childbirth back in 1931. Landon hadn't heard if the man had remarried, so he was a little nervous as he asked, "I don't believe I know what you're referring to, Mr. Gracey."

"This man wants to take Shar on the road. He says she'll be a big star in gospel music someday, and he wants to give her a leg up."

Could it really be true? Had he really lost his love because he was a day late in coming to visit? He closed his eyes and prayed that Shar would want to stay there with him.

5

$\mathcal{M}$other Barnett, why on earth are you still here? I would have thought you'd be home resting your legs by now," Shar said as she grabbed her purse and prepared to leave the church.

"Chile, didn't I tell you that these old knees wasn't bothering me today?"

"Oh yeah, I forgot."

"I stayed to help these young girls put the sanctuary back to right while you was downstairs cleaning the kitchen. But I'm headed home now." Mother Barnett held a smile that was as wide as the ocean.

Shar knew why she was smiling like that. Mother Barnett still believed that something good was going to happen that day. As Shar thought about that, she'd come to the conclusion that Mother Barnett had good reason to think like that. The old woman had only had two other no-pain days in the entire time that Shar had known her. On the first no-pain day, Pastor Landon had delivered his first sermon as the new pastor of United Worship Center. On the other no-pain day, Brother Wilson had stood up and testified that he and his family were about to be thrown out on the street because he didn't have the money to pay his rent. But he'd found a crisp one hundred dollar bill lying on the street as if the Lord Himself had left it there just for him. The whole church rejoiced because Brother Wilson and his family wouldn't be on the streets.

As they walked out of the church together, Mother Barnett told Shar, "I'm going home to put the light in the window for Herbert."

Pastor Landon's encouraging words had helped Shar to cheer up a bit after Thomas Dorsey left the church without so much as a wave good-bye. But, in truth, walking with Mother Barnett had helped her more. Because if she could still be putting a light in her window in hopes that old no-account Herbert Barnett would come back home after being gone so long, then who was she to be down in the mouth just because Thomas Dorsey didn't take notice of her?

She was happiest when she sang praises to God. So if God intended for her to stay an apprentice at that beauty shop, shampooing heads and sweeping the floor during the week and then helping mama with the washing and ironing on the weekend, she would do it with a smile on her face, as long as she could open her mouth and sing God's praises every Sunday morning. She didn't need to be like Mahalia Jackson or Rosetta Tharpe, singing to hundreds and even thousands of people at a time. And anyway, she wasn't special like that. All Shar really wanted right then was to earn enough money to get her mother to a doctor. Her mother refused to take money out of the household for frivolous things like having a doctor take a look at her. "I'd rather use my home remedies and keep my money to pay the rent," Marlene had told Shar. But her mother's made-up concoctions didn't seem to be working for that cough.

"Hey, Shar, you looking mighty pretty today," Rodney Oldham hollered out as she passed him on the street.

Shar just rolled her eyes. Rodney was a pretty boy who hung out on the streets with his good-for-nothing friends, doing nothing but gambling and getting into trouble. If she married him, Shar had no doubt that she'd be putting a light in her window just like Mother Barnett. So she ignored him and tried her best to stay out of his way, while she prayed that Landon would soon make up his mind about him and her. Shar's Daddy had only courted her mama for three months before he knew that she was the one.

"I know you heard me, Shar Gracey. One day you gon' take that nose of yours out the air and realize that you ain't no better than nobody else," Rodney said as he followed behind her.

"Never said I was any better'n you. I just don't like you, and I wish you'd leave me be."

"Oh, well excuse me for breathing." Rodney waved his hand toward the street and moved out of her way. "Don't let me stop you from gettin' somewhere in life. But while you're going, just remember that you just as poor as the rest of us."

Rodney hadn't told her nothing new. As far as Shar was concerned, she was born poor, and she would stay that way until the day she died. Her father had big dreams about going north. He promised them that things would be better, that she would be able to sing in Chicago and wouldn't be restricted by nothing and nobody. Her mama told Shar that she was sure to find a husband with a good-paying job and then move on up in the world. But the only moving they had done was when they put their raggedy old furniture in their raggedy old house that sat right smack-dab in the middle of the Black Belt. And the only singing Shar had done was at church. Shar was tired of being mad about their plight in life. She kicked at a few rocks on the street . . . time to just accept things as they were and find happiness the best way she could.

At least that's what she told herself as she opened the front door to her house and walked in. But when she saw her mom and dad sitting with Thomas Dorsey and Landon, Shar's heart took a leap in the direction of hope again. "Wh—what's going on?" she stammered.

Her father stood up and pointed at Thomas Dorsey. "He wants you to join his choir. Didn't I tell you, gal? Didn't I tell you that your day was a-coming?"

Her mama stood up and pointed at Landon. "Pastor Landon wants to marry you, chile. Don't go running off, following no pipe dreams, when you got a man here that wants to make a life with you."

Her mother had never had patience for all the music talk Shar and her daddy shared. Marlene couldn't carry a tune, so she didn't understand the dreams that Shar and her daddy had about making something of themselves in the music business. Marlene just wanted to make sure that Shar found a good and honorable man to marry, and she wasn't about to let Johnny Gracey's pipe dreams spoil that.

But Shar had been dreaming about singing and about marrying Pastor Landon for so long now, that she couldn't hardly believe either dream was about to come true, let alone both. In the entire year that she had been courting him, Landon had never so much as hinted that he was thinking about marriage. He didn't act like Rodney, making all his catcalls at her as she passed him by, or any of the other men who'd been interested in her. Landon had always treated her with kindness . . . like a lady. And now he was at her house, holding onto those flowers he'd promised her. She opened her mouth and timidly asked, "You want to marry me?"

Landon handed her the flowers. "I had hoped to be able to ask you myself, but yes. I do want to marry you."

"But why? I mean . . . you never let on." She had been dreaming about being with him for so long but never in a million years thought it would come true. Pastor Landon was an educated and well-traveled man, and why would he want to spend time with her?

Landon stood, hat in hand. "You're pretty special to me, Shar Gracey. I've prayed about this. And you're the one for me."

Johnny waved Landon's comment off and then said, "Mr. Dorsey thinks you're special too. His choir needs someone with your strong vocals. And you could even make some money to help with your ma's medical bills."

Marlene's eyes bucked as her hand went to her hips, "Johnny Gracey, you're not fightin' fair."

Shar turned her attention to Thomas Dorsey. "You want me to travel? I thought your choir performed Chicago."

"We do, but we also go on the road for extended periods of time. I will be leaving in three weeks and would love for you to come with us."

With wonderment in her voice, Shar asked, "I would get paid?"

Thomas nodded. "Your pa told me that y'all need money to get your mama to the doctor. My choir members don't get paid, but if you're willing to sell my sheet music after each service, I can pay for that."

Shar turned to her mother. "And you would go to the doctor?"

"I would make sure of it," Johnny Gracey said, while giving his wife a look that dared her to defy him.

But Marlene wasn't done matchmaking. "I've got home remedies, Shar. You don't have to concern yourself about me. You just worry about getting yourself down the aisle. Every preacher needs a good wife."

Blushing, Shar turned away from her mother to cast her gaze on Landon, the man she had been dreaming about marrying ever since that first day he walked her and her mama home. She turned to Thomas Dorsey and said, "Thank you kindly for wanting me in your choir, Mr. Dorsey. But do you mind if I speak with Pastor Landon first."

Her daddy stepped closer. "What you gotta speak with him about? Didn't I tell you that your sanging voice was gon' take you places?" Johnny's eyes misted as he added, "It's the only thang I ever had to give you. But I'm mighty proud that you've got a chance to get out of here and see the world with it."

Shar's daddy and most of his brothers and sisters could sing like songbirds. He'd always reminded Shar that she got her voice from his mother and that she wasn't gon' waste her talent like the rest of the Graceys had. Shar had assured her daddy that she wouldn't waste what the good Lord and Grandma Gracey had given her.

She turned back to Landon. He was so handsome and kind and everything she ever wanted in a man. At six feet, he stood taller than most of the men she knew. Shar always liked the way his trim mustache looked against his smooth chocolate skin. She wanted to marry this man like she wanted to breathe. But would Landon wait for her? Would he allow her to do this tour so she could earn enough money to help her family?

"Pastor Landon is not going to wait around forever for you, chile. You go running off to see the world because of some pipe dream of your daddy's and you'll miss out. Hear what I'm telling you, Shar?"

"Yes, Mama, I hear you." She then asked her daddy, "Do you mind if I speak with Pastor Landon on the porch?"

Johnny waved them off. "Go on, but be quick about it. Mr. Dorsey is an important man, and he don't have all day for you to be diddling around."

Landon walked Shar out of the house. Once they had taken their seats on the stoop he said, "I didn't know your dad was so set on you singing."

"That's all he's ever talked about since I was a kid and he discovered I could sing. He said that his mama wanted to sing, but got beat so bad trying to save her youngest son from a lynching that she lost her voice."

"You never told me that."

"I don't like thinking about Grandma Gracey having her beautiful voice beat out of her. I never heard her sing because I hadn't been born when it happened, but my daddy said that the world lost something special indeed, when Grandma Gracey's voice left her."

"Do you really have to go, Shar? You already sing in the choir at church, and I'm sure you could find other churches in Chicago to sing at also?" Landon said.

"But Mr. Dorsey is going to pay me."

"Is money so important, Shar? Don't you care at all about the fact that I want to marry you?"

"You know I care," Shar said quickly. "Any woman would be right pleased at the thought of being the wife of Pastor Landon Norstrom. I am mighty proud that you asked my parents for my hand."

"Then stay here with me, Shar. I'd treat you like a princess. I can promise you that."

Shar's eyes became misty at Landon's promise to treat her like a princess, but she didn't respond.

Landon got the hint. "There's more that you're not saying, isn't there? I need to know what I'm up against."

She closed her eyes. Wishing that she wasn't poor and colored and needing to decide between love and money. But she wasn't Cinderella, and no matter how bad she wanted it, no princess fairytales was coming her way. She was Shar Gracey, the daughter of a woman who was too poor to go to a doctor. "My family needs the money. My mama is sick. I can feel it in my bones. But she won't go to a doctor because we don't have the money."

"I know a doctor who I can get to check your mama out. He does house calls, and if I let him know what's going on, he might be able to work out a payment plan."

"What about the medicine, Landon? If she needs medicine, can you pay for that too?" She lifted a hand to halt his answer. "I can't ask you to do that. My daddy wouldn't take your charity."

"We could take up a collection at the church."

Shar shook her head. "Most of the folks at the church just as bad off as we are. I can't see burdening them with our problems."

Landon put his arm around Shar. As he touched his forehead to hers, they both let out a long-suffering sigh.

Tears slid down Shar's face as she asked, "What are we going to do?"

"I can't answer that for you. All I can do is love you and hope that you choose me."

Shar pulled away from Landon and grabbed hold of the rail as she made her way down the steps. She didn't know why life was so unfair to her, but life ain't never gave a dang about what she wanted. "What kind of choices do I have?"

Landon didn't get up, didn't respond, just kept his eyes on her, looking and waiting.

Pointing toward the door, she said, "If I go in there and tell Mr. Dorsey that I'll go on that tour with him, my daddy will be over the moon with joy and my mama will get the medicine that she needs. But then I lose you." She paused for a second and took a deep breath. "But if I say no, I won't go on the tour, I'll stay right here and marry you. I'll be happy, and you'll be happy, but then my mama might die." She turned away from him and whispered to herself, "How can I live with that?"

She thought about Mother Barnett saying that somebody was going to get some good news today. At that moment, she couldn't help but wonder if her good news was sitting in the house talking to her parents about the tour or if he was directly behind her, waiting on an answer as to whether or not she would become his wife.

6

*A*s the week progressed and Shar still hadn't made up her mind whether she should stay or go, her parents started in on each other. Things became so contentious between her parents that Shar sat on the porch rather than go in the house most evenings. But sitting on the porch didn't stop her from hearing the arguments. Even now as she tried to set her mind on other things Shar could hear her daddy saying, "If that Pastor Landon really loved Shar like he claims he do, he'd wish her well and promise to be waiting when she gets back."

"And why should he do that?" Marlene yelled back.

"Why shouldn't he? What kind of man, claiming to love a woman, won't let down his pride so that she can have the things she wants out of life?"

"You that kind of man, Johnny Gracey." Marlene's voice was filled with accusation and venom. "You promised to love me and see to my happiness and Shar's happiness, but you're breaking my heart and you don't even care."

"Marlene, now that's not fair. All I ever strived for in life was to do right by you and Shar. But the two of us together barely bring in enough money to pay the rent on this house. How we going to afford the care you need without Shar bringing in some extra money? You think I want you to sit here and die just so Shar can run off and marry that preacher that you been throwing her on for over a year now?"

Shar felt as if she was being pulled in a hundred different directions. She and her daddy had always been close. He'd told her on countless occasions that she was the apple of his eye. But her vacillating over this decision was causing him to look at her differently. Her mama was mad at her for even considering going on this tour. And Shar hadn't heard a peep out of Landon since Sunday afternoon. She'd never dreamed in a million years that her prayers would get answered like this.

Shar couldn't take anymore. She got up off the stoop, getting ready to headed to the church. They was having a fish fry this Friday, so she hoped that she would be able to catch up with Landon and talk this out. She felt like a poster child for the phrase, be careful what you pray for because you just may get it . . . and then be forced to choose between two blessings.

Before Shar could get off the porch, her mama stopped arguing with her daddy because a coughing spell overtook her. It sounded so awful that Shar opened the front door and raced to her mama's side. "What's wrong with her, Daddy?"

Marlene was struggling to hold herself up as her body was being ravished with a cough that she couldn't stop or control. Johnny took his wife's arm and sat her down on the couch.

"Now do you see what your constant bickering has done?" Shar barked at her father.

Marlene lifted a hand as she struggled to regain her voice. "Not his fault."

Shar looked at her daddy. She saw fear in his eyes. His wife was suffering, and he couldn't do a thing about it. She turned her eyes back to her mama, and for the first time since all these coughing spells began, Shar noticed how much weight her mother had lost. "Mama, do you want me and Daddy to get you to the hospital?"

Marlene shook her head as she got up off the couch. "I'll be fine. Just need to rest is all."

Shar followed her mother. Marlene got in her bed. Shar put a blanket around her and then sat down next to the bed. Marlene closed her eyes, looking as if the coughing had zapped all the energy out of her body. She sat there rubbing her mama's head while she slept, remembering all the times that her mama had done this same thing for her when she was feeling poorly. She would return the favor, and nothing more needed to be mulled over.

As tears rolled down her face, Shar's heart was breaking with the knowledge that even though her prayers had been answered, she was still Shar Gracey and life just wasn't gon' roll over and let her be happy.

"Looks like you done made up your mind. Am I right about that, baby-girl?"

Her daddy had come into the room with them. Shar nodded.

"Do I want to hear this decision of yours?" he asked.

She nodded again as she wiped the tears from her face. "I suspect you right, Daddy. If Landon really loves me, then he'll wait until I get back from this tour."

Johnny clapped his hands. "Did you hear that, Marlene?" Marlene's eyes fluttered, but she didn't respond. "And I don't care what you got to say about it, because I'm getting you to the hospital no sooner than Shar gets herself on that tour bus."

After having a five-day pity party, Landon realized that he didn't want to lose Shar, even if it meant that he would have to get in line behind her singing career. He loved her, and if he hadn't made it clear enough the last time they spoke, Shar Gracey was the only woman for him. With hat in hand, Landon made his way back over to the Gracey house.

Johnny opened the door and came out on the porch with a suspicious look on his face. "No use trying to talk her out of doing what she was born to do, Reverend. Does God tell the rooster not to crow or the lion not to roar?"

"Now, Johnny, I know you don't attend church or have much interest in the things of God like me and Shar."

"What does my not wanting you to stop my daughter from pursuing her dreams got to do with me not attending that church of yours?" Johnny folded his arms around his belly, waiting on an answer.

"Nothing, I didn't mean it like that . . . " Landon shook his head. "Look, I'm not here to argue with you or to stand in Shar's way. I was just hoping that you would allow me to see her one more time. Is that possible?"

"Well I don't know about that." Johnny puffed out his chest, showing that he was every bit the man of the house and his word was law around there. "Shar has a real chance of getting out of here and making something of her life. And I just don't believe that the good Lord blessed her with a voice like that, just so she can hang around here, helping her mother with the washing.

"So if I let you talk to Shar, I want you to give me your word as a man of God that you won't be putting no thoughts of marriage and babies in her head."

Landon didn't understand why Johnny was so dead set against Shar and him getting married. Didn't every father want marriage and a happy home for his children? "Look, Mr. Gracey, I can promise you that I won't try to stop Shar from doing what she wants to do. But you need to understand something. I love your daughter and have been dreaming about marrying her for at least a year now. I want to do right by her."

"Then let her go on this tour so she can help her family out," Johnny demanded.

"I will. Now can you please let me speak to Shar so she doesn't leave town without me at least saying good-bye?"

Begrudgingly, Johnny opened his front door and hollered inside, "Shar, get out here, gal. Pastor Landon wants to talk to you."

Shar rushed to the front door. She stepped out on the porch with her daddy and Landon. Joy shone across her face at the sight of him. "How are you doing today?" she asked.

Landon smiled. "I'm better now that I have you in my presence." Landon then turned back to Johnny who had just rolled his eyes at Landon's statement. "Do you mind if Shar takes a walk with me?"

"Just around the corner and back, that's all the time y'all need to talk," Johnny said as he stepped back into the house. He then turned back to Shar and said, "Don't stay gone too long. Your mama might be needing you."

"Okay, Daddy, I won't be long." Shar stepped off the porch and started walking down the street with Landon. "I never expected that you'd come back by the house. I was getting ready to go by the church, but then Mama had another one of her coughing spells."

"Is that right," Landon said, allowing his chest to puff a bit at the knowledge that Shar was still thinking about him. As they rounded the corner, Landon said, "To tell you the truth, Shar, this situation has been on my mind all week. I could barely concentrate to write my sermon."

"I don't want God mad at me for troubling your mind, Landon. Please get your sermon done and preach a grand message this Sunday. I surely need to hear something grand to stop my heart from aching like it's been doing."

Her mind was made up. Landon could see it all over her face, but he couldn't stop himself from asking. He had to hear the words fall from her lips. He stopped walking, looked into her eyes as he asked, "You've made up your mind, haven't you?"

"This hasn't been easy for me, Landon."

"I don't doubt that."

Shar lowered her head, shuffled her feet, and then spit it out. "The thought of losing you is breaking my heart, but I have got to go."

Overcome with emotion, Landon grabbed hold of Shar's hands, not caring who saw the preacher holding hands with the lady he intended to marry. "I just got to let you know that I'm not going nowhere, Shar Gracey. I'm going to be right here waiting until you return. And when you return home, the first thing I'm going to do is ask for your hand in marriage again."

"Oh, Landon, do you really mean it?"

He let go of her hands and started back on their journey down the street. "As sure as the day is long, I mean every word." He stopped again and looked into her eyes. "I love you, Shar. Been loving you for a long time now, and I believe that our love will survive."

Tears sprang to Shar's eyes. "I love you too, Landon. But I never imagined that you felt the same way about me. Never imagined that you would love me enough to let me go for a spell."

"I've been trying to put my house in order. I just opened a savings account down at the bank. I wanted to show your daddy that I'd be able to take care of you. So that once you come back, you'll never have to leave my side again."

"I have no doubt that you'd be able to take care of me. I'm just thankful that you're willing to wait for me to go and do what I need to do for my mama. I promise you that when I come back home, I won't be thinking about anything but becoming Mrs. Landon Norstrom."

"And Shar . . . "

They had resumed walking, rounded the corner, and headed back to her house. "Yes, Landon?"

"So that we don't miss each other too much, maybe we should exchange letters."

"I would love that."

He reached into his pocket and pulled out a small Bible with a black leather-bound cover. "I want you to take this with you. Whenever you feel sad or alone, just remember that God is always with you and I will be with you soon enough."

They were in front of her house again. She took the Bible from him and then wrapped her arms around him, hugging him tight and taking in the scent of him. She would carry his scent along with her on the journey.

*

Shar had her suitcase on top of her bed, folding up her dresses and piling them in one by one. As she did so, she realized that she was truly leaving home. She wouldn't be seeing her mom or dad or even Landon for a while, and her heart began to ache a bit.

She began singing "What a Friend We Have in Jesus." Her mother opened her bedroom door and came in humming the same song—"What a friend we have in Jesus, all our sins and griefs to bear. What a privilege to carry everything to God in prayer."

"Shar, chile, you are singing my song," Marlene declared as she began folding some of the clothes on Shar's bed and placing them in her suitcase.

"I know you like that song, Mama. I was just thinking about how much I'm going to miss you and everybody else, and the song just bubbled up in my heart until I had to sing it."

"I'm going to miss you too, baby. I just don't know what I'm going to do without you around this house."

Shar looked at her mama. She had stayed up late last night getting the washing done for Mrs. Jackson, and then she had come to Shar's room to help her pack. Marlene picked up Shar's undergarments and began folding them. Shar moved them out of her mother's reach. "You don't have to help me with this, Mama. I can see that you're tired."

"Tired or not, I'm not letting my child go off into this world without first making sure you've at least got clean undergarments and your dresses that need stitching get it." Marlene sat down on the bed. "Now, if you're concerned about how tired I am, I'll just sit here and help you with the folding while stretching out my legs."

Her mama amazed her. She was so strong, even when she was weak. Marlene Gracey would sooner die than ignore the needs of her family. She would miss her mama every day that she was gone. But she would remain strong because her mother needed her. "Okay, Mama, you can help me all you want, just as long as you prop your feet up while you're doing it."

Shar worked with her mother for the next hour on what should and shouldn't go into her suitcase. When they were finished and Shar was latching the suitcase up, Marlene asked, "Are you sure this is what you want to do?"

"Of course it is, Mama. Why do you ask?"

Lifting herself up and planting her feet on the floor, Marlene looked her daughter in the eye and said, "You and your daddy got big dreams . . . bigger dreams than I've ever even thought of having. I'm not faulting you for that." Marlene walked around the bed and put her hand on Shar's arm. "But if all you got is dreams and your man done left with some other woman, then what do you really have to hold onto? I'm just worried that these big dreams your daddy's got for you is gon' cost you the love of a good man like Pastor Landon."

Shar sat down on the bed, and her mother joined her. "Look at you and Daddy. He once told me that from the moment he laid eyes on you, nothing could stop him from making you his wife. Now if Landon feels that way about me, then he'll be here when I get back, right?"

"A man has got his pride, whether he be a preacher or a janitor. You just remember that I told you that."

7

The Tour
1935–1937

"Shar, gal, get over here and help me sell this sheet music," Sallie Martin, Thomas Dorsey's business manager yelled.

"Coming." Shar ran over to Sallie and took the sheet music out of her hand. "Sorry 'bout that Mrs. Sallie. I got lost in the words of this song and just about forgot what I was supposed to be doing."

"You ain't getting paid two dollars a week to read this here sheet music. You getting paid to sell it."

Shar's mama had now been diagnosed with tuberculosis. So Shar was thankful to be able to help sell the music sheets to earn money for her mother's medication. "I know Mrs. Sallie, but the words of 'Never Turn Back' just drew me to it. I just know that Mr. Dorsey will let me sing it if I keep practicing." Shar patted her chest while clearing her throat. "Listen to this," she said as she sang:

I started out for heaven
Such a long time ago
For the world of temptation
Made my journey hard and slow

"Whatcha think?" Shar asked after she finished.

"I think you have a very beautiful voice, Shar Gracey. But you don't know nothing 'bout never turning back or dealing with no hard journey. There just ain't enough heartache in you to deliver that song to an audience the way it ought to be delivered."

"I know I'm young, Mrs. Sallie, but what does that have to do with me singing a song like this?"

Shaking her head at how naive Shar was, Sallie said, "I can respect talent. Lord knows I'm a better saleswoman than a singer any day of the week. But I keep on singing because I've got a story to tell. So, if you still got something to sing about after some no-count wants to lay up at your place drinking and gambling all hours of the night, and you have to struggle your way through . . . and you're two seconds from giving up, then I'll come hear you sing this song. Until then, go sell this sheet music to our customers, okay, gal?"

On that note, Shar walked away. She had heard talk that Sallie was separated from her husband because of his penchant for gambling and drinking. And although she could admit that dealing with a man like that could make a woman's way hard and cause her to want to give up, she didn't agree that she had to go through something like that in order to sing that song. But she kept those thoughts to herself and just sold the sheet music as she was told.

Shar had been touring with Thomas Dorsey's choir for a year by then but still hadn't been allowed to sing a solo. Mr. Dorsey gave the solos either to Sallie Martin or to half-living-right Rosetta Tharpe. Whenever Rosetta could drag herself out of the Cotton Club or whatever other nightclub she chose to sing her blues songs in, she'd show up at one of the churches they were singing at and Mr. Dorsey would let her lead his songs.

That Mr. Dorsey would prefer Rosetta over her drove Shar crazy. She could understand why Mr. Dorsey allowed Mrs. Sallie to sing his songs . . . even if she was hard on the ears; Mrs. Sallie could sell his sheet music like nobody's business once she finished singing. But Rosetta sold her own records after church service. And what's more, that woman wasn't even trying to live right. It was shameful, just shameful the way Rosetta would beg pardon from her church and promise to sing only gospel music, but the minute the Cotton Club called, she would back-slide right back to her sinful jazz music.

"I'll take a copy of the song Rosetta sang tonight," a portly gentleman said as he anxiously stood in front of Shar.

"That would be the 'Old Ship of Zion,'" Shar told him as she pulled that sheet out of her stack and handed it to the man. He handed her a quarter and then went on about his merry way.

"Well, I guess that answers that," Shar said to herself as she continued to walk around the fellowship hall selling copies of "Old Ship of Zion" and realizing that what Rosetta sang, sold. That made Shar more determined than ever to get Mr. Dorsey to let her lead his songs. She needed to show him that what she sang would also sell . . . and that she didn't have to be double minded like Rosetta to make a name for herself.

That's what Shar admired about Mahalia Jackson. Folks in the choir liked to spread petty gossip about her, but they were just jealous. Mrs. Mahalia had God's ear for sure, and she didn't swing back and forth from the nightclub to the church to make a living, either. The nights Mahalia sang with Mr. Dorsey's choir, they'd sell out of his sheet music.

"Come on, gal. I swear you do more daydreaming than selling," Sallie said as she ushered Shar out of the church building.

"I've made some good sales, Mrs. Sallie."

"Yeah, but you could have made more if you had approached the people, instead of waiting for them to come sniffing around you."

"Okay, Mrs. Sallie, I'll do better in the next town. I promise."

"Let's just go. We're booked into a hotel tonight, and we need to get over there and check in before nightfall."

"But we haven't eaten yet," Shar protested. They'd missed meals before because a restaurant owner refused to serve them or the store they stepped into to get some meat for sandwiches wouldn't serve coloreds. Shar was completely fed up with the eating situation on this tour. She didn't have much while living in Chicago with her parents, but food had always been on the table. The sisters at the church they sang at today had cooked ham, green beans, yams, and bread pudding, and Shar wasn't leaving without getting a plate.

"We got to get over to that hotel before they just up and decide not to rent those rooms to us."

"But why can't we grab a plate before we leave?"

Sallie was about to object again, but Thomas Dorsey walked over to them and said, "Come on everybody, let's get us a plate. Never know, this might be our last meal for the day."

If that's the case, I'm getting two plates, Shar thought as she walked toward the kitchen, not even looking back to see if anyone else was following. Since she'd left home, Shar had lost ten pounds. She was homesick and knew that played a part in her weight loss, but most of it came from being denied food. So, when they had someone offering them free food, Shar wasn't about to turn it down.

Mr. Dorsey was spending the night at the pastor's house, so he didn't want to offend them by having his choir grab plates and leave. They sat down and ate the food at their leisure. A couple members of the choir—Emma Jean Parson and Matthew James—sat down with Shar.

"Girl, I'm glad you pitched a fit about us eating. This food is good," Emma Jean said.

"I wouldn't care if it was good or not. I'm starving and don't have no money to get nothing to eat with," Matthew said.

"Tell me about it," Shar agreed.

"At least you get paid for selling the sheet music. Mr. Dorsey don't let everybody do that," Matthew complained.

"I had to do something to earn money or I couldn't come. My mama is sick and needs medication."

"Oh, Shar, I'm so sorry to hear that," Emma Jean said.

Matthew picked up his plate and stood in a huff. "I got problems, too. Shar ain't the only one who needs money. If Mr. Dorsey wants me to keep playing the guitar, I need to get paid, too." With that said, Matthew sat down at the next table.

"Don't let him get to you, Shar. Matthew complains about everything."

In the year that they had been touring, Shar had gotten used to Matthew's mood swings. She knew that people were jealous of the money she was earning and called her the teacher's pet behind her back. But Shar didn't feel like any kind of teacher's pet since she still hadn't been allowed to lead a song or sing a solo.

A man walked over to Shar's table. He was dressed in his Sunday best, hair slicked back and shoes polished. He stuck out a hand in Shar's direction. "I'm Deacon Morrison."

Shar shook his hand. "I'm Shar Gracey," she said and then turned back to her food.

Deacon Morrison sat down next to Shar and started chatting her up. He told her that he was a widower looking for a good woman to make his wife. He smelled like Old Spice, just like Landon smelled on Sunday morning. Shar didn't want to be rude, especially since the food was so good and filling, but sitting there smelling Deacon Morrison's cologne made her long for Pastor Landon Norstrom. Shar stood up. "I'm sorry Deacon, but I need to get a piece of that bread pudding before it's all gone."

Shar hustled over to the dessert table as if getting a piece of that bread pudding was the only thing on her mind. But in truth, Shar's heart was racing with thoughts of Landon. She and Landon had been trading letters twice a month since she'd been on the road. But the last few months, even though she sent Landon three letters, he'd only sent her one in return. She knew that Landon was busy. He had a church to run, and he was diligently working on a project to help colored people get decent housing. But each night as she went to sleep, Shar wondered if she had missed her chance at happiness.

"Whatcha daydreaming 'bout now, gal?" Sallie said as she advanced on Shar.

Startled, Shar turned toward Sallie. "I—I was just—"

Sallie lifted a hand, halting Shar's explanation. "Save it. Wrap up that bread pudding and let's go."

Shar did as she was told and then followed Sallie out of the church. Deacon Morrison ran out the door behind them. "Miss Shar, Miss Shar," he yelled.

Shar stopped walking, but she really wanted to run away from this man with his Sunday-suit-wearing, Old-Spice-smelling self.

"I brought you another piece of bread pudding."

Shar lifted the napkin in her hand. "I already have a piece."

"Well, now you have two. You can eat one tonight and the other in the morning before you all get on the road."

"Thank you, Deacon Morrison."

"Come on here, Shar. We got to get to that hotel before it gets too dark," Sallie yelled from the bus.

Shar was so tired of hearing how dangerous it was for coloreds to be caught out after dark in the South. If it was so dangerous, why on earth did they even bother to tour down there? She got on the bus and sat down with the rest of the choir members as they rode down the rocky road toward the grand hotel that the church had booked them into. There was usually a boardinghouse or a friend of a friend that allowed the choir to spend the night in most of the towns they performed in. But every so often they came to a town that didn't have any boardinghouses or friends that could take them in. Once, they even slept on the church floor because the only hotel that was in that small town refused to rent rooms to colored people. But no matter how bad their sleeping arrangements were from town to town, nothing would stop them from spreading God's good news. Like Mr. Dorsey said, "The gospel is just good news."

They arrived at the hotel, and Shar put her bread pudding in her bag. She then slung the bag around her back and got off the bus with the other choir members. Stan, the bus driver, walked ahead of them as he attempted to go into the hotel. But a white-haired man with the meanest scowl that Shar had ever seen came barreling out the door before Stan could lay a finger on the knob.

"Get on away from 'round here," he said as he held up a thick tree branch.

Stan held up his hands. "Hold on, sir. You got us all wrong. We supposed to be here. Pastor Barnes of the church down the street made reservations for us."

"Then he should have told us that he was trying to rent rooms for a bunch of jungle bunnies and I would have let him know that we don't have no rooms available."

"We're not trying to cause no trouble, sir. We just need a place to lay our heads. We'll be gone by first light of morning," Stan said with hat in hand and head bowed low.

"I said get." He waved the stick at them. "Unless you want me to take this here stick to you."

Another man came barreling out of the hotel looking madder than a bull in a bullfight. "What's going on out here, Joey?"

Joey pointed his stick at them as he said, "A bunch of coloreds trying to get inside the hotel."

"What?" The man's nostrils flared as he looked at Stan. "You trying to cause trouble, boy?"

With his head still bowed, careful not to make eye contact, Stan said, "No trouble at'all. We just want a room for the night."

"Sleep outside with the dogs where you belong," Mr. Angry-bull-face said.

These men were acting as if their very presence would defile the place. Shar wanted to do or say something, but it felt as if she had a mouth full of molasses and her feet were glued to the ground.

Matthew James, the guitar player, stepped up. He grabbed Stan's arm and began pulling him back. "Come on, Stan, I'd rather sleep outside than to stay somewhere we ain't wanted."

Shar could see that the man with the stick didn't like that comment. But before she could get the molasses out of her mouth and warn the group, the man lashed out at Matthew.

"We don't take kindly to uppity negroes around here," the man said as he swung that big thick stick. The stick connected with the back of Matthew's head, and he went down like he'd just received a one, two punch from Joe Louis.

The man with the stick kept hitting Matthew, while his friend started kicking him so hard that Shar feared Matthew's ribs would break. Her father had told her that he left the South because he was tired of seeing young boys hanging on trees for the crime of being colored. When he'd said that to her, Shar had wondered how anyone could simply stand around and watch something as horrific as that happen without doing anything about it. But as she looked around at her choir members and saw that they were all watching the beating that Matthew was getting without saying or doing anything, she realized how it happened . . . fear closed mouths and paralyzed feet.

But Shar could stand the silence no more. She opened her mouth and screamed at the men. She shouted so loud that the man with the stick stopped hitting Matthew and turned toward her. The hatred Shar saw in his eyes startled her. She'd never met this man before . . . never done anything to him. "Stop it! Stop it!" Shar shouted at them again and again.

As she rushed toward the man, her fear was stripped away by the idea of being hated for nothing. She wanted to claw that man's eyes out and give him a reason to hate her. The man raised the stick in her direction. It was covered in blood . . . Matthew's blood. "You're killing him," Shar screamed as she continued to advance.

Sallie and Emma Jean grabbed Shar's arms and pulled her back toward the bus. "No, I've got to help Matthew."

"How you gon' help him? By getting whooped on the head, too?" Sallie asked as they drug Shar kicking and screaming onto the bus.

"No, no. Let me go. Let me go." Shar jerked and pulled. She had to break free . . . had to help Matthew.

"Hush, chile, they're bringing him," Sallie said as the other choir members surrounded Matthew to block the men from hitting him again. They picked him up and ran to the bus. "Let's get out of here," Stan yelled as he closed the door on the bus and sped off.

Emma Jean and Shar worked furiously at stopping the flow of blood coming from Matthew's wounds. They didn't have any towels, so choir members gave their old shirts. Emma Jean dunked some of the shirts into a bucket of water and began wiping the blood away from the cuts and bruises Matthew had all over his head, back, and arms. Shar cut up the other shirts and tied them around Matthew's head and arms. They also tied several shirts around his midsection to stop the bleeding from cuts on his back and stomach. All of this was done as their bus driver drove as fast as he could to get them as far away from that Mississippi hotel as possible.

Matthew moaned and groaned as they moved him around. But when Shar lifted his right arm so that she could bandage it, Matthew yelled like he was being beaten all over again.

"It's broken," Emma Jean told Shar.

Tears flowed down Shar's face as she thought of the pain that Matthew must be in. She was ashamed of herself for the way she'd just stood there with her choir members watching the beating. "I'm sorry, Matthew. I'm so sorry. We all should have been on that ground with you."

"Hush, gal," Sallie said as she brought some more shirts to them. "If it hadna been for you screaming and hollering the way you did, those men would have killed Matthew. So you hush that crying. He's bruised, but he'll live."

"But his arm is broke," Shar bellowed through her tears. "How can he play the guitar with a broke arm?"

"Mmph, he's alive, and that's all that matters." Sallie put the shirts down and went back to the front of the bus to give instructions to the bus driver.

They drove late into the night until they came upon a church building. They parked in the pathway next to the church, and Sallie told everyone to get some sleep. But Shar couldn't sleep. She and Emma Jean sat up in order to keep an eye on Matthew. He seemed to be breathing a lot easier since Shar and Emma Jean made one of the shirts into a sling and put his arm in it.

"Why are people so evil?" Shar asked Emma Jean as they sat up watching Matthew.

"I can't explain it," Emma Jean whispered, shaking her head. "My mama once knew a white woman who was like an angel to her. Treated her more like a sister than an employee."

"Maybe that woman just didn't show your mama her true feelings. Maybe she really thought that your mama was an animal and needed to sleep outside, just like those evil men at that hotel."

"No way. Mrs. Lila was good to me, too. When my dad died and my mama couldn't pay the rent, she stepped in and paid it for us. She wouldn't have done that if she thought we were no better than animals, now would she?"

The look on Shar's face said she didn't believe a word Emma Jean said.

"I'm serious, Shar. People like Mrs. Lila are the reason why I sing. We bring hope of better days to people when we sing."

Shar didn't say anything. She turned toward the window and looked into the darkness. She wanted to go home so bad that she felt like getting off the bus and walking all the way back to Chicago . . . back to her mama and back to Landon. Tears streamed down her face as she realized that if she didn't hurry up and figure out the reason why she wanted to sing, she would leave the tour and be forced to find some other way to pay for her mama's medication.

8

As Landon finished reading Shar's letter his heart filled with sorrow. He wanted to drop everything and go to her. Shar seemed so distressed, but who wouldn't be after witnessing someone being beaten to within an inch of his life? He put the letter on his desk, stood, and walked over to the bay window.

As he looked out of his window, he could see the dilapidated and overcrowded homes that his people lived in. With more coloreds migrating from southern states every day, Landon knew that something would have to be done to help, not only the people in his church, but coloreds all over Chicago. The newly established Chicago Housing Authority wanted to build high-rise projects and throw a bunch of colored people in them, but Landon wasn't so sure that was the answer. Low-income housing would change the mentality of his people and keep them in poverty-stricken conditions.

He wanted home ownership outside of the Black Belt for the people. And he had finally gotten a test case to work with. Joseph and Marva Barnes had moved from Mississippi to Chicago five years ago. They had both graduated from college and held good jobs. Joseph worked for the steel industry, and Marva was a school teacher. The Barneses had been living with Marva's parents since they arrived in Chicago so they could save enough money to purchase a home.

They found the home they wanted, but the owner refused to sell it to them because they would be the first colored couple in the neighborhood. Landon figured it was way past time for the advancement of colored people and that was why he decided to turn to the NAACP for help with the matter. Walter F. White, the secretary of the NAACP, was speaking at the Ebenezer Baptist Church that night, and Landon intended to be there. He'd tried to schedule a meeting with Mr. White. So far he hadn't heard back, but Landon would not be deterred.

He would go to that meeting, speak with Walter White, and then get on the road first thing in the morning. He needed to get to Tennessee, where Shar and the Dorsey choir were supposed to be performing for the next week. "I'm coming to see about you, Shar, just hold on," he said as he continued to stare out at the intolerable conditions the people of the Black Belt were forced to live in.

There was a knock at his door, then Nettie Johnson opened it. "I got it!" she said as she practically ran into his office.

Landon turned toward his new secretary. Nettie had been a member of his church for years, but as membership increased in recent months, he found that he couldn't handle everything himself. Nettie had been working with him for two months so far, and she had managed to bring some organization into his life. "What's got you so excited, Miss Nettie?"

She handed Landon a small slip of paper. "I just got off the phone with none other than Mr. Walter F. White, and he is willing to give you about five minutes after his meeting at Ebenezer tonight."

Landon grabbed the paper and stared at it. Walter White's name was on the paper, but the telephone number had a

Chicago area code. "Is this the telephone number to where he's staying at tonight?"

With an I-got-the-victory smile on her face, Nettie said, "It sure is."

"I've been trying to reach this man for weeks but haven't been able to get to him. How on earth did you get this number?"

Nettie pranced around the room, strutting like a fat rat with the keys to a cheese factory. "My cousin's boyfriend's aunt lives next door to the couple who took Mr. White in for the night."

"Well aren't you quite the investigator," Landon said as he got so excited he pulled Nettie to him and gave her a quick hug. He put the number in his pants pocket. "I won't call unless I miss him at the meeting, but thank you so much."

"This is going to work, Pastor Landon. I can feel it."

He headed toward the door, opened it, and then turned around, shaking his head in bewilderment. "I could kiss you, Nettie Johnson." As the words came out of his mouth, he knew it had been a mistake. Nettie was his employee, and he had no romantic designs on her. He had just been so thrilled at how tenaciously she had pursued Mr. White. After that, Landon knew that he and Nettie would be able to accomplish any goal they set their minds to.

As Nettie stood in Landon's office watching him walk away from her, she wished that he would be a man of his word and open that door back up and give her a kiss. But she knew that wasn't going to happen any time soon, so she busied herself with cleaning his office. Pastor Landon was a dynamic preacher and a born leader, but he had no organizational skills at all. That was the reason she quit her job two months ago and came to work at the church . . . well, that and because she loved him and wanted him to succeed in everything he laid his hands to.

Nettie sat down at Pastor Landon's desk to organize the papers he had scattered all over the place, but the first paper she picked up was a letter from Shar Gracey, and it froze her to the core.

> My Dearest Landon,
>   I must be the biggest fool to ever leave Chicago. I miss you and ma and pa so much that some nights I cry myself to sleep. I don't feel as if I'm doing much of anything while I'm touring and traveling on these wicked roads. Mr. Dorsey still hasn't let me lead a song. We sleep outside more than we are offered a room for comfort. And last night, two white men almost beat Matthew James to death . . .

Nettie could read no more. She put the letter down as she realized that she would have to do something drastic to get Landon's mind off of Shar Gracey. She just didn't know what in the world she could do. So, she prayed for a miracle. Just one little miracle that would finally turn things in her favor.

Landon sat through the meeting and listened intently at everything Walter F. White had to say. White was so fair skinned that he'd often been mistaken for a white man. This aided his success as secretary of the NAACP and his primary cause, which was to stop the lynching of colored people. Lynching had been outlawed, but the South was hard to tame and the Klan refused to stop killing.

Landon was impressed with White, but not just because of his ability to argue against lynching. White had been instrumental in blocking the segregationist Judge John J. Parker's nomination by President Herbert Hoover to the U.S. Supreme Court. And Landon didn't know any other colored man who could lay claim to something like that.

Based on his speech, Landon could tell that White was very passionate about his purpose. The man would stop at nothing until he had accomplished his goal. But every so often Mr. White's speech turned to the Jim Crow laws of segregation. It was right there, that Landon hoped he and Mr. White could do some business. Although Jim Crow laws were not necessarily in effect in Chicago, his people had nonetheless been segregated to the Black Belt and were expected to live in unsanitary conditions. It was for this very reason that more children in the Black Belt were dying than in any other part of Chicago. And Landon was passionate about that.

When Walter White finished speaking, the deacons passed the collection plate around. Landon put three dollars in the plate. He was a regular contributor to the NAACP and considered it an honor to help fund this cause. After the benediction was stated, Landon got out of his seat and walked to the front of the church. White was standing by the front pew, shaking hands and talking with people as they passed by him. Landon sat down on the front pew and waited for the line to dwindle down.

Once White had shaken the hand of the last man in line, Landon stood back up and walked over to him. "I'm honored to finally meet you, sir. My name is Landon Norstrom."

White shook his hand while asking, "You and I are supposed to meet tonight, am I right, Pastor?"

Landon nodded. "Yes, we are."

"Well, Pastor Norstrom, you sure have a persistent secretary."

Landon smiled. "She's very passionate about our mission."

"And what is your mission? Or better yet, what kind of help do you need from me for your mission?"

Landon looked around the sanctuary. There were still too many people in the room for him to speak freely. He hated feeling paranoid, but some colored people were so jealous of the advancement of anyone other than themselves that they got in the way and made trouble before any real progress could be made. "Is there someplace where we can speak privately?"

White turned to Pastor Jones and asked, "May we use your office for a moment?"

Pastor Jones patted Walter White on the shoulder. "Sure thing. It's yours for as long as you need it."

They went into Pastor Jones's office and Secretary White closed the door. They sat down in the two worn leather chairs in front of the desk. "Now, what do you have going on that you think we can help with?"

Landon leaned forward, excited to have an audience with a man that he admired greatly. "I've been working with the people in my community on housing. The white folks in this city have us living on top of each other in deplorable conditions."

"Yeah but so many of our people migrated to Chicago that there isn't enough housing for everyone. From what I hear, the housing authority will be putting up high-rise apartments to help with this problem," Secretary White said.

"You are correct about that, but I don't think those high-rises are the answer. Those apartments are meant to house low-income people."

"A lot of our people can't afford to pay the high prices these homeowners are renting their homes for. That's why so many are sharing houses. Shouldn't they receive some type of help by way of low-income housing?"

"Low-income housing might be the answer for some of our chronically unemployed. The depression has hit our neighborhood the hardest. But some of our people can afford better. They want to own nice homes just like anyone else. A couple in my church have spent years saving money in order to buy a nice home. They are educated and professional.

"So, I thought they would be the perfect test case for moving our people out of the Black Belt. But when they tried to purchase the home of their choice, the owner refused to sell it to them."

"What reason did the owners give for not wanting to sell the home?" White asked.

"They said that they didn't want to anger their neighbors by selling their home to a bunch of coloreds."

"That certainly is troubling, but to be truthful, Pastor Norstrom, our brothers and sisters in the South are still doing far worse than the people in the Black Belt. Your community is worried about housing, while I'm still trying to stop the lynching that's going on in the South."

"I know that you are dedicated to the problems in the South, and I commend you for the job you're doing on that. But I know that you also agree with me that separate is not equal. And if we are being denied housing strictly because of color, that isn't right."

"I agree that it's not right, Pastor Norstrom. But what can the NAACP do to help?"

"I want to sue the city of Chicago."

White shook his head, "I don't know if that's a good idea. There's no precedent to say we'd win the case."

"What about the case that Charles Houston and that Thurgood Marshall just won in Baltimore, Maryland?"

"Thurgood asked Charles to help him with that case. Donald Murray's case was perfect for Maryland because he was more than qualified to attend that university. And Judge O'Dunne agreed with us. He ruled that Murray had been rejected solely on the basis of race."

"The Barneses' case is perfect for Chicago. This family is professional. They have been good citizens in the community, and they have enough money to buy the house. I'm telling you, this case is a winner." Landon was excited just thinking about what a case like that could mean for the people in his community.

Secretary White quietly contemplated Landon's words and then said, "Okay, I'll tell you what . . . Charles will be in Chicago next week. I'll tell him to put you on his calendar. If you can convince him to take on your case, then I'm in."

Charles H. Houston was counsel for the NAACP. This was more than Landon could have hoped for. "Thank you so much, Secretary White. And if he doesn't already have a place to stay, I have a spare bedroom in my house."

"We appreciate that, Pastor." White stood up, signaling that the meeting was over.

Landon stood and shook White's hand. "You won't regret this. Tell Attorney Houston that I look forward to meeting with him next week." As soon as those words were out of Landon's mouth, he realized that he hadn't planned on being in Chicago next week. He'd wanted to leave town in the morning in order to travel to Tennessee. But Landon knew that there was no way he would be prepared for a meeting with the great Charles H. Houston if he was traveling back and forth instead of putting this case together.

Landon really wanted to go to Shar and make sure she was okay. His heart sank when he'd read her letter. She sounded as if she were headed into a depression, and he couldn't bear to think of the deplorable conditions in which she was living. But Shar had willingly decided to go on the road, while the people in the Black Belt wanted out but couldn't get out. He owed it to them to stay there and help bring them out of the so-called Promised Land.

As he sat down to write Shar another letter, he prayed that she was comforted by his words of love and adoration. Each of his letters had explained the situation in Chicago, so he hoped she understood that only the business of God could keep him from her at this time. As soon as he had a handle on what he hoped would become the *Barnes v. Chicago* case, he would go to Shar and bring her back home with him.

9

In the week since Matthew's beating, Shar had been inconsolable. They had traveled to Tennessee in order to take Matthew home. Once they arrived, they located several boardinghouses because Mr. Dorsey decided to stay and perform at a few of the local churches. But Shar's heart wasn't in it.

She had written to Landon and told him how she was feeling. She'd even told him where she would be staying in hopes that he would come see her, or at least write to her. But so far, he hadn't done either. Tears rolled down Shar's face as she contemplated the fact that she had stayed away from Landon too long. And he had lost interest in her, or maybe he'd even found someone else to love. Shar couldn't blame Landon for that . . . what man would wait around for months on end for his woman to come back home?

The way she was feeling right then reminded her of how low she'd felt after being knocked out of the Miss Bronze America competition after placing in the semi-finals. Shar's mother had spent the last bit of money they had to purchase the material for Shar's dress. She had wanted to win that competition to pay her mama back, but instead they had fallen further behind in their bills and had to take on more day work to make ends meet. "It's not fair," she whispered.

"What's not fair?" Emma Jean asked as she came into the room she shared with Shar.

Startled, Shar jumped. She then sat up in bed and pulled the cover close to her chest. "Don't you knock?"

"We share this room, remember? Although, you do seem to be in it a lot more than I am. What's going on, Shar? Have you been crying again?"

Shar turned her head and wiped the tears from her face.

Emma Jean sat down on the edge of the bed. Her voice was sympathetic as she said, "Look, Shar, I know that what happened with Matthew was awful, but it could have been worse."

"How could it have been worse? Matthew's arm is broken, and he can't play the guitar."

"He's still alive and his arm will heal. In the meantime his brother, Nicoli James, has stepped in and offered to play the guitar for us."

Shar grabbed some tissue and blew her nose. "I didn't know Matthew had a brother."

"He showed up last night." A big grin spread across Emma Jean's face as she added, "And girl, he is so handsome, I could hardly remember the words to the song we were singing for drooling over him." Emma Jean then began fanning herself as if she needed to cool down.

Laughing as she watched Emma Jean fan herself, Shar said, "Nobody is that handsome." Although she remembered drooling over Landon Norstrom a few times while sitting in that choir stand back home.

"You just need to get out of this bed and come see for yourself."

The laughter stopped as Shar thought about the days that she had spent as a prisoner of the boardinghouse she was in.

She'd stayed in that bed for the last three days, only getting up to use the bathroom. "I don't know, Emma Jean. I feel bad that you all are out singing every night, and I'm stuck in here. But every time I think about leaving, I imagine all these terrible things happening to us."

"Well, nothing has happened to us these last few days. Maybe God will provide peace for us during the rest of the tour. Just look at this nice boardinghouse we're staying in. If God didn't help us find this nice lady, then who did?"

"Mrs. Smith is nice to us," Shar agreed.

"You know what I think?" Emma Jean asked.

"What?"

"I think God has placed Mrs. Smith into your life to be your angel."

"What do you mean?"

"Open your eyes, Shar. Mrs. Smith didn't shut the door in our faces when we asked to rent the room. Matter of fact, she seems to be waiting on you hand and foot. Bringing you break-fast and dinner when you don't get up to get it yourself."

"I didn't ask her to do that."

"That's just what I mean. Mrs. Smith did that stuff for you, simply because she can tell that you're hurting and wants to help."

Shar's eyes filled with tears again. "She has been trying to make me smile. I think she feels bad about what happened to us in Mississippi."

"In case you haven't noticed, Mrs. Smith is white."

"Yeah, so?"

"These is good white folks. That's why I say she is your angel. I'm telling you, Shar, God directed us to her house."

When Shar didn't respond, Emma Jean said, "Come on, girl, get out of this bed and let's go. We're singing at a Baptist church, and you know they won't allow our musicians to play. So we are going to need all the best voices in the choir tonight."

Shar admired Emma Jean. She had a beautiful voice and knew why she wanted to sing: in order to bring hope to God's people. Shar knew that her voice was beautiful also. She loved gospel music, but she couldn't say with total conviction why she wanted to sing. Did she want to help people . . . bring them hope, like Emma Jean? Or did singing gospel music bring hope to her only? "I don't know if I'm ready to come back to the choir tonight," she finally said.

Emma Jean stood up. "Suit yourself. But if you keep lying in this bed, you won't be able to sell that sheet music for Mr. Dorsey."

Emma Jean had a point. She might not know why she had chosen to sing gospel music, but she did know why she was on this tour. "You're right. I need to clear my mind and get back to work. Wait for me downstairs. I'll be ready in thirty minutes."

Shar climbed out of bed. She then walked down the hall, got into the shower, and decided to forget about her troubles. However, forgetting about her troubles also meant forgetting about Landon. Because his absence in her life was troubling her more than she ever thought possible.

As the warm water caressed her body, Shar turned to the one person who she knew she could request an audience with any time of the day or night. "Dear Lord, I feel so weak right now. I don't know what to do, and I don't have anyone but you to turn to. I need You to help me." As she said those words, she thought about the unanswered cry for help that she had sent to Landon. She was comforted with the knowledge that God would never ignore her.

Getting out of the shower, Shar put on her best dress and headed downstairs. Emma Jean was waiting for her by the kitchen because they were not allowed to sit in the living room.

Nor were they allowed to enter or leave out of the front door of the home of these good white folks. She and Emma Jean left out of the back door and walked the two miles to the church they were singing at that afternoon.

By the time they made it to Marsdale Baptist Church, Sallie looked like she was about to lose her mind from worry. When Shar walked through the door, she breathed a sigh of relief and said, "Thank God. Gal, I was hoping that you'd get your act together and show up here tonight."

"I hope I'm not too late, Mrs. Sallie. I didn't think you'd be selling the sheet music until after service."

"Don't worry about the sheet music. Mahalia is stuck in Chicago. She won't be able to sing tonight, so Mr. Dorsey wants you to sing. I was just getting ready to send someone after you."

Shar couldn't believe what she was hearing. She had traveled from city to city, state to state with this tour for over a year and had not once been allowed to lead a song. And then on the night that she had all but decided to stay in bed and cry her eyes out, she gets the opportunity to lead a song that Mahalia Jackson was supposed to sing. "Will I be singing 'Never Turn Back'?" Shar asked with excitement in her voice.

Sallie laughed, "How many times do I have to tell you that you don't know enough about life to sing that song?"

"B-but that's the one I had been practicing."

"Now you can practice this one." Sallie handed her the sheet music and then said, "And hurry up. You've got an hour."

Shar looked down at the sheet music and was astounded to see that the song she was supposed to lead was "Precious Lord, Take My Hand." This was the song Mr. Dorsey wrote after his wife and newborn died within days of one another. Mr. Dorsey had been in St. Louis when he received the telegram about his wife dying in childbirth. He rushed home only to discover that the baby had died also. As the rumor went, Mr. Dorsey locked himself in the house and almost had a nervous breakdown. But while he was alone, pouring out his heart to God, he wrote the song "Precious Lord, Take My Hand."

Mr. Dorsey was in the sanctuary with the rest of the choir rehearsing the songs. Shar didn't want to embarrass herself in front of him and the choir by trying to lead a song she had never practiced before, so she rushed outside. She stood behind the church and began to sing . . .

Precious Lord, take my hand.
Lead me on, help me stand.
I am tired, I am weak, I am worn.

As she sang the words, Shar realized that either Mr. Dorsey or Mrs. Sallie knew exactly how she had been feeling these last few days . . . tired, weak, and worn. She had even just prayed and told God that she was weak and needed help. She was feeling this song, like it was a part of her soul. Tears streamed down her face as she opened her mouth and belted out . . .

Through the storm, through the night,
Lead me on to the light,
Take my hand, precious Lord
Lead me home.

"Bravo, bravo," a man said while clapping his hands and walking toward her.

Shar had closed her eyes as she sung the last verses of the song. She hadn't seen anyone standing behind the church building and was startled when he started clapping. "I'm sorry, I didn't know anyone was coming back here."

"You don't need to apologize to me. I was the one listening in on your performance."

Shar wiped the tears from her eyes. As she did that she was able to clearly see the man walking toward her. He was gorgeous. High yellow with shiny black hair that had been parted down the middle and slicked back. With that thin, trim mustache he looked like a colored Clark Gable.

He stuck his hand out to her, "I'm Nicoli James, Matthew's brother."

She shook his hand and said, "I'm Shar Gracey." Oh my God, Emma Jean was right. This man is too fine. Shar normally didn't go for high yellow men. They were much too pretty for her taste, but something in Nicoli's dark eyes mesmerized her.

"Well, Miss Shar Gracey, you sing like an angel. I almost raised my hands and shouted hallelujah."

He was still holding her hand. She slid it out of his grip and stepped around him. "I guess I'd better get back in there. I need to practice this song with the choir."

"Honey, trust me, you don't need no practice. Even Mahalia Jackson, on her best day, never sounded as good as you do singing that song."

"I don't think Mr. Dorsey feels that way. He rather likes the sound of Mahalia's voice. When she sings, I sell twice the number of sheet music than I do on any other night," Shar told him with conviction. She thought he was kind to compliment her so, but she didn't need him lying to her about sounding better than Mahalia.

"All right, you go on in. I'll be listening for your sweet voice once the program gets going."

As Shar turned to walk away, she wondered why Nicoli wasn't headed back into the church with her. No one else was behind the church building, and Nicoli wasn't practicing his guitar; he didn't even have it with him. Besides, Marsdale Baptist wouldn't allow him to play it today anyway. But she didn't know him well enough to butt into his business, so she didn't ask any questions.

Shar went into the sanctuary with the rest of the choir members and began practicing the songs with everyone else. When she added her voice with the others, Mr. Dorsey suddenly held up his hands and stopped the choir from singing. He turned to Shar and said, "Now I know what has been missing these last few days. Nice to have you back, Miss Gracey."

Wow! Did he just say that her voice made the difference in his choir? Shar was truly humbled to hear Mr. Dorsey say that, since she hadn't heard a word of praise from him in months. "Thank you, sir. I'm happy to be back."

"All right, now let's finish this rehearsal before the members start showing up for the afternoon service," Thomas Dorsey said.

They rehearsed three more songs and then broke for prayer. Nicoli walked into the sanctuary as they were getting ready to hold hands and bow their heads. He came and stood next to Shar and grabbed her hand just as Mr. Dorsey began the prayer. Shar had to admit that she didn't hear a word of Mr. Dorsey's prayer because she could hear nothing over the loud flutter of her heart as Nicoli squeezed her hand.

10

Chicago Defender—June 6, 1936
The Problem of Better Housing
By Robert R. Taylor

No single group has a greater stake in the benefits
to be derived from a sound national housing program
than the Negro. He will be one of the chief benefi-
ciaries of a well-administered housing plan because of
several obvious reasons:

First, the Negro is an underpaid worker and his
wages are generally too low to warrant his paying
a normal economic rent for housing. Second, most
properties occupied by Negroes are owned by absen-
tee landlords, whose sole interest is to extract the
maximum revenue while offering minimum services
and maintenance.

Third, racial discrimination forces Negroes to
accept disgraceful housing facilities, which are almost
always located in decaying or slum districts. Fourth,
in bargaining for the use of property the Negro is
denied advantages accruing from the application of
the fundamental laws of demand and supply because
of the restricted residential zone in which he is
huddled . . .

Landon and Robert had parted ways a few years back on the housing issue. Robert believed that Negroes would be helped if more low-income housing projects were built. But Landon believed that low-income housing would increase the Negroes' dependence on the government and stifle economic growth. However, Landon agreed with everything Robert had to say in his article. Especially the part about Negroes being denied their bargaining rights for better housing because their buying ability was restricted to certain residential zones. Homeownership outside of the Black Belt was the key to opening the community's eyes to better days that were just on the horizon.

Landon was scheduled to meet with William Toliver in a few minutes. He had hoped the NAACP chief counsel, Charles H. Houston, would be meeting with him today. But Houston was knee deep in another board of education case like the one he'd just won in Baltimore with Thurgood Marshall. Landon understood what the primary interest of the NAACP were, however, he intended to do his very best to convince Attorney Toliver that decent housing for colored people in Chicago was just as much a civil rights issue.

There was a knock on his office door. Landon yelled, "Come in."

Nettie opened the door, grinning from ear to ear. She skipped into the room with her hands behind her back. "So, how are you feeling on this most important day?"

"I've just been sitting here praying for God to open Mr. Toliver's eyes so that he can see that we need their help."

"I have faith in you, Pastor. You'll convince him."

"From your mouth to God's ears," Landon said while pointing heavenward.

"Well, I guess we'll soon see because Mr. Toliver is here. Are you ready for the meeting?"

"I pray that I am."

"I'll send him in," she said as she began walking out of the office.

Landon picked some envelopes off his desk and handed them to Nettie. "Can you put these in the mail today?"

"Sure thing, boss." She closed the door behind her.

Landon rubbed his hands together and lifted his head toward heaven. "Lord, You and You alone have seen me and my people through a mighty long list of injustices. Help us with this one as well."

As Landon finished his request to his Lord and Savior, his door opened, and William Toliver walked in carrying a brown leather briefcase. Landon stood up and shook the man's hand. "Thank you for coming to see about us, sir."

"It's my pleasure, Pastor Norstrom. The NAACP is very interested in the plight of colored people in Chicago. We have heard of your struggles and want to help. But we need to make it clear that our resources are still very thin."

Landon understood what he was saying. Toliver was a southerner. And many southerners were still migrating to Chicago, believing that this was some sort of Promised Land for colored people. But Landon was going to show Toliver a land that Moses would have been ashamed to lead his people into. The Black Belt wasn't flowing with milk and honey, but with trash and baby-killing debris.

Landon put on his hat and coat and said, "Let's take a walk. I'd like to introduce you to a few people." They stepped outside of the church onto State Street. The Black Belt consisted of about thirty blocks of small dilapidated houses. Young and old men hung out on porch steps or the corner grocer or they just walked aimlessly up and down the streets. Trash was piled high in front of most of the homes. Rats the size of cats could be seen nibbling on the trash as they walked down the street.

A rat scurried toward Toliver. The man jumped as the rodent passed by him to get to a pile of trash on the other side of the street. Toliver said, "Don't you all have mandatory garbage collection requirements in Chicago?"

Landon smiled. He hadn't even knocked on his first door and the man was already getting the picture. "They say their resources are limited, and we are last on their list. So we can go weeks without seeing a garbage truck."

They turned the corner and walked past a few houses until they were standing in front of a one-story, single-family dwelling that had seen better days . . . much better days. "This is the home of Mr. and Mrs. James and Penny Flowers. They are allowing us to look through their home today because they believe it will help you folks at the NAACP see what's really going on. But Mr. and Mrs. Flowers are proud people. They've worked hard for what they have, so try not to say anything against the home. Let's just let them guide us through it and tell us what they need help with. Okay?"

"I'm not here to make snap judgments. I want to observe and take my finding back to the home office," Toliver said with conviction.

"Well, okay then, let's go." Landon knocked on the door and then waited until it was opened. "Good day, Mrs. Flowers." He gave the older woman a hug. "Thank you for your willingness to help with our cause."

"It seems like everybody's got some cause or another these days," the old woman said as she stepped aside to allow Landon and William Toliver into her home. "But if you young folks wasn't always on your soapbox, I reckon wouldn't much get done."

They took off their hats and stepped in. "God has blessed you with a right understanding, Mrs. Flowers. And we sure appreciate you," Landon said. He then turned toward his guest and told Mrs. Flowers, "This is Mr. William Toliver. He's an attorney with the NAACP."

"Well ain't we steppin' in high cotton today. We got a pastor and a big time lawyer in our home. Would you gentlemen like a cold glass of water?"

"You're very kind to offer, but I need to get Mr. Toliver through our neighborhood as quickly as possible. So, if you don't mind. We'd just like to see the house and get going to the next."

"All right, Pastor. Well let's get started," she said as she began to slowly move away from the door.

"Where is your husband?" Landon asked.

"Oh, James went down to the church to stand in the bread line. He hates doing it, but he lost that good factory job a month ago, and well," she hunched her shoulders as she said, "we still got to eat."

Landon put his hand on Mrs. Flowers's shoulder. "My church has been putting together food baskets for displaced workers. I'll make sure you get one of those packages this week."

Her eyes got misty as she said, "Thank you, Pastor, we sure can use it." As she began walking through the house, she added, "James and I have worked nearly 'bout all of our lives. We ain't never asked nobody for nothing. But this here depression has hit us hard."

"You're not alone there, Mrs. Flowers. About fifty percent of the colored population lost their jobs due to this depression. But I believe that things are about to turn around. We're only a few short years from 1940. Going into a new decade has to be a sign of things turning around for us," Landon said with hope in his heart and conviction in his voice.

They walked through the house as Mrs. Flowers showed them holes in the floor as the floorboards had rotted out. There were buckets of water on the floor in the living room, kitchen, and both bedrooms. Mrs. Flowers said that the buckets were there to catch the rain from the leaking roof. There was another bucket underneath the sink. The pipes were leaking.

After stepping over buckets and holes in the floor, Toliver turned to Mrs. Flowers and asked, "How long have you lived here?"

"We were in a boardinghouse the first three years after we arrived in Chicago, but we've been in this house for two years come this spring."

Toliver's mouth hung open. When he regained his voice he said, "You've been in this house less than two years, and you have all these problems?"

"The previous tenants let me keep their buckets. The roof has been leaking for a while now, but the owner won't fix it. But believe it or not, we're the lucky ones."

"Why would you say that?" Landon asked, wondering why anyone who'd been forced to live in such conditions would consider themselves lucky.

"We have running water and plumbing," Mrs. Flowers told them matter-of-factly.

As they toured some of the other homes they discovered that it was exactly as Mrs. Flowers had said. Many of the residents of the Black Belt had no running water or plumbing. They were forced to do their business outside. After touring about five homes and viewing the conditions on the outside of the homes, Landon figured William Toliver had seen enough. "Let's head back to my office."

Once they were seated in Landon's office, Toliver said, "Okay, I see that the conditions are bad. I'm used to seeing homes in such poor conditions in the South, but I honestly thought you all had it so much better."

"Some of us do. There are homes in the Black Belt that are in good condition and well maintained, but those are few and far between. We have about eight or ten people per household and that's fine for the citizens who can do no better. We're not asking the government for a handout. What I want is to be able to get decent housing for families who will be able to afford the homes and maintain them."

"And you've already tried this with one couple?"

"That's correct. They are the reason I need help from the NAACP. The Barnes family has the perfect case to bring to trial. They are educated, with good jobs and money in the bank. They saved for years to be able to buy a home. They hoped that by the time they had enough money to purchase a home that things would be different and they wouldn't be forced to buy a home in the already overcrowded Black Belt."

"But the home owner refused to sell to them because they're colored," Toliver finished Landon's statement for him.

"Yes. So, what do you think? Can you help us?"

Toliver leaned back in his seat and rubbed his chin as he pondered the situation. He then leaned forward and said, "I'll tell you what. If you can get me at least ten cases like this, I might be able to convince Mr. Houston to go to trial."

"Here's the thing, Mr. Toliver, I'm just not sure if I can come up with ten eligible couples who have saved enough money to purchase a home."

"There has to be nine other credit-worthy people in this town with good jobs. You'll just have to find them."

"And what if I can't?" Landon asked as if he was Abraham pleading with God about his ability to find ten righteous people in Sodom and Gomorrah.

Toliver stood up and put his hat back on. "You have to. This place is still considered the Promised Land by most colored southerners. So, if I'm going to convince the NAACP to exhaust our resources on a Chicago case, we have to have ample proof of discrimination."

Landon stood up and walked Toliver out. When they were at the front door of the church, Landon shook the man's hand. "I thank you for your time. I hope to see you again real soon."

"You get us some more qualified couples who've been refused housing outside of the Black Belt and we will go to bat for you."

As Landon stood at the door watching Toliver walk away, his shoulders slumped with the knowledge that it would probably take him years to find nine more qualified colored people.

"What's wrong with you? I thought the meeting was going good." Nettie asked as she walked up behind him.

"He wants me to find several more qualified cases before we move to trial."

"So, I ask again, what's wrong?" Nettie didn't understand why Landon seemed so dejected.

Landon had never discussed his personal life with Nettie and didn't feel comfortable doing so now, but he really needed to unburden himself. He turned to her and said, "I had planned to leave town after my meeting with Mr. Toliver. I have a good friend who needs me. But now I feel as if I will be letting so many people down if I leave at a time when there is still so much to be done."

"Well, we already have one couple. The Barnses are perfect. So, all we need to do is find a few more."

"Nine more," Landon corrected her.

"Okay, well then we'll find nine more people interested in home ownership. That shouldn't be too hard to do," Nettie said with her normal eager-beaver attitude.

But Landon wasn't catching her fever this time. He told her, "We're in the middle of the worst depression this country has ever seen. It won't be so easy to find nine gainfully employed colored people with enough money saved to purchase a home." He rubbed his temples as he said more to himself than anyone else, "I really need to go see about Shar."

Nettie put a hand on Landon's shoulder. She gave him her best I'm-here-for-you smile as she said, "If you don't mind me saying so, Pastor Landon, you simply can't be all things to all people. Now we have babies dying at a higher rate on our side of town than any other part of this city because of the poor conditions they live in. We need to get as many people out of here as possible. Then once this area isn't so crowded, we can get it cleaned up for the remaining residents."

Landon knew Nettie was right. He had a duty to this community. What he was doing would save lives. He just felt so bad about letting Shar down. He knew she wanted to see him, but she would have to be content with receiving another letter from him for now. Landon was on a mission from God and couldn't turn back now, not even for love. He just hoped that Shar would be patient with him.

11

Shar could hardly believe how things had changed. Ever since the night that Mahalia couldn't make it to Tennessee, Shar had been leading Mr. Dorsey's songs at every event. And then she would come out to the fellowship hall and sell the sheet music like nobody's business. Shar was actually happy again and enjoying the tour as she hadn't before. In truth, though, she didn't think her newfound enjoyment had much to do with the fact that she was leading songs, but more to do with the fact that Nicoli was now on the tour and putting a smile on her face.

Shar turned from her seat in the choir stand and looked back to where Nicoli was standing, strumming his guitar and looking every bit like the music man he was born to be.

"If you don't concentrate on this song and stop staring at that man, Mr. Dorsey is going to throw you out of the choir," Emma Jean warned as she nudged Shar with her elbow.

They were singing "Old Ship of Zion." Sallie was the lead on the song, so all Shar had to do was to sing the backup with the choir. It was one of those repetitive songs, so it wasn't hard to keep track, even though her mind was somewhere else.

Sallie sang, "I got on board early one morning . . . I got on board."

And then the choir sang, "It's the old ship of Zion. It's the old ship of Zion. It's the old ship of Zion."

Sallie sang, "I got on board early one morning . . . I got on board."

And then the choir sang, "Ain't no danger in the water. Ain't no danger in the water. Ain't no danger in the water."

Mr. Dorsey banged on the piano and Nicoli played his guitar like a man with a story to tell, then Sallie took off. She talked to the audience, engaged them in the story while the congregation got happy. They stood up and clapped their hands. Shar forgot about everything but the anointing that was flowing through the room. She got so happy, she started shouting in the choir stand.

When service was over Shar found herself selling nothing but "Old Ship of Zion." Sallie put her foot in that song, and Nicoli's guitar-playing took it to another level. Musicians rushed to buy the sheet music because they thought they'd be able to recreate what just happened in service at their own church. But there was only one Sallie Martin. And there definitely was only one Nicoli James.

"How much longer do you have to sell this stuff?" Nicoli asked as he came up behind her.

Shar jumped. She hadn't seen Nicoli and thought he was outside, doing whatever he did behind church buildings. "You scared me, you sneak."

He grabbed her hand. "Go for a walk with me?" Nicoli asked.

"I can't. I have to do my job." Shar pulled her hand away and looked around the room, making sure that no one was watching them.

"From what I hear, they only pay you two dollars a week, while Sallie is already up to about ten dollars a week."

"Sallie does a whole lot more for Mr. Dorsey than I do. I'm grateful that I am making anything at all. I need the money to send back to my parents."

Nicoli's eyes bugged out of his head as he asked, "You're doing all this work and you don't even get to keep the money?"

Shar shook her head as she turned to a customer and sold another copy of "Old Ship of Zion." When she turned back to Nicoli she said, "My mama has tuberculosis. She needs medicine. What's left over helps with the bills."

"Nicoli James, if you don't leave that gal alone so she can sell that sheet music, I'm gon' skin you alive," Sallie barked as she pulled Nicoli away from Shar.

Shar giggled as she watched Nicoli being hauled away by the very forceful Mrs. Sallie Martin. She then got back to the business of selling the sheet music. By the time she had finished and everyone had left the church, Shar had sold a hundred sheets of music. Seventy of those had been "Old Ship of Zion."

When they arrived at the boardinghouse they were staying at for the night, the woman informed them that she only had two beds left. So, the women shared the beds, while the men were stuck sleeping on the bus. This was the part of touring that Shar didn't like. The uncertainty of where she would lay her head made her ill at times. She knew for certain that if Nicoli hadn't joined the tour when he had, she would have gone back home by now.

After dinner, Shar, Emma Jean, and a few other choir members sat in the parlor practicing some of their songs. When they finished practicing, everyone left the parlor except Shar, Geraldine, and Emma Jean. The three of them stayed so they could gossip and giggle.

In the midst of giggling over a crack Geraldine had made about Sallie Martin, Emma Jean spilled her lemonade on her blouse. She and Geraldine then went upstairs so that Emma Jean could change.

That's when Nicoli approached Shar again and asked, "You want to take that walk now?"

"We don't know anything about this area."

"If you've seen one colored neighborhood, you've seen them all. And besides, I'm about to go crazy just sitting around here."

Hesitantly, Shar said, "I don't know. Mr. Dorsey don't like for us to go off on our own."

"Girl, you sound like a broken record. Every time I talk to you, you always telling me what Mr. Dorsey or Mrs. Sallie said." He shook his head as if he was disappointed in her. "I'm gon' have to leave you alone and find myself a real woman." He started to walk away.

Shar put her hand on his shoulder. "Wait. Don't be like that. I'm twenty years old, so I am a woman. I just don't want to get into no trouble."

"How you gon' get in trouble when you're with me?" As Nicoli said these words he puffed out his chest like he was a big bad kind of man that didn't nobody mess with.

"Oh, so I guess you're not afraid of nothing?" Emma Jean asked with challenge in her voice as she walked back into the room.

He turned to face her and said, "I'm not afraid of you."

Emma Jean put her hands on her hips and let her backbone slip as she swayed her ample hips from side to side. "I don't think you're afraid of me at all, Nicoli James. You just don't know how to handle a woman like me."

What was Emma Jean doing? Shar watched the woman shamelessly flirt with Nicoli. She had half a mind to tell Emma Jean how ridiculous she looked, flirting with a man who wasn't even thinking about her. But Shar glanced over at Nicoli, and he seemed more interested than she expected.

"Shar is the only scaredy cat in here. I've been trying to get her to take a walk with me, but she won't do it." Nicoli turned toward Shar as he asked Emma Jean, "What about you, Emma? Are you afraid to take a walk with me?"

Emma Jean strutted over to Nicoli and hooked her arm in his. "I sure am not. Let's go."

⁊

Shar hadn't spoken to Nicoli or Emma Jean since the day they walked out of the boardinghouse together. But it wasn't as if Emma Jean cared. She had been whispering behind Shar's back all week, telling everybody about how she stole Nicoli away from Shar. Truth be told, Shar was mortified. Nicoli had taken her mind off of Landon and the fact that she hadn't heard from him in over a month.

But now Nicoli had abandoned her, just like Landon had. Shar began to wonder if her lack of male companionship meant that something was wrong with her.

"Why in the world are you walking around here looking so down in the mouth?" Sallie asked Shar as they pulled up to the church they would be performing at that day. "You've been begging for your opportunity to lead some songs for over a year. Now that you're leading songs, you seem just as miserable as you were before."

Shar walked off the bus with Sallie. "I'm sorry, Mrs. Sallie. I've got a lot on my mind."

"Well, you better get it off your mind, if you want to keep leading these songs."

"What does the way I'm feeling have to do with my singing?" Shar protested.

"These congregations we sing to ain't no dummies. They can feel your mood. So, if you're depressed while singing a praise song . . . instead of uplifting their spirits, you're just going to depress the people. And if they're depressed, they sure won't be buying no sheet music."

When Shar first began leading songs, the sheet music was selling like ice water on a hot summer day. But once Emma Jean started messing with her, Shar noticed that the sheet music for the songs she led hardly sold at all. She had lost her inspiration and that was all there was to it. As the choir members walked into the church, Shar hung back. "I need to go pray, Mrs. Sallie. I'll catch up with you all in a minute."

On the side of the church building, there was a concrete bench. Shar sat down on it and looked heavenward. She desperately needed to feel God's love right here and right now. Landon Norstrom had given up on her, even though he'd pledged to love her for a lifetime. And more recently, Nicoli James had also walked away from her so that he could be with someone more adventurous. Shar just didn't know what was wrong with her. Her mama and dad had always said that she was the prettiest girl this side of New Orleans, but maybe men needed more than a pretty face.

Shar just didn't know what she was missing, or if she even needed to be concerned with stuff like that. So, with her head lifted she said, "Lord, I'm so confused. I feel like I'm letting You down. I'm supposed to be singing to glorify You, but I just keep thinking about my problems. I want things that I can't have, and I just need to get over it and go sing with an uplifted heart."

She took a deep breath as she tried to get her body to line up with what she knew was right. She was there to sing and to send money back home . . . not to go on walks and sit up all night talking her head off with some gorgeous guy who wasn't thinking about her two minutes after he left her presence. "Thank you, Lord, for helping me see the light. I know what

I have to do. So, I'm gon' head on into this church to sing for Your glory."

She stood up, and as she turned around to head inside the church, she came face to face with Nicoli James. "Oh, I'm sorry, I didn't know anyone else was back here," she said as she stepped around him.

"I didn't want to interrupt you. It seemed like you had a mighty powerful message to get to the Lord."

Shar didn't answer him. She hung her head and started walking.

Nicoli ran over to her, grabbed her arm, and turned her around. "Don't be like that, Shar. You haven't said a word to me all week and I miss the sound of your voice."

"I don't know why you'd be missing the sound of my voice when you've got Emma Jean whispering in your ear." The minute Shar said those words she wanted to swallow them back. She sounded like a cackling hen, and no man liked that in a woman.

"I'm just friends with Emma Jean. But I was hoping for much more than that with you, Shar Gracey." His hands traveled up her arm and back.

A sensation went up Shar's spine that she'd never felt before. She instantly knew that no good would come from what she was feeling, so she snatched her arm away from Nicoli. "You're a slick talker, Mr. James. But I know about men like you. You're only after one thing."

"You're wrong about me, Shar. For years, I've been looking for one lady that I could give my all to. I thought you might be the one. But if you won't even give me a chance . . . " His words trailed off as if he'd run out of things to say at the mere thought of not being with Shar.

With hands on hips, Shar demanded, "How can I give you a chance when you running around here with Emma Jean?"

"I told you that I'm just friends with that girl. Emma Jean don't mean nothing to me."

She harrumphed. "Well, then maybe you ought to tell that to her. Because she thinks she's something." Shar pointed at the concrete bench she'd just been sitting on and said, "I just got finished praying to the good Lord, asking Him to help me forget about you, Nicoli James. So, that's what I aim to do." She turned and strutted away from him.

Shar was able to get in a few minutes of rehearsal before service began. Then she sat real still and listened to every word of the reverend's message, hoping that he would have some words of wisdom that would cause her to stop thinking about Nicoli James. But the message that night had been about being a servant and allowing God to use the talents He'd blessed you with. She was already doing that, so Shar hadn't seen where the preached word helped her much that night.

Not wanting to witness Emma Jean and Nicoli getting cozy in the back of the bus, Shar rushed to the bus before the other choir members walked out of the church and slid into a window seat directly behind the bus driver. She turned her head toward the window and kept her eyes on the church building. Shar wasn't about to give Nicoli and Emma Jean the satisfaction of watching them get on the bus together.

As the people started getting on the bus, Shar didn't turn around so she didn't know who was on the bus yet. Then the driver yelled at someone. "Hey, are you coming with us or staying here?"

"I'm coming," Shar heard Nicoli reply.

"Well, then get on the bus. We don't have all day to wait on you."

Shar kept her face toward the window as Nicoli got on the bus. Emma Jean was probably right behind him, or they might even be holding hands as they scooted their way down the narrow aisle of the bus. No way was Shar going to watch that display.

She held her breath as someone walked up to her seat then sat down next to her. Shar couldn't help herself. She turned to see who was in the seat next to her and saw that it was Nicoli.

The look on his face was sorrowful as he said, "I never should have took that walk with Emma Jean. I'm sorry, Shar. Can you give me another chance?"

Shar opened her mouth to give him another tongue-lashing. But as she gazed into those deep, dark, and beautiful black eyes of his, she found herself saying, "You better be for real this time. Do you hear me, Nicoli?"

"Yes, ma'am," he said with a mock salute. As the bus pulled off, Nicoli put his arm around Shar's shoulder and leaned back into his seat.

12

Landon knocked on the door and then took his hat off as he waited for it to be opened. Harvey Peterson, one of his parishioners, opened the door and invited him in. "Thank you, Harvey. I appreciate you and Helen making time for me this evening," Landon said as he walked in.

"Not at all. Helen and I are honored that you would come to our home."

"Don't just leave Pastor standing in the doorway. Bring him on in here so he can have a seat," Helen called from the living room.

"You heard the lady. Let's go sit down," Harvey said as he walked into the living room.

As Landon sat down, Helen asked, "Would you like a cold glass of water?"

"Thank you, Mrs. Helen. That's mighty nice of you."

Harvey sat down across from Landon and slapped his leg. "So, what's this important business you want to discuss with us?"

Helen walked back in the room, handed Landon the glass of water, and then set a coaster on the coffee table in front of him before sitting down next to her husband.

Landon took a sip from his glass and then set it down on the coaster. He clasped his hands together as he turned toward his hosts. "You all know that I've been working with several people in the community to do something about our housing situation."

"And we thank you for what you've been doing, Pastor. Not many people seem to care about the conditions we're forced to live in," Harvey said.

"I hate going outside because with the trash collection constantly backed up, it just stinks so bad out there," Helen said.

"Mr. Taylor is working on a housing project that will help low-income families. But I think the best answer for some of our gainfully employed residents is homeownership."

Harvey shook his head. "I wouldn't buy this house if the landlord offered me money for it. The roof is leaking, the furnace is broke, and there are a host of other things wrong that the landlord refuses to fix."

"I'm not talking about buying these houses. The depression has hit the white folks just as hard as it's hit us. A lot of them have lost their homes and the bank has them up for sale."

Helen lifted a hand. "Now wait a minute, Pastor. You didn't live in Chicago when the Irish attacked the coloreds because they thought we was muscling in on their turf, but I did. And I never want to see bloodshed like we saw that summer . . . colored and white men dead in the streets for nothing. No siree, I don't want to relive that."

Holding up a hand, Landon reminded her, "That happened the summer of 1919. Things are different now. More of our people are holding public office, and I'm working with the NAACP on this." Landon didn't mention that he needed to find ten cases of housing discrimination before he'd actually have the full force of the NAACP on his side.

"Well, what do you want from us?" Harvey asked. "We don't have the money to buy one of them bank-owned homes."

"But you do have jobs. Harvey, you've been trimming my hair down at that barbershop of yours for three years. Even with the depression, folks still come in for a shape up." Landon turned to Helen and added, "And your beauty salon is getting more business than any other salon on State Street."

"What difference does that make? With the high rents we pay for this house and our shops, we're always just as broke as a homeless man begging for spare change," Harvey said.

"But if you were able to purchase a home at a reasonable price, you'd be able to save some money, right?"

"Of course, but the bank and nobody else is going to let us have one of those houses," Helen said with conviction. "I've tried that several times and I've got the permanent scars to prove it."

"But we have to give it a try, Sister Helen. We owe it to our children and grandchildren."

Helen didn't respond.

Harvey said, "So, what's your plan?"

Landon knew that he had no choice. He would have to tell them the entire plan if he had any hope of getting them on board. "You're right," Landon said. "I don't believe that the bank is going to let us buy those homes without a fight. So right now I'm looking for at least ten people who have every qualification the bank needs for homeownership. We are then going to attempt to purchase those homes I told you about. But when the bank or the homeowner says no, that's when we'll get the NAACP involved."

"And just how are they going to get involved?" Helen asked with skepticism in her voice.

"We'll go to court and sue for discrimination."

"And you think the courts don't already know that we're being discriminated against?" Harvey asked.

"It's not about them knowing. It's about providing them with so much evidence that the situation can no longer be ignored."

Harvey stood up. He walked to the window in his living room and looked outside. His eyes filled with anger at the sight before him. When he turned back around, he told Landon. "I think our children would enjoy living in one of them nice homes."

The blood drained from Helen's face as she stood. "This is just going to cause trouble, Harvey. We don't need to get involved. We have a good life. Just leave it at that."

Harvey rushed to his wife's side and pulled her into his arms. "This isn't going to be like 1919, Helen. It's been almost twenty years since all that violence occurred. You and our children deserve better than what we've got here." He stepped out of their embrace, put his hands on her shoulders, and looked her in the eye. "I couldn't rightly call myself a man if I didn't at least try to get my family a piece of this American dream."

Landon didn't think he would ever forget the intensity in Harvey's voice as he declared the dream he had for his family. Landon believed they could go all the way. He stood up and put out his hand. Harvey shook it. "You won't be sorry, Harvey. We're doing something that's going to matter, not just for us, but for generations to come." With that, Landon left the Peterson's house. With their help, he now had two case studies . . . just eight more to go.

As he stepped outside, Landon glanced down the street at John and Marlene Gracey's house. He thought back to the day that he'd stood outside their home and begged Shar to stay with him. He could really use her help right now. He missed Shar in the worst way. Some nights he lay awake remembering how beautiful she looked in that shimmering white dress. He still thought she should have won that contest. But winner or not, she was still Miss Bronze America in his book.

He hadn't heard from Shar in weeks, so he wasn't privy to her upcoming schedule. Landon decided to stop by her parents' house to see if they knew where she would be next. He had spent weeks trying to come up with more case studies with no results. He felt good about getting the Peterson's on board. But he'd feel even better if he could see Shar's smiling face.

He knocked on the door, and Marlene answered. She was holding a cloth to her mouth as she said, "Well, hello there, Reverend."

"How've you been doing, Mrs. Marlene?"

"I've been better, that's for sure," she said as she closed her front door and stepped out onto the porch. "I would invite you in, but I don't want to spread this tuberculosis." She coughed.

"Are you taking your medicine?"

"I am, but it don't seem to be getting rid of this cough none."

In Landon's haste to find out about Shar, he'd forgotten about Marlene's diagnosis. Knowing the Graceys as he did, he knew they would feel awful if Marlene spread TB throughout the community. "I don't want to keep you. I just stopped by to find out if you've heard from Shar. I want to go see her, but I don't know what city she's going to be in next."

Marlene's brows furrowed as she asked, "She didn't tell you?"

"Tell me what?"

"She's been in town for three days. The choir is singing at Pilgrim Baptist Church for the National Convention of Gospel Choirs that Mr. Dorsey puts on every year."

Shar was in town and hadn't come to see him. The news hit him hard . . . left him breathless.

"Are you okay, Reverend?"

"Thanks for telling me, Mrs. Marlene. I hope you feel better soon." He walked off the porch without saying another word.

The Pilgrim Baptist Church was located on the South Side, in an area that James J. Gentry, a local theater editor dubbed Bronzeville. The area had been so named because of the brown skin of the residents. The church was on Indian Avenue, and as Landon made his way to the church he kept wondering why Shar had stopped writing to him and why she hadn't informed him that she would be in Chicago. He'd been writing to her twice a month for over a year, but she hadn't written him in over a month. So, he had no idea where to send a letter. Had Shar been gone so long that she'd forgotten about him? Landon prayed that wasn't the case. He just didn't know what he'd do if Shar wasn't a part of his life.

The church was filled to capacity by the time he arrived. Landon took a seat in the back and waited while one choir after another sang. Mahalia Jackson sang "Precious Lord, Take my Hand." Rosetta Tharpe sang "Search Me Lord." Landon was enjoying himself as one singer after the next gave praise to the Lord. Then Shar grabbed the microphone. She began singing, "I'm Going to Live the Life I Sing About in My Song." And just like every other time that Landon heard her voice, he was swept away.

He closed his eyes and listened to the sweet sound of her voice. He could spend a lifetime listening to Shar sing praises to God. Landon imagined heaven's angels standing around Shar, helping her harmonize and singing background for her. As Shar finished her song, he opened his eyes and for the briefest moment thought he noticed Shar and the guitar player staring at each other.

When the service ended, Landon went in search of Shar. She was in the fellowship hall selling Thomas Dorsey's sheet music. He walked up behind her, tapped her on the shoulder, and as she turned around said, "Hello, stranger."

"Landon . . . " She dropped the sheet music and then bent down to pick them up. Landon bent down to help her. As they stood back up, she said, "I didn't think you'd come tonight."

"Your mother told me you were in town. I wouldn't have missed this for anything in the world. It still takes my breath away to hear you sing to the glory of God."

"But you stopped writing. I thought you were too busy to worry about some silly concert."

Landon was confused by that comment. He'd been writing to Shar ever since she left town. "I didn't stop writing. You're the one who stopped writing to me. I've been wondering why I hadn't heard from you."

"This just doesn't make any sense, Landon. I have sent you one letter after another, but I never received a response to them." She lowered her head and then continued, "I just assumed that you had lost interest in me."

They were standing in the middle of the fellowship hall, people all around them, but Landon's eyes were fixed on Shar. "How could you think I'd lost interest in you, Shar? I love you. Don't you know that?"

Shar lifted her hands to her ears. "Don't say that. Please don't say that."

"What's wrong?" Landon pulled her hands away from her ears as he asked, "Why don't you want to hear how I feel about you?"

Shar looked around. Uncomfortable with all the people in the fellowship hall, she grabbed Landon's arm and walked him outside. They stood at the bottom of the steps, and then she told him, "I don't deserve your love."

"Why would you say that?"

Shar kept her head down. She didn't answer him.

The front door of the church opened and a man stepped out with two plates of food in his hand. He said, "Hey, babe, they're feeding us tonight. I got you a plate."

Shar was still standing there with her head down. She didn't respond to the man who had just called her "babe." So, Landon turned to him and said, "Hello, I'm Pastor Landon Norstrom."

The man walked down the stairs, handed one of the plates to Shar, and then stuck his hand out to Landon. They shook as the man said, "I'm Nicoli James, Shar's fiancé."

13

"What's gotten into you?" Nettie asked as she ran into Landon's office after hearing loud banging and clanging sounds.

"I can never find anything in this office," Landon barked.

Nettie picked up the file drawer that had been pulled from the cabinet and thrown on the floor. She put it back where it belonged and then said, "I try to keep everything in order for you. Just tell me what you're looking for and I'll find it."

Landon sat down behind his desk and rolled his eyes in agitation. "I was working on my sermon for Sunday service. But I couldn't concentrate, so I decided to work on the housing project, but I can't find the file on the homes that are up for sale."

"I left that file on your desk." Nettie moved a few pieces of paper and then picked up the file and handed it to him.

Landon took it but then flung it back down on his desk. "What's the use? I've been beating my head against a wall for this project for so long and still haven't come close to getting anyone into a home yet."

"What are you talking about? You've found two eligible people."

"And I need ten. So what does that tell you?"

Nettie put her hands on her hips and gave Landon a disapproving look. "It tells me that you've got eight more to go. But based on your attitude I think you need to step back and take a break."

Landon sneered at the thought. "I can't step back. It was so all-fired important that I help people who don't even want to help themselves that I put everything I wanted on the back burner." To himself, he added, now I have nothing but this project.

"Go home, Pastor Landon. You need to get some rest."

Landon's mind had drifted back to Pilgrim Baptist Church, where he'd stood on the front steps of that church and had his heart ripped out of his chest as Shar beamed up at her fiancé.

"Did you hear me, Pastor?"

"Huh? Did you say something?"

"Go home. You've been here working all day. Don't stay late tonight. You need some rest."

Landon put his face in his hands as he tried to calm himself. When he looked up, he decided. "You're right. I've been working on this project for too long without a break. I'm going home and getting some sleep."

"I think that's an excellent idea. Get you some rest, and I'll see you tomorrow."

Landon jumped out of his seat and headed toward the door. His hand was on the knob, but he remembered something and then turned back around. "Hey, Nettie, when I give you my letters to mail, have you ever not had enough postage to mail all of the letters?"

"No, why?"

"A friend said that she hasn't received my letters lately."

Nettie hunched her shoulders and with wide-eyed innocence responded, "I can't imagine why anyone would have problems receiving your mail, but I'll check with the post office."

"Okay. I'll see you tomorrow." But the minute Landon stepped outside, he dreaded the thought of going home. Sitting down on the church stoop, he tried to figure on something to do this evening. Going to an empty house to spend another night with nothing but his passion for the community to keep him company wasn't on his to-do list. So he walked the neighborhood. Landon desperately needed to remind himself of what he was fighting for.

He'd been working so hard for the past few months, trying to do right by the people in the community that he'd let down the one person he wanted to spend a lifetime with. But Landon was having a hard time understanding how Shar didn't know how he felt about her. Maybe the truth was, Shar knew and didn't care.

She wanted Nicoli James and that was all that mattered to her. Now Landon needed to figure out what mattered to him. And as he walked block after block of the Black Belt, his conviction for his mission in life grew stronger. The men, women, and children in this neighborhood needed him, and he wasn't going to let them down.

He headed home. Turning on to his street, Landon became a bit perplexed. Although it was dark out by that time, his street appeared to be lit up like a Christmas tree. He kept walking down his street, and as he got closer to his house, Landon realized that it wasn't lights from a Christmas tree that lit his street, but a burning cross that had been erected in his yard.

So now they've come after me, Landon thought. He had seen crosses a-plenty in the South. Erected whenever the Ku Klux Klan thought a colored man had gotten too big for his britches. Landon shook his head as he thought about the day Shar's father had told him he was a day late and a dollar short. That's how he felt about this attempted intimidation from angry people who wanted things to stay the way they were.

They should have burned this cross in his yard before Shar kicked him in the teeth with her betrayal, because now he was too numb to care about it. He walked past the cross, opened his front door, went inside his house, and flopped onto his bed without taking his street clothes off. The rains came and quenched the fire outside, but the one burning in Landon's heart would be much harder to get rid of.

"What's this I hear about you and Nicoli getting engaged?" Mahalia asked as she took a seat next to Shar.

Shar rolled her eyes. "Nicoli was just jealous because my pastor came to see me the other night, so he told him that we were engaged. But I've only been seeing Nicoli for a few weeks."

"Just like a dog, marking his territory," Mahalia said.

"What territory?"

"Girl, you too wet behind the ears to know what Mahalia is talking about. That's why you don't have no business with that snake," Sallie said.

Shar ignored Sallie. She didn't have much good to say about any man. She told Mahalia, "Nicoli didn't mean anything by what he did. He knew that Pastor Landon had hurt me by not responding to my letters, so he was just trying to let him know that I done moved on."

"I've met Pastor Landon. I even had a few conversations with him concerning what he's trying to do with the housing situation in Chicago. He's a good man. Are you sure you want to mess that up?" Mahalia asked.

"Pastor Landon is the one who messed up. He left me in the lurch without so much as a by-your-leave. I can't sit around and wait on him to save the world. I need someone in my life right now."

Mahalia stood up. But before she left she said, "Now, Shar, you're younger than me, and where you're going, I done all ready been. So I'm gon' tell you straight. That Nicoli James don't have the same love for gospel music as we do. He's just like my first husband, always looking for the money and trying to see how the things in your life can benefit him."

Shar shook her head emphatically. "Nicoli isn't like that, Mahalia. I don't have no money, but he still wants to be with me. He loves me."

Mahalia sat back down. "I thought you just been seeing him for a few weeks?"

"That's right. I can't explain how it happened. I just know that he loves me and I love him right back."

Sallie rolled her eyes heavenward. She tapped Mahalia on the shoulder. "Come on, let's go practice. You can't open a closed mind."

As the two women walked away from her, Shar suspected that they thought she was the biggest fool who'd ever come north. But as Nicoli sauntered over to her, put his arms around her, and pulled her into a loving embrace, Shar stopped concerning herself with what other people thought. However, she did have a bone to pick with Nicoli. She pulled out of his embrace and sulkily asked, "Why you going around here telling everybody that we're engaged?"

"I thought we were."

"How? You never asked for my hand in marriage. And besides, we've only been going together for three weeks. We can't just up and get engaged."

The look on Nicoli's face was serious as he told her, "It don't take me two years to decide what I want, Shar. I'm not that pastor friend of yours who wants you one minute and then leaves you high and dry the next."

Sometimes, Shar wished that she had never mouthed a word of her and Pastor Landon's business. Nicoli seemed to delight in telling her just how little Pastor Landon cared about her. But maybe he was right. And maybe she needed to be with someone who knew his mind and had no trouble acting on it. "All right then, Nicoli, we're engaged. But we need to keep this just between us until we talk to my ma and pa about it."

He held up his hands. "Whatever you say, baby, whatever you say."

❦

Nettie knocked on Pastor Landon's front door. When he didn't answer, she tried the knob. It was unlocked. She thought it strange that Pastor Landon wouldn't lock his front door when there had obviously been a cross burned in his front yard the night before. She and her parents had heard about it first thing that morning, so Nettie made it her business to come and check on him.

"Pastor Landon," she called from the entryway.

He didn't answer.

She called again, "Pastor Landon? Are you here?" Please God, don't let him be dead. With little concern for her own well being, Nettie rushed through the house in search of Landon.

"If you're in here, please speak up, Pastor Landon." Desperation dripped from Nettie's voice as she made the plea.

Landon yelled from the back of the house, "Who's there?"

"It's me, Pastor. Nettie."

"Oh."

She heard the disappointment in his voice, but she didn't care. She was just grateful that the Klan hadn't strung him up or shot him and left him for dead in his own home. "We heard about what happened last night, so I came to see if you were all right."

Landon walked into the living room. He had on a long terry-cloth robe, pajama pants, and house shoes. "Why aren't you dressed?" There was distress in Nettie's voice as she viewed the disheveled look of her pastor.

"I think I'm going to stay home today. I need to rest."

With hands on hips Nettie took charge. "Stay home if you like, but you are going to sit yourself down in this kitchen so I can fix you some breakfast and then you can lay back down if you want to."

Landon sat down as he was told but said, "If I'da known you were this bossy I don't think I would have hired you."

As she scrambled eggs, Nettie smiled as she said, "You sure would have hired me. Believe it or not, you need me. And by the way, I already had that hideous cross removed from your front yard. It's going to take a while for the grass to grow back, but that's all the damage you received."

Landon rubbed his temples. "I forgot about that cross."

"How could you have forgotten about something like that?"

He laid his head on the table. "I had something else on my mind."

"Sit up, Pastor. That's enough moping around. I'm going to take care of you, and you're going to be just fine."

Landon turned around and looked at Nettie as if seeing her for the first time. "So you're going to take care of me, huh?"

"That's what I said." She put the eggs on his plate and then handed it to him. Nettie then stood behind him, smiling as he took the first bite.

14

They were on their dilapidated bus headed to Memphis for another concert. Shar leaned her head back against the headrest and closed her eyes, hoping that she'd be able to get some sleep during the bumpy ride.

"Hey baby, can I talk to you for a minute?"

As Shar opened her eyes to the sound of Nicoli calling her "baby," she almost wanted to put her finger to her lips and shush him. They were supposed to be engaged, but Nicoli still hadn't received her dad's permission, so it just didn't seem right and proper for Nicoli to be so casual with her. But nothing she said ever stopped him from doing exactly as he pleased, so Shar decided to just go with the flow. It was exciting being with a man like Nicoli, someone who took chances and wasn't always doing what was expected of him.

"I've been thinking about some things." Nicoli adjusted himself in the seat. "Now as far as I can tell, it's been your voice that has been carrying this choir from town to town."

Shar's eyes grew wide as she looked around trying to determine if anyone else heard Nicoli's bold claims about her voice.

"Don't talk like that, Nicoli. Mr. Dorsey has plenty of great singers in his choir. I'm just grateful to be here."

"Okay, okay, baby. I love your modesty, but you need a manager, somebody who will look out for your best interest . . . cause ain't nobody else doing it."

"Why you talking like this? We're just gonna make the other singers mad, and then Mr. Dorsey's gonna put me out of his choir."

Nicoli leaned back in his seat and stared at Shar as if seeing her with new eyes. "You aren't putting on, are you? You really don't know how special you are. Matter of fact, if I was managing you, I'd make sure that Dorsey gave this choir the right billing. We should be calling it," he lifted his hands in the air and spaced them apart as if viewing marquee signage. "I can see it now: Shar Gracey and the Thomas Dorsey choir."

Now she did shush him. "Hush all that foolish talk." Her family was depending on her. They needed that little bit of money she was able to send home. Shar couldn't afford to anger Thomas Dorsey with Nicoli's foolishness.

"Baby, you've got to trust me." He put his arms around her and leaned in closer as he said, "And here's something else I been pondering. We need to start putting our money together so I can get some things going for us."

The bus drove over a pothole, which shook the bus and jerked Shar out of Nicoli's embrace. She turned to him with concern in her eyes. "I don't have any money, Nicoli. I send everything I make home to my parents."

"But now that we're engaged, I think we need to be more concerned about us, rather than your folks back home."

Shaking her head vigorously, Shar spoke up, "My mama needs that money. She's in poor health, and if I can't send money home, who knows when she'll be able to get to a doctor."

"Calm down, baby." He put his arm around her again and pulled her back toward him. "I just wanted to find a way to help us, but I would never jeopardize your mama's health."

Shar breathed a sigh of relief. Nicoli wasn't trying to take money from her family; he just wanted to make things happen for them. She couldn't blame him for his ambition, now could she? "Thank you for understanding, Nicoli."

The bus stopped. Shar turned to look out the window, thinking that they had reached the farm they were all spending the night at. Shar wasn't looking forward to getting off the bus, because they wouldn't be spending the night in the farmhouse. That night, they would be sleeping in the barn with the livestock. Her home in Chicago was drafty and creaky, but at least she didn't have to share it with animals.

"Oh my God!" Nicoli shouted as he slumped down in his seat.

Shar heard the fear in Nicoli's voice and watched as he slunk down in to the seat next to her, but she couldn't grasp what was causing all the fuss. Then a rock crashed through the back window. As Shar reflexively glanced toward the back, she was shocked to see white men running toward the bus carrying rocks and sticks and yelling hateful, ugly things at them.

"Get down, girl. Do you want them to blow your head off?" Nicoli yelled.

In slow motion everything was coming into focus for Shar. They were being attacked by mad, hateful men.

"Why are we just sitting here?" someone yelled from the back of the bus.

"The engine cut out on me. I'm trying to get it going," the bus driver screamed back at everyone as the bus began to rock back and forth.

"They're shaking the bus."

Terrified, Shar whispered to Nicoli, "Do something. Stop them." But as Shar looked into Nicoli's eyes, she saw the same horrified look that colored folks got when they experienced hate from white folks that had no reason to hate them. In a world where a colored man could get lynched just for looking like he wanted to say something back to an up-to-no-good white man, Nicoli was powerless and so was she.

They pounded on the bus and screamed, "Get out of here, niggers."

"No jiggaboos allowed on this street," another angry, hate-filled man screamed at them.

Hank, the bus driver, stood up and grabbed his baseball bat. Shar lifted a hand to try to halt him. "Don't go out there, Hank. Those men are full of hate. They'll kill you."

Hank huffed, gripping the bat tighter. "I got no choice, Shar. The battery done shook loose again. Got to clamp those plugs back on it so we can get moving."

"Them fools out there gon' clamp something on top of your head if you go out there," a woman shouted from the back of the bus.

Nicoli leaned over to Shar and said, "Stay right here. No matter what happens, don't get off this bus." He then stood up, straightened his brown button-down shirt, and balled his fist.

It looked to Shar as if he was gathering strength from some place down deep inside of him as he prepared to walk off the bus with Hank. The old hateful white men on the outside of the bus were still chanting and spewing evil, but that didn't seem to bother Nicoli.

"Hank won't get his head knocked off if us men go out and help him," Nicoli said as he turned a challenging eye toward the two men seated in the middle of the bus and then another at the front.

"You talking big now, but that's just how Matthew got his arm busted up," Pete, the piano player, said.

Nicoli grabbed Pete by the collar and barked in his face. "Keep my brother's name out of your mouth."

"Are you two going to fight, or are you going to come outside and help me get this bus started?" Hank asked as he opened the double doors, took a deep breath, and marched outside.

"I'm coming," Nicoli said as he let go of Pete's shirt.

Shar wanted to beg Nicoli to stay on the bus with her, but as the other men got up and walked off the bus with him, she turned her eyes toward heaven and prayed for the safe return of Nicoli and all the rest of the men who were determined to face this injustice head-on.

"Get back on that bus," one of the white men demanded as Hank lifted up the hood.

Hank leaned his bat against the grill of the bus and ignored them as he adjusted the corroded plugs on the battery.

"Did you hear me, nigga? I said git." The white man bent down, picked up a big rock, and threw it at Hank.

Nicoli blocked the rock. "He's just trying to fix the battery. We will be leaving your upstanding town as fast as we can, believe me."

Hank put the hood down, and the men formed a semicircle around Hank as they attempted to get back on the bus.

"You shouldn't have stopped here in the first place. We don't want your kind around here," Shar heard one of the white men say. The next thing she knew, fists were flying, and people were running this way and that. As Shar looked out the window in horror, she saw Pete fall to the ground. A couple of the men pushed their way back onto the bus. Hank and Nicoli grabbed hold of Pete as the white men kicked and punched him. They took a few punches themselves as they lifted Pete off the ground and shoved their way back onto the bus.

Hank pushed the lever, closing the doors so no one else could get onto the bus. He pumped the gas pedal and then turned the ignition. The engine turned over slowly, but as Hank pumped the gas again it finally roared to life.

Shar let out a loud, "Thank you, Jesus," as the bus started moving. The men walked back to their seats; she sat back down next to Nicoli. He had a cut above his eyebrow. Shar lifted her index finger and attempted to wipe away the blood, but Nicoli turned away from her. She looked to the front of the bus and saw that Hank was using his left hand to drive the bus while his right hand held a bloody rag against the back of his head.

Two of the choir members were tending to Pete's wounds, but no one said a word. Even the engine, which had been roaring its way from city to city, seemed to quiet down a bit. Shame was plastered on the menfolk's faces. They kept their eyes averted, not looking at any of the women for the longest time. They had just witnessed the men being attacked for no good reason. They had to just take their lumps and run back inside the bus because each one of them knew that if they so much as raised a hand to one of those white men, the town sheriff would have ignored how beat up they were and hauled them off to jail, accusing them of starting a fight.

Shar closed her eyes as a tear drifted down her face. At home, sheltered by her parents, she'd never known just how much evil was in the world. It was starting to get to her, causing her to feel so much hate in her heart that she might just burst open with all the evil thoughts roaming through her mind. She didn't know how she could go before another church and sing praise songs when she had so much hate in her heart. But the saddest thing about it was that she didn't even know if she still wanted to sing praises to God. How could she, when He was allowing people to treat them in such an ill manner?

15

"What's got you looking so sad," Mahalia asked as she sat down next to Shar in the fellowship hall of the church where they were about to sing.

With slumped shoulders and her hand under her chin, Shar said, "I'm just not feeling well today."

"Did Nicoli do something to you?"

Shar saw the look of anger on Mahalia's face. She so appreciated that Mahalia was protective of her, just like her mother would have been. But Shar lifted a hand and shook her head. "Nicoli didn't do nothing to me, Mahalia. I'm just not feeling so good about being on the road and all."

Mahalia put an arm around her. "I know that you're still shaken by what happened on that bus. But you can't let ignorant people like that get to you. We've got to press on."

With her head lowered, Shar admitted, "I don't know how to do that."

Plopping down in the seat next to Shar, Mahalia put her hand beneath Shar's chin and looked her in the eye. "Girl, colored folks been figuring out how to do this or that since time began. We're not a people who just give up and lay down so somebody can walk all over us."

Shar turned away from Mahalia. She didn't have the strength to lay her burdens down and keep on moving forward. She needed time to figure out who she was and if what she was doing even mattered in the whole grand scheme of things. "You don't believe me? Well, all I can tell you is I'm still out here striving even after having to become a beautician to make ends meet when my first few records didn't sell worth nothing." Mahalia stood up. "I'm back out here, riding from town to town, singing in tents and churches."

"But what I don't understand is why you keep striving. What good is all this praise-singing when there is still so much injustice in the world?"

"God gave us these voices for a reason, Shar Gracey. When I sing I bring hope to people who have little hope. Your voice does the same thing. But if you don't know that yet, maybe you need to take a little time off and seek God about the call that is on your life."

Shar shook her head. "I can't take time off. I need the money."

Putting her hands on her ample hips, Mahalia sternly said, "Then buck up and get ready to go out there and sing your heart out for this tent revival." Mahalia turned and started walking toward the tent where the choir would be singing that night.

Shar got up and began following behind Mahalia with her head hanging low like a disobedient child being forced to do something she didn't want to do. As she moved closer to the tent, she kept wondering if she could really sing about hope when she didn't feel much hope. She stopped.

Mahalia turned around. "What's wrong now?"

Shar pointed toward the tent and looked as if she was about to upchuck her supper. "I can't go in there . . . not tonight."

"Then go on back to the farm and hide away in that barn." Mahalia waved her hand in the air, shooing Shar away.

At that rebuke, Shar wanted to change her mind, show Mahalia that she wasn't made of mush but sterner stuff. She remembered the little girl she used to be, who belted out "Amazing Grace" for the first time at the age of six . . . remembered how everyone at church stood and applauded . . . remembered how her heart leaped at the opportunity to sing God's praises. Her heart wasn't singing tonight, because she just didn't know what good her voice would do for all the people around her who had so little but needed so much.

With tears falling down her face, Shar took Mahalia's advice and began the long walk back to the McGinn's farm. The road was rocky, and Shar's left shoe had a hole in the bottom of it, so she had to stop every so often and shake the pebbles out of her shoe. About the fifth time she stopped to shake the pebbles out, she glanced down an alley and caught a glimpse of Nicoli hunched over and throwing something on the ground while four other men formed a circle around him. Shar put her shoe back on and made her way down the alley in a huff.

Shar couldn't believe what she was seeing. "Nicoli, Nicoli," she screamed as her hands went to her hips. "What in the cotton-picking world do you think you're doing?"

Nicoli was bent down on the ground, snapping up the dice he'd just thrown when Shar started screaming his name. He threw the dice back down and stood up.

One of the other guys snapped his finger and said, "Seven."

Nicoli smiled as he made his way toward Shar. He grabbed her by the arm and walked her back out of the alley. "What are you doing following me here?"

"I didn't follow you. I saw you as I was shaking the pebbles out of my shoe."

"Why aren't you down at the tent revival, getting ready to sing?"

Shar snatched her arm out of Nicoli's grip. "Don't you talk to me like I'm some child that you can tell where to stand and where to go. I want to know why you are in this alley shooting craps with these men." Shar's nostrils were flaring by the time she finished.

"Hey, Eddie, I'll get with y'all later."

Holding the dice in his hands, Eddie stood up with a puzzled look on his face. "But you're winning."

Nicoli waved that comment off and turned back to Shar. "Do you want me to walk you back to the tent revival?"

"No. I want you to tell me why you're shooting craps."

Rolling his eyes, Nicoli said, "Don't start with me, Shar. We need money, and I'm going to get it for us the best way I can."

She pointed toward the alley. "We don't need money that bad. My mama says that a gambler is worse than a thief. Because a thief mostly robs people he don't know, but a gambler robs his own family with the money he throws away."

"That's just foolish talk." He put an arm around her shoulder as he started walking her back toward the tent revival. "I'm trying to make money to help build your singing career. I'm not taking from my family like some thief."

"My mama says—"

"Girl, will you stop telling me all the things your mama has filled your head with since the day you were born? You're a grown woman now, Shar. And we have to figure things out on our own."

Shar pulled away from him and put her hands on her hips. "Sounds like a bunch of nonsense to me, Nicoli. My daddy would skin me alive if I married some gambling man."

"I don't want to argue with you, Shar. Just let me walk you back to the revival. We can talk about this on the way."

Shaking her head, she told him, "I'm not going back to the revival. I'm going to the McGinn's farm."

"Aren't you supposed to be singing tonight?"

"I don't feel good, and I don't want to talk about it. Just walk me back to the farm, okay?"

He put his hand in Shar's. Their hands swung as they walked toward the farm, but Nicoli didn't say anything for the first five minutes of their walk. When he finally did open his mouth again, he said, "If you're tired of singing in that choir, I got a lead on a nightclub that would pay you good money to sing."

Shar pulled her hand out of Nicoli's grip, stopped dead in her tracks and started shaking her head. "Nicoli James, I know you are not suggesting that I take my God-given gift of singing and parade it before a bunch of drunks and whoremongers?"

"Now just wait a minute and hear me out before you reject my idea outright." Nicoli took a deep breath and then trudged on, "You don't want me gambling. Okay." He threw his hand in the air. "I won't gamble anymore, but we gotta be realistic. Thomas Dorsey ain't paying us no kind of decent wage, so we gotta find another way to make our money."

Frustrated, Shar stomped her foot and then grabbed hold of Nicoli's arm. "This is crazy talk. I could never be like Rosetta Tharpe. Haven't you noticed how some of the church members treat her when she travels with us?"

With a lifted brow and a look of confusion on his face, Nicoli said, "Everybody loves Rosetta. What are you talking about?"

"I hear what they say about her. They think she sings devil music. And I'm not going to do that, Nicoli. I just won't." She let out a loud, frustrated scream as she took off running toward the farmhouse.

$\mathscr{L}$❤

"I can't believe it," Nettie said to Landon as Mr. and Mrs. Thompson walked out of his office. "You have really been working hard on this and now we have our sixth family."

Despite trying to appear unmoved by the situation, a smile lined his face. "I'm thankful that God is answering my prayers, but I still need to find a way to get the down payments that will be needed to purchase these homes. So far only one out of the six families has been able to save any money, and they only have five hundred dollars."

"That's like a million dollars to most of the people around here," Nettie reminded him as she sat down in the chair in front of his desk.

Landon nodded. "It's a mountain all right. But my God gives us the strength to climb mountains."

"I'm just so thankful for you, Pastor Landon. When you came to pastor this church, you told us that you were here to help make our lives better, and you haven't given up on that promise." Nettie's voice caught as emotion overtook her and a tear drifted down her pretty brown face. "I-I just wanted you to know that I'm proud to be working for a man as humble and kind as you."

"Hey, what are the tears for?"

Lowering her head as more tears flowed, Nettie wrapped her arms around her stomach and cried as if she was standing in a doctor's office and had just been told that her father only had a few months of life left in him.

Landon had counseled many crying women, but never one he worked so closely with. He stood, rushed around his desk, and lowered his knee to the ground as he bent in front of Nettie. "What's wrong? Please tell me what's got you so upset."

Nettie put her hands over her eyes trying to stop the steady flow of tears. She wiped her face and then stood up. She wiped her hands on her dress then backed away from Landon. "I'm sorry, I feel like such a fool."

He stepped toward her. "But why? Did I say something to upset you?" Landon was truly confused. One minute Nettie was congratulating him for getting closer to his goal, and the next she was crying as if she was at a funeral.

She wiped a few errant tears from her face and then looked up at Landon. "It's not you, it's me."

Landon didn't know what to do. Nettie was breaking down right before his eyes. He wanted to wrap his arms around her, but he wasn't sure of his place. He was Nettie's pastor, but sometimes when she looked at him, he saw a longing in her eyes . . . like he was seeing now.

"I can't keep working for you, Pastor. I hate to leave while we're making such progress, but I don't see any way around it."

"But I don't understand. If I haven't done anything to you, then why do you want to leave?"

Nettie closed her eyes and turned away from Landon. She gripped the edge of his desk as she seemed to strengthen herself for what she needed to say. She took a deep breath and then, with her head held high, turned back to him and said, "I'm in love with you, Landon."

Struck dumb by her declaration, Landon didn't know what to say. His heart was still so damaged by Shar's betrayal that he didn't know if he was ready to trust another woman with his heart so soon.

"You don't have to say anything. I know that you're still stuck on Shar Gracey." She moved toward the door and put her hand on the knob.

Landon reached out to her. "Wait, don't leave." He'd come to depend on Nettie. She was in this struggle for good, affordable housing for colored people with him. Having a woman by his side who shared his dreams and vision counted for something, didn't it? No, he didn't get the same feeling of fireworks and butterflies as he did when Shar was near him, but he couldn't discount what he and Nettie shared. "I don't want you to quit your job. You're right about my feelings for Shar, but she is engaged to someone else, and I need to move on with my life."

Nettie took her hand off the doorknob and turned back around to face Landon. "I-I didn't mean to be so forward with you, Pastor Landon. I'm not trying to force you to do anything you don't want to do. I just wanted you to know." She put her hand over her heart and with a shaky voice declared, "I can't bear to work with you, feeling the way I do about you and knowing that your heart will always be with Shar."

Landon walked over to Nettie. He took her hand in his and gazed into her tear-soaked eyes. He saw love for him in those eyes. He couldn't honestly say that he loved Nettie, and he didn't want to hurt her. But he liked what he was seeing so he asked, "Would you like to have dinner with me tonight?"

16

Mahalia tried to warn her about Nicoli and now Shar was beginning to wish she'd had the good sense to listen up. After Shar caught him gambling in the alley, Nicoli had turned into somebody she didn't recognize.

Mahalia left the tour and went back to Chicago. Then the choir left Tennessee and headed to St. Louis. That's when things went from bad to worse. Nicoli got caught drinking and Mr. Dorsey fired him. That same night, it seemed as if Mr. Dorsey's mind was someplace else. People said he got like that from time to time, ever since losing his wife and child some years back. The tragedy had taken a toll on his heart and mind. But Sallie assured them that things would be put back to right in no time at all.

Shar understood, but she still felt as if she had been abandoned in a city she knew nothing about. On top of that Shar's daddy had just sent her a letter about her mama's worsening condition. She was now in the hospital. He thanked Shar for the money she'd been sending home and told her that without that money, he doubted that he would have been able to convince Marlene to go to the hospital. But with Mr. Dorsey still laid up with an aching heart, they just weren't bringing in much money from his sheet music. She had no idea how she would be able to keep sending money home.

Shar was an emotional wreck as she sat in the parlor of the boardinghouse they were staying at while singing at the St. Hope Church of Christ's revival. Every time she saw the name of the church they were singing at, Shar felt as if God was mocking her. As if she was lying to herself and everybody else in that church house when she stood up to sing about things she knew so little about.

"What are you so down in the mouth about now, gal?" Sallie Martin asked as she and Rosetta Tharpe came into the room and sat down on the sofa in front of her.

"Things just don't feel right with Mr. Dorsey out of commission." Instead of talking about her own problems, Shar decided to deal with the other thing that had been on her mind all week. "I feel so bad for him. One man shouldn't have to carry so much sorrow."

"You sho' right about that. Thank God I have never been tested like that. Just don't know if I could pass such a test," Rosetta said.

"We all have our own cross to bear . . . some, more than others," Sallie said sorrowfully.

Sallie was right, and Shar was beginning to see Nicoli as her cross more and more each day. He continued to try to shape her singing career the way he wanted it to be. And Shar just didn't know how she would ever be able to please Nicoli and God at the same time. When Shar was a child, her father filled her head with dreams of doing big things with her singing, but so far all Shar saw was despair and hopelessness all around her. "It just never seems to get better," were the words that fell out of Shar's mouth before a lone tear drifted down her face.

"It is a crying shame indeed," Sallie agreed, thinking Shar was still talking about Dorsey's predicament. She slapped her knee and then stood up. "But we don't have time to sit around moping about it. Mr. Dorsey wants us down at that church singing and selling his sheet music. So, let's go."

"As they say, the show must go on." Rosetta stood, joining Sallie.

Shar had returned to the group two nights after she'd caught Nicoli gambling. She'd gone back to the place they had been staying in Tennessee and pulled out the Bible that Landon gave her. She'd turned in the Bible to Jeremiah 29:11 and read, "For I know the thoughts that I think toward you, saith the LORD, thoughts of peace, and not of evil, to give you an expected end."

Shar wasn't sure what her end would be like, but somehow the thought that God already knew brought comfort to her. She'd rested her mind and just kept on singing God's praises. She stood with Sallie and Rosetta and headed down the street to hear the word of God and praise His name in song.

The revival was electrifying that night. Minister Johnson brought the house down with his message of overcoming and becoming a people who could walk down the street with heads held high because we are somebody. After hearing that soul stirring message, when it was time for the choir to sing, Shar got up and sang "Amazing Grace" like she had never sang it before.

Everybody was on a spiritual high as they walked back to the boardinghouse. Shar felt like shouting right on the front steps of the boardinghouse. As a matter of fact, as her choir went inside, Shar stayed behind to just stare up at the stars and wonder at how amazing God was. That he could move her from despair to joy in a matter of days was beyond her comprehension.

As she continued to look at the stars, Shar steepled her hands and prayed to God, "Lord, I don't know why I'm not strong like Sallie or Mahalia. I don't know why I can't just do Your will without questioning You about all the hardships we been facing. But I am trying to change my ways."

Her surroundings were beautiful. The colorful leaves danced on the trees. Shar wanted to join them in the dance. But there was still something in her way, blocking her blessing. Shar didn't know how to move it and didn't know for sure if she truly wanted it moved. "Lord, I sure could use some guidance."

"Shar, Shar, help me."

At the sound of her name, Shar jumped and ran for the front door. She had never before heard the audible voice of God in answer to one of her prayers, and Shar doubted very seriously that the Lord would be asking her for help. She put her hand on the doorknob, getting ready to turn it when she heard the whispery voice again.

"Help me, Shar."

"Nicoli?" Shar turned slightly and saw a figure in the shadows on the side of the house.

Dragging his left leg and holding his arm against his side, Nicoli came into view. "It's me."

Shar walked back down the porch steps and went to Nicoli. As she got closer to him, her steps were halted as she caught a glimpse of his face. She gasped and then rushed over to him and lightly touched his swollen and bloody face. "What happened to you? Who did this?"

"They're going to kill me, baby."

Looked to her like Nicoli had taken the beating of his life, like if he had taken one more blow there wouldn't be no life left in him. It was then that she wondered if she could live in a world that did not include her Nicoli. She didn't know what kind of fool that made her, but she didn't care either. Nicoli was hurt. He needed her. "Who wants to kill you? What's going on?" She was torn and panic-stricken as she pulled him closer to her.

"I owe a lot of money to," he winced, and with a sharp intake of breath, he sat down on the ground as if his legs wouldn't hold him one second longer, "really nasty guys."

Stepping back and putting her hands on her hips, she demanded, "What have you been doing, Nicoli? Didn't we agree that you wouldn't gamble anymore?"

With remorse in his eyes, he lowered his head. "I know, I know, baby. But I had no choice. I've been trying to raise enough money to get back to my hometown so I can introduce you to my family." Raising his head and looking like a raccoon about the eyes, he told her, "And anyway, a colored man don't have too many options. It's not like I'm ever going to be able to go to college and get me one of those fancy jobs."

"That's just an excuse, Nicoli. Colored people been going to college for years now, and I'm right proud of the accomplishments that have been coming our way, thanks to colored people out there making a difference." As she said those words she thought of Landon and the difference he was trying to make in her neighborhood. The difference between the two men couldn't have been clearer.

"I don't see none of those so-called fabulous colored folks putting food on our table. I've been crawling under every rock I can find to earn enough money to take care of you, but you don't appreciate nothing I do. Now people want to," his voice broke off as he said, "kill me."

Her heart lurched. She took her hands off her hips and sympathy coated her words. "I don't understand. They already beat you up. If they wanted to kill you, wouldn't they have done that when they had a chance?"

"They're giving me two days to come up with the money."

The door to the boardinghouse opened, and Sallie leaned out and hollered, "Shar, who you out there with, gal? Get on in this house."

Shar turned toward the house and yelled back, "It's Nicoli. He's been hurt bad. Come help me get him in the house."

Sallie stalked over to them. She took one look at Nicoli sprawled out on the ground and said, "Shar, if you've got any sense, you'll get yourself in that house," she pointed toward the boardinghouse, "and don't look back."

"I can't just leave him out here like this. He needs our help."

Scowling like a pit bull, Sallie pointed an accusatory finger in Nicoli's face. "If you care anything about this girl, you'll get outta here and leave her alone."

"Me and Shar is getting married." Nicoli pulled himself off the ground, and while hunched over, he breathed fire in Sallie's face. "I'm not leaving her alone just because you don't like me. You got no say so when it comes to me and Shar."

"It's not that I don't like you . . . I don't like what you stand for. You a able-bodied man who don't want to work hard for what you get . . . you just want money to rain down on you from heaven above. I know all about your kind, and you ain't no good."

"You don't know nothing about me." Nicoli limped toward Sallie, trying to get closer to her.

Shar stepped in between the two and put her hands on Nicoli's chest, pushing him backward. "Please don't argue like this."

"You heard what she said," Nicoli pointed at Sallie. "She thinks you're too good for me."

"You got that right," Sallie said, not backing down.

Still holding Nicoli back, Shar turned to Sallie. "Go back in the house, Sallie. I get that you don't want Nicoli inside, so just let me talk to him and then I'll come back in, okay?"

"I don't like it, Shar. And I don't think your mama would want you out here late at night with this rabble-rouser."

"I won't be long. Just give me a minute, okay?"

Shaking her head as she turned back toward the house, Sallie said, "If you're not in this house in five minutes, I'll be coming back to get you. And I won't be alone."

As the door slammed shut, Shar told Nicoli. "You've got to go. Sallie will come back out here and beat you with a stick if you don't do as she says."

"Girl, ain't nobody scared of Sallie Martin but you."

"Please, Nicoli, just go and I'll see you tomorrow."

"I can't just go, Shar. I need your help, and this time you can't say no, not if you truly love me."

"What can I do? I don't have any money to give you."

He grabbed hold of her arm and shook her. "Think, Shar. You don't have money, but you do have that wonderful voice that can make us all the money in the world if we play our cards right."

As she stepped back, Shar's eyes grew. "I know you're not talking about what I think you're talking about."

He reached out for Shar, fear in his eyes. "It's the only way, Shar. You love me, don't you?"

Did she love him? Shar had thought that she was in love those first few weeks when Nicoli was wooing her and on the day that he announced that they were engaged. But that was a different Nicoli. The beat-up gambler standing before her now was some other Nicoli. And Shar didn't know if she wanted to love this Nicoli anymore.

When she didn't answer, Nicoli ran his hand through his hair and twisted his lip as he backed up. "Okay, I know that

I have been difficult lately. But you don't want to see me dead just because I've been gambling, do you?"

"Trying to fill me full of guilt ain't going to work. I didn't put those dice in your hand. So why should I go against everything I believe just to help you out of this jam?"

"Shar, it's really no big deal. The man I owe the money to owns a nightclub and he told me that he will forgive my debt, if you will sing in his club this weekend."

All her life she thought her voice was given to her so that she could praise God. Could she really use her voice for something other than praise to God?

"If you don't help me, baby, I don't know what I'm going to do."

The look on Nicoli's face was a mix of fear and sorrow. He got back down on his knees and crawled to her. She could see the pain reflected on his face with each movement, even before the tears bubbled up in his eyes. "I got no where else to go, Shar. I done burned every bridge I had." He was now directly in front of her. He leaned his head against her stomach and let out a gutteral cry that sounded like an animal howling at the moon. "Please don't let me die."

Closing her eyes, Shar wished she was back home in Chicago with her mama and daddy protecting her and showing her the way. She'd prayed for God's help and all she'd gotten in return was Nicoli, leaning and depending on her. Lifting his head off her stomach, she stepped back so she could look him in the eye.

"Are you gon' help me, Shar. I promise, if you do this, I'll never ask you for another thing as long as we live."

Shar looked toward the boardhouse, knowing full well that she should do as Sallie said, but before she could stop herself she was saying, "I'll do this on one condition."

Light came back into his eyes as he got back onto his feet. "Anything, baby, anything."

"You've got to stop drinking and gambling."

"After what happened tonight, you don't have to worry about me no more, Shar. I'm going the straight-and-narrow way from now on." He crossed his heart with his finger to add emphasis to his pledge.

"You better mean it this time, Nicoli, because I'm not going to live the rest of my life getting you out of jams that you got no business being in."

17

Landon walked down The Stroll with Nettie as they headed to one of his favorite eateries. A few years back Landon never would have escorted a lady on State Street between 26th and 39th streets, because that was where the action was. That section of State Street had been packed with colored people night and day. But back in the early '20s it had been mostly men lining the streets. At night the lights blazed and the sidewalks were crowded with people attending the jazz clubs and those who just wanted to gawk at all the activity. During the daylight hours people lined the streets while loitering, gossiping, and just watching the people. But that was before the Savoy Ballroom opened on 47th and South Parkway in 1927. Now most of the nightlife was over by the Savoy, so Landon felt comfortable walking those streets with Nettie.

Nettie's eyes were wide and curious as she glanced around her surroundings. She grabbed hold of Landon's hand as they walked into the restaurant and said, "I've never been down this side of State Street before. My mom said it was too wild and loose over here for a young lady, but it doesn't seem like much of anything is going on."

Landon wanted to kick himself. Why hadn't he considered Nettie's feelings before taking her to dinner? "If you're uncomfortable here, we could always go somewhere else," he told her.

Patting his shoulder, she lightly pushed him forward, further into the small restaurant. "Didn't you say this is one of your favorite places to eat?"

"They have the best meatloaf and mashed potatoes I've had the pleasure of sampling in the Chicago area."

"Well then let's grab a seat so I can check out the menu."

"But I don't want you to feel uncomfortable. I should have asked you where you wanted to eat, before making a decision in the first place." Landon was bothered by what he had done because in his heart he knew for sure that if it was Shar he was taking out, he would have fallen all over himself to make sure that everything was to her liking.

Nettie wrapped her hand around Landon's arm. "I only commented about the area because my mama had warned me so severely about hanging out around here. But things seem fine to me. I don't think she would be alarmed at all to know that I was having dinner with my pastor over here."

"Well as long as you're okay, then I'm okay." Landon escorted Nettie to an empty table in the middle of the restaurant. He pulled the chair out for her, and Nettie sat down.

When Landon was seated across from her, Nettie told him, "I've only kept company with one other man, Pastor, and all he ever did was sit on our porch with me. So believe me, I'm thrilled to be out to dinner with you."

"Do me a favor, Nettie."

"What's that, Pastor?"

"Since we are keeping company and all, call me Landon when we aren't at church, okay?"

Smiling, with a look of adoration in her eyes, Nettie put her hand on top of Landon's as it lay on the table. "Sure, I can do that, Landon." She said his name as if trying it out to see how it felt on her lips.

"Hey, Pastor Landon, you back for some more meatloaf and mashed potatoes?" a server asked as she stood in front of the table grinning at him.

"You better know it, Patty. And you can throw some peas and cornbread on my plate too," Landon moved his hand from Nettie's and glanced toward her as he said, "Patty, I'd like to introduce you to Miss Nettie Johnson. She and I work together at the church. She's my right hand, isn't that right, Nettie?"

The light dimmed a bit in Nettie's eyes as she turned to Patty and said, "Yep, I'm his assistant." She got a bit more animated as she declared, "And we're doing mighty important work that's gonna be felt all through the Black Belt."

"I know all about the work you and Pastor Landon have been doing. My ma and pa are having dinner here tonight. I told you about them, remember, Reverend?" She pointed to a table near the back of the room where an older, distinctly well-dressed couple sat.

Landon turned toward the table and then asked, "Are they still having trouble buying that house?"

"The bank manager told them flat out that he wasn't loaning money to no coloreds trying to move in a white district."

Landon shook his head, wondering when the day would come that they would be known simply as a man or woman and not be judged first by the color of their skin.

"Well these bank managers won't be able to treat our people like that for much longer. Not once Pastor Landon and the NAACP get through with them," Nettie said with great pride.

"That's what I told my parents. Would you mind speaking with them tonight?"

He glanced at Nettie, and she nodded. Landon then turned back to Patty and said, "Of course, please ask them if they'd like to have their dinner at our table."

"I sure will," Patty said hurriedly. But just before leaving the table she turned back to Nettie and asked, "Do you know what you want to eat?"

Nettie lifted her hands, indicating that they were empty. "I don't have a menu." She then waved at the air. "Just bring me what Landon is having."

"Two meatloaf specials coming up."

"Oh, but instead of peas, I'll have some corn, please," Nettie told her.

Patty left the table and rushed over to where her parents were seated.

Looking over at Nettie, Landon wondered if he had made a mistake bringing Nettie to a place where the people knew him and knew what he was trying to do in the community. "I'm sorry about this. I had no idea that her parents would be here tonight."

Nettie waved the apology away. "I don't mind, Landon. This is what we are about." She leaned closer to him and added, "And those two look like they might have some money saved up for their down payment."

Landon smiled. He had a partner in Nettie. She cared about his cause and had made it her own. As Frank and Judy Joseph sat down at the table and enjoyed dinner and fellowship with them, Landon discovered that he had, indeed, found his seventh couple who were not only willing, but also well able to purchase a good home.

As they began their trek home after a successful business meeting/date, Nettie said, "Didn't I tell you those two would have a down payment to put down on their house?"

"You were so right." Landon grinned from ear to ear as they walked down State Street. "But I still can't believe that they managed to save fifty-five hundred dollars. I don't know anyone with that kind of money."

Nettie put her hand on Landon's arm as she said, "God is blessing our work, Landon. You will get all ten couples that the NAACP needs for their case, and God will provide a way for us to get all the down payment money that we need." She lifted her hands as if in praise to God. "I feel it. I believe and I know it's going to happen."

Landon glanced over at Nettie. Her enthusiasm was electrifying, and Landon was beginning to grab hold of it and forget about his need to know where all the money would come from. Hope was filling Landon's heart; his life's work would be realized.

Nettie started clapping her hands and singing a praise song. She nudged Landon. "Come on, sing with me."

Landon wanted to close his eyes in order to block out the pain entering his heart. He had been having such a wonderful time with Nettie, feeling as if she might be a kindred spirit. But as he listened to her sing the song Shar had sung the first day he saw her, Landon began wondering if he had done the right thing when he decided to keep company with Nettie.

If a simple praise song could cause his heart to ache for Shar Gracey, he probably wasn't ready to keep company with anyone. He saw Nettie safely to her door, and then as he walked home, he let his mind drift a few years back. But instead of hearing Nettie's voice, Shar was singing and he was falling in love all over again.

In an attempt to shut his mind off from dreaming foolishness, Landon tried to concentrate on Nettie and the beautiful evening they had shared. Living in the past would get him nowhere fast. Shar was engaged, and he needed to get over her.

But telling himself those simple truths didn't stop Landon from wondering what Shar was doing and if she was thinking about him, just as he was thinking about her that night.

Walking into the speakeasy was like stepping into utter darkness. The lights were dimmed, with a spotlight on the small dance floor. Men sat at the bar, guzzling down alcohol and laughing like hyenas. They all seemed to be having a good time, but Shar felt an undercurrent of something she just couldn't put her finger on. All she could think of was that these must be some of the same men Nicoli gambled and drank with. And Nicoli didn't seem to be having so much fun when she saw him the other night.

Nicoli guided her toward the back of the club to a small dressing room. "Mr. Marson wants you to get ready in here," he told her.

"What do you mean, 'get ready'? Am I going to practice with the piano player or something?"

"No, Shar, Mr. Marson wants you to wear something similar to what his other singers wear on stage. He told me that one of his girls will be bringing you a new outfit."

Shar looked down at her clothes. She had on an olive colored two-piece gown. The jacket buttoned from her neck down to her waist, and the hemline of the skirt brushed against the floor. The dress had been handed down to her from her mother, who'd received it second hand from her mother. Shar had worn the dress to church on countless occasions and had even received a few compliments on how well maintained the dress was. "What's wrong with what I have on?"

Nicoli took her by the hand and walked her over to a chair so she could sit down. "I like everything you wear. And if it was up to me, you could go out on that stage tonight exactly as you are. But Shar, these guys mean business. To tell you the truth, I don't know what Mr. Marson would do if you denied his request."

Becoming alarmed, Shar asked, "You think he would do something to me?" What had she gotten herself into?

"Don't look like that. I don't think he would do anything to you. I just don't want to find out the hard way."

"Find out what?"

He put a hand over her mouth to shush her. "Look, Shar, I know I let you down, but I promise that if you get me out of this jam, I'll never put you in the middle of my gambling problems again."

Putting her hands on her hips, Shar glared at Nicoli. "Are you telling me that you're going to keep on gambling, even after getting beat up and forcing me to sing in this . . . " she stretched forth her hand, trying to find the words, "this house of ill repute?"

"Calm down, Shar, that's not what I meant at all."

"Just what do you mean, Nicoli? Because I don't want to live my life on pins and needles, wondering what you're going to get us into next."

Someone knocked on the door. Nicoli put his hand on the back of the chair Shar was sitting in and said, "Come in."

The door opened, and a petite, freckle-faced young woman came into the room holding a white ostrich feather fan in one hand and the most God-forsaken-looking dress in the other hand. The woman hung the dress on a coatrack and then turned to Shar and said, "I think this will fit you."

Shar stood and made her way to the coat stand with her hand covering her mouth as she viewed the black chiffon flapper dress with the very low "v" neckline. The dress was showered with black sequins and tiny rhinestones. It looked expensive, and Shar was afraid to even touch it.

The woman said, "Try it on."

Looking around the room as if trying to find a place to hide, Shar said, "I can't wear that."

The woman waved her concern away. "Do you know how many women would kill to be in a dress like this?" She took the dress off the hanger and laid it on her arm so Shar could view the label. "This dress was made in France. Now how many colored women outside of Josephine Baker get to slide into something that came out of France?"

The woman was right. The dress and the ostrich feathers did indeed look like something Josephine Baker would strut in as she dazzled European audiences. But Shar wasn't anything like Josephine Baker. Shar was a gospel singer and that was all she'd ever wanted to be. "But I don't sing like Josephine Baker or any of the other women who sing in this club. I sing gospel music," was all Shar could think to say in protest.

The woman laughed. "Daisy Little, one of your so-called gospel singers, was in here just last week, wearing a dress shorter than the one I'm letting you wear."

Nicoli put his arm around Shar as he told the woman. "Just leave the dress, and I'll make sure she puts it on before she goes out on the stage."

The woman turned to Nicoli. "She got the first-time jitters or something?"

"Yeah, you know how it is. Just give me a few minutes to talk to her, and we'll be ready to start the show in no time. All right?"

Handing Nicoli the ostrich feathers and dress, the woman said, "Good luck," as she walked out of the room, laughing her head off.

When the door closed, Shar put her hands over her face and burst into tears.

Nicoli laid the dress and feather fan on a chair and wrapped his arms around Shar. "I'm sorry, baby, I didn't mean to make you so sad."

"I-I can't do this, Nicoli."

Pulling back, he wiped the tears from her face and then kissed her forehead. "I need you to be strong for me. You can't break down like some scared little know-nothing girl. You're a grown woman, and you can handle this. My life depends on it," he reminded her.

Shar was getting so tired of hearing about Nicoli's troubles—troubles that he brought on his self—and now she had to come behind him and clean the whole mess up. Would the rest of their lives be like this? Could she truly be happy with an impetuous man like Nicoli?

"My mama would skin me alive if she saw me in a dress like that." Pointing at the dress, she added, "No decent lady would go out in public dressed like that."

"I am so tired of listening to you whine." He stepped back and bore down on her with cold dark eyes. "We've got a lot riding on this performance, so you need to stop all this crying and get in that dress."

"I don't have anything riding on this performance. I told you that I don't want to sing in places like this. And now I see that Mahalia was right about you. You're just like her ex-husband, always looking for ways to make money rather than appreciating what God blesses us with." Shar grabbed her purse and began walking toward the door.

Nicoli took hold of her arm and squeezed it. "You're supposed to be my woman. You just can't leave me in the lurch like this."

"Let me go, Nicoli. You're hurting my arm." She tried to twist out of his grip, but the more she moved, the tighter his grip became. "Let me go," she begged, hating the sound of her voice.

"I'll never let you go. You and me belong together. Get that through your thick head and you'll be just fine."

Tears glistened in her eyes and she tried to lift his iron grip one finger at a time. "Why are you doing this?"

"Me?" he asked incredulously. "I'm not the one going back on my word. You said you would help me, and you're not getting out of here until you do exactly what you said you would do." As he let go of her arm, he picked up the dress and shoved it at her. "Put this on and then get yourself on that stage. I'll be outside waiting on you."

Tears streamed down her face as Nicoli closed the door behind him. She stood there rubbing her arm and looking at the bluish purple mark that was beginning to form. Her mind drifted back to the day Landon came to see her when the choir was in Chicago. She thought about how she allowed Nicoli to put his arm around her and tell the most honorable man she had ever known that she was engaged. And right then she knew that she was the biggest fool the world had ever known.

18

Stepping onto that stage, Shar was as nervous as she'd ever been. The flapper dress she wore showed her knees, and way, way too much of her bosom was hanging out for all to see. Shar felt like a showgirl as she opened the ostrich feather fan all the way, so that it covered her from the tip of her shoulder to just below her knees.

But Shar was thankful that the fan covered her knees because they were shaking. Totally out of her element in that environment, Shar only knew a few secular songs and that was because the lady next door to her parents' house played her blues songs while hanging her wash out to dry. One of the songs was by Bessie Smith. It wasn't very ladylike, so Shar stood in front of the mic, looking out at the audience in the dimly lit room wondering what she should do.

"Move that feather so we can see you, girl," one of the men at the bar yelled.

"Forget seeing her. I thought she was supposed to be singing something," another man hollered from the back.

Shar's eyes darted across the ballroom, looking for Nicoli, hoping and praying that he would come and rescue her.

The piano player banged on the keys trying to get her attention. He was seated to the left of her on the floor just below the stage. Shar looked down. "What do you want me to play?" he asked.

She quickly racked her brain, but when she could come up with nothing else, she told him, " 'Mama's Got the Blues' by Bessie Smith."

"Now you're talking." The piano player smiled as his fingers tapped the keys.

Having no choice but to do something now that she was on stage, Shar opened her mouth and began belting out the only song she thought would satisfy this crowd.

Some people say that the weary blues ain't bad
But it's the worst old feeling that I've ever had

The crowd started clapping and yelling, "Sing that song . . . girl, you know you got some chops on you."

A portly man seated at one of the tables in the front of the room, got out of his chair, rushed up to the stage, and leaned over and grabbed hold of Shar's ankle. "I'll hold your aching head, baby."

Shar jumped back, moving away from leering hands. She looked around for Nicoli as she held the feather closer to her body. When she spotted Nicoli, he was seated at a table in the back giving her the evil eye while a scantily dressed woman whispered in his ear.

He was getting mad again. Remembering the way he'd gripped her arm in the dressing room, Shar was terrified of what Nicoli would do to her if she stopped singing, so with tears brimming in her eyes she continued. She sang every word of that song even as tears rolled down her face. She kept singing until she was done. She then stood there with her head bowed low, feeling ashamed of herself and everything she stood for.

One by one the men and women in the room stood up and applauded. They started screaming, "More . . . more."

The piano man hollered up at her, "You don't want to say no to this crowd. Just start singing, and I'll follow your lead."

She didn't want to sing another blues songs and didn't think she could make it through another one if she tried. Her stomach was turning, accusing her of betraying her beliefs. She had no business in a place like this . . . dressed like this . . . singing songs like this.

"You've got to do something, girl. These cats will lose their mind if you don't give 'em what they want," the piano player hollered up at her.

But Shar didn't care anymore. She stepped down from the stage, walked over to Nicoli, ignored the woman seated next to him, and said, "I'm leaving. I should never have agreed to do this."

He stood. "You can't just walk out of here. Mr. Marson wants you to sing a set."

Shar wasn't going to be intimidated by him one second longer. He'd hurt her arm in the dressing room, but she doubted that he would try anything like that in front of a room full of witnesses. She pointed at the woman next to him. "Tell her to go up there and sing while these dirty old men paw at her and make all sorts of God-awful comments." Shar threw the Ostrich feather at Nicoli.

"You're jealous over Lucy." He looked from Lucy to Shar, still holding the feather. "We're just friends, girl. Now stop acting crazy and get back on that stage."

"No," Shar said as she huffed her way toward the door.

As she reached for the door handle, a hand gripped her around her upper arm, and she was instantly paralyzed, thinking that Nicoli was about to beat on her in front of all these people. Why oh why hadn't she listened to Mahalia?

"I'm sorry, little lady, but I can't let you leave out of here in that dress. I had it shipped all the way from France."

That wasn't Nicoli's voice. A chill went up Shar's spine as she turned around and faced the man who'd had Nicoli beaten to within an inch of his life, and now she wondered if he planned to do the same to her.

"I'm Joe Marson," the big and burly man who looked like he could outbox Joe Louis said.

"I'm sorry, sir. I wasn't trying to steal the dress." She looked down at herself and shook her head as she told him, "And believe me, I certainly don't want to walk the streets in it."

Mr. Marson laughed.

Shar was surprised by the laugh and was beginning to think that maybe he wasn't such a bad guy after all. She leaned into him and asked, "Do you think I could go back to the dressing room and get my clothes?"

"You certainly can," he said with a smile.

Shar thanked him and made a move to go to the dressing room.

Joe Marson then put one finger up and said, "But, since I have already paid Nicoli for this performance, I'm going to need you to sing at least one more song, before I let you into that dressing room tonight." His eyes became cold and unyielding, but the smile was still plastered on his face.

Shar wanted to refuse, but that chill was going up her spine again. This man was dangerous, and she knew it with every fiber of her being. She wasn't about to argue with him. So, she got back on that stage and did as she was told. When the song ended, the crowd started begging for more again. Mr. Marson motioned for her to keep singing. By the third song, Shar was getting into the rhythm. The piano player was working with her, and the crowd didn't seem as rowdy. So she closed her eyes and began to feel each song as she belted the words out.

After the fifth song, Mr. Marson walked to the edge of the stage and held out his hand to her. Shar put the microphone in its cradle and walked off the stage and sat down at Mr. Marson's table.

"Well, I'll say this, Miss Shar Gracey, you have a voice that other singers would kill to have."

Shar reckoned that he was giving her a compliment but didn't know if she liked the thought of anyone contemplating murder just to have her voice. "I'm thinking that other singers are happy with the voice God gave 'em."

Marson shook the table with his big belly laugh. "You are a caution. I bet you keep Nicoli in stitches."

"She sure does, Mr. Marson. Funniest girl I ever met and the prettiest too." Nicoli pulled up a chair and sat down at the table with them. He tried to put an arm around Shar, but she brushed it off.

"I was just getting ready to invite this little lady to sing at my club for the rest of the weekend."

Shar shook her head. "I can't come back in here. I sing with Thomas Dorsey's choir."

"I know Dorsey. We used to call him Georgia Tom when he was playing his piano in the juke joints. So, I doubt if he will condemn you for trying to earn a little money." Marson leaned back in his seat, looking from Nicoli to Shar waiting on an answer.

"What do you mean? How can I earn money?" Shar was suddenly very interested in the conversation.

"I can pay you ten dollars a night."

Nicoli jumped in. "Since I'm Shar's manager, I need to advise her that she shouldn't settle for anything less than twenty-five a night."

"Nicoli, what are you doing?" Shar asked. She wasn't sure if she wanted to come back to this club. Even though Mr. Marson tried to make her feel better about it by reminding her that Mr. Dorsey had once played in nightclubs and juke joints, she still wasn't comfortable with any of this. However, Shar did like the sound of that money. And she didn't want Nicoli messing anything up for her before she could decide what to do.

Nicoli put a hand on her shoulder. "This is a conversation for us men. Let me handle this."

Shar wanted to roll her eyes at that. But she didn't interrupt again.

"I'll let her put a tip jar out. If she sings like she did tonight and then makes nice with the customers, she'll make some good tips."

Nicoli said, "Deal," then shook Marson's hand.

On the walk home, Nicoli couldn't contain his joy. "You did it, Shar. You showed them what I've known all along."

"And that is?" Shar asked tight-lipped. She hadn't forgotten about the woman he'd been whispering with in the back of the room.

"That Shar Gracey is going to be somebody. You're on your way. And I'm going to be your manager so you don't get cheated."

"It sure looked like you were doing a little cheating of your own tonight. I guess this is what you do behind my back at these clubs." She folded her arms around her stomach as she kept walking.

"You need to stop being so jealous. I ain't got time for nobody but you in my life. And I sure wouldn't be cheating with Lucy. That girl don't have nothing on you."

"I don't care if her name is Lucy or Emma Jean or whoever else you want to cozy up with. I'm getting plum tired of the way you're treating me."

Nicoli took hold of Shar's arms and stopped her from walking. "Look at me, Shar."

She averted her eyes. Nicoli talked her into too much stuff when she looked at him.

"I'm serious, Shar. Look at me. Look me in the eye and tell me that you can't see how much I love you. I ain't never been with a woman like you. And I don't want to be with nobody but you."

She turned to him, but truth be told, Shar couldn't tell what his eyes was saying. But the words were melting the ice from around her heart.

"I swear for God, that meeting you has changed me. You're the best thing that ever happened to me . . . do you hear me?"

"I hear you. I just don't know if what we're doing is right."

"Nothing could ever be righter," Nicoli said as he bent his head and softly kissed Shar as if she was treasured and precious.

Coming up for air after that kiss, Shar was a little disoriented and confused. Did he love her? Was he good for her? Was she just being a worrywart? She lightly punched Nicoli's shoulder as she said, "I just better not catch you with that woman again. That's all I'm saying."

He put an arm around her as they continued their journey. He asked, "So have you decided to take the gig so we can earn some money for our future?"

She shook her head. "I will go back to that nightclub this week, but I'm sending all that money to my family." She wanted to add that she wasn't leaving any money behind because Nicoli would just gamble it away but kept that part to herself.

Although Shar was hesitant to admit it, she actually enjoyed herself at the nightclub the second and third night. But on the fourth night, she snapped back to reality as Lucy walked into the club and started whispering in Nicoli's ear again. Shar was on the stage singing a Billie Holiday song, "These Foolish Things."

She tried to finish her song without bursting into tears, but it was becoming too much for her to bear as she watched the loose woman climb on Nicoli's lap, put her arms around his neck, and kiss him like he belonged to her. Shar's heart felt like it wanted to stop right then and there. So she had to turn away from Nicoli in order to press on and finish the song even as tears rolled down her foolish face.

When her set was over, she got off the stage, determined that this was the last time Nicoli would make a fool out of her. She saw him for who and what he was. He didn't mean her a bit of good and couldn't hold onto a promise if his life depended on it. Wiping the tears from her face, she was getting ready to confront Nicoli, but then she noticed that he was no longer in his seat. Instead of worrying herself about him, she went straight to Mr. Marson and stuck out her hand. "Can I have my money now? I'm leaving."

"I thought you liked it here?" Marson asked.

"It's just time for me to go." What was wrong with her? How had she gotten so comfortable in this place?

"I gave your money to your manager."

She turned and looked for the tip jar on the piano. Every other night, she'd had a couple of dollars in that jar once she'd finished singing. Tonight it was empty. "Why'd you give him my money? I was planning on sending it to my mama."

Marson lifted his hands, indicating that her problem wasn't his problem. "I'm not no referee. The man said he was your manager so I gave him the money. If you want it, go get it from him."

Shar wasn't about to stand there arguing with a big burly man like Mr. Marson. If Nicoli had money in his pocket, then Shar knew exactly where he had taken off to. She grabbed her handbag out of the dressing room and then headed out of the back door. The darkness of the alley made her hesitate, but then she heard the voices of rabble-rousers and started walking in the direction of the noise. As she rounded the corner, she came upon four men hunched over. Nicoli had just shot the dice, and he popped his finger as the dice rolled onto the ground.

"Nicoli." Shar yelled his name, not even surprised at where she'd found this promise-breaker.

Nicoli turned to face her. He pointed at the door. "Get back in that club. You ain't got no business back here."

Holding out her hand, Shar said, "Just give me my money so I can go."

"Look at you, acting like you're the only one working in that club. Who do you think got you that gig?"

"I don't want to hear it, Nicoli. Give me my money so I can get away from you and your lying, cheating ways."

Grabbing her arm, he said, "All of this nagging you do is getting old."

She snatched away from him. "Just give me my money so I can go."

"Go on and give the girl her money and let's get back to the game already," one of the men said.

"Mind your business," Nicoli yelled over his shoulder.

With one hand on her hip, Shar kept her hand stuck out, letting Nicoli know that she wasn't in the mood for no discussions.

Nicoli went into his pocket, pulled out ten dollars, and handed it to Shar.

She looked at it. "This is not the right amount. I earned at least forty dollars plus tips this week. Where's the rest of the money?"

"Takes money to make money. I've been out here trying to double it for us."

"I never asked you to double my money. I asked you to stop gambling, drinking, and cheating." Shar was so angry she wanted to spit. Instead she blew out a frustrated sigh as she stomped her foot, then rolled her eyes to high heaven and started making her way out of the alley.

"Where do you think you're going?"

"Away from you," she hollered back.

"Okay, I get it. You're angry. Go home and cool off. You'll be back once you think about how much money we can make together."

She didn't respond. Just kept walking. A woman could only play the fool for so long. And this was it for Shar. She was tired of crying and arguing with Nicoli. She made her way out of that alley without looking back. She couldn't bear to see him bent over, throwing those dice onto the ground one more time.

Her head was all messed up and jumbled with the things she'd seen and done since leaving home. Her mind drifted back to United Worship, thinking about the time she sat in the pews listening as Landon preached about Better Days. She wondered if he still believed in the messages he preached. She wanted to believe . . . wanted to hold onto some part of what used to mean something to her.

But she couldn't ponder on it for long, because in the darkness of the night, Shar lost her footing and scraped her knee as she fell onto the dirt path. Getting up, she dusted herself off and then turned this way and that. Her mind was running a mile a minute as she tried to figure if she'd made a wrong turn when she'd left the club by way of the alley.

All Shar could think to do was to keep walking until she ran into something that was familiar to her, but then it started raining. She stopped walking, lifted her head toward heaven, and asked, "Really? Do you really have to rain right now?" She looked around again, trying to figure out the best way to get back to the farm. But it was dark, and the rain was disorienting her.

Standing on the corner as thick raindrops plopped on her head, totally ruining the press and curl job she'd scraped up the money to get done a few days ago. Shar was having a hard time making her way, but she knew she couldn't just stand in the rain all night, so she clutched her handbag to her chest and got back to walking, hoping that she was going in the right direction.

She heard footsteps behind her and tried to hurry along, while trying to figure out which way she needed to go. The footsteps became louder and faster. For fear that someone from that alley had followed her out of the club looking to fulfill evil intentions, she started running. When the person behind her picked up the pace as well, Shar screamed.

She looked around hoping to find someone to help her, but the rain had probably driven most of the residents inside because the street was empty. But that didn't stop her from crying out, "Help, help."

A hand wrapped around her mouth. She bit down on it and kept screaming.

"Shut up," the man hollered as he reached for her handbag.

He's going to rob me. No, dear Lord, don't let him take my money. Didn't Nicoli already steal enough of it. "No, leave me alone." Shar tried to yank her handbag out of his grasp, determined to hold onto the little bit she had to contribute to her mama's care.

"Let it go."

"No." Shar didn't know if she was emboldened by the rain or if she simply didn't want to lose one more thing that night, but she took her fist and swung at the man as she once again tried to yank her handbag strap out of his hand.

The guy ducked out of the way of her fist and then pulled on the bag again. When Shar wouldn't release it, he picked up a rock and smashed her in the head with it. She released the handbag, and as she fell to the ground and began slipping into total darkness, Shar wasn't seeing no better days ahead, only fleeting hope and utter despair.

19

Landon felt awful for having contemplated a relationship with Nettie before getting Shar out of his system. He wasn't the sort of man to lead women on, and certainly not women in his congregation. If word started getting around that he was this love-'em-and-leave-'em kind of preacher who broke the hearts of the young women in his church, he'd never live it down. And any good he did for the community would always be tainted by his undisciplined personal life.

But Landon also wasn't blind to the fact that he needed Nettie. She was on his team, and he was so grateful to have someone by his side who believed in the mission God gave him. However, he refused to pretend that he felt something that he didn't. As far as Landon was concerned, doing something like that would be cruel. And he never wanted to be cruel to someone as sweet and loyal as Nettie.

So there he was wearing out the flooring in his office as he paced back and forth, trying to figure out how to tell Nettie that their date was a mistake and he wanted to step back. Landon hadn't had a whole lot of practice with women, since he'd been spending most of his time on his ministry and waiting in vain for Shar to return home. He wouldn't do that to Nettie. He wouldn't be able to look himself in the face if he allowed Nettie to wait around, hoping that his feelings would change.

A knock sounded at his door. Landon stopped pacing, turned toward the door, and took a deep breath. "Come in."

The door opened, and a smiling Nettie walked in carrying a healthy slice of crumb cake in one hand and a cup of coffee in the other. "My mother was at it again. She knows how much you love her crumb cake, so she wouldn't let me leave the house this morning without bringing you a slice."

"Your mama is a blessed angel," he said as he took the cake and coffee from Nettie. Landon sat down behind his desk, took a sip of his coffee, and bit into his cake. "Mmm, if this isn't the best crumb cake I've ever tasted, then I'm a monkey's uncle."

"Oh, and before I forget, my mother sends her thanks for you getting me home at a decent hour last week." Nettie winked at him. "But she also said that if we wanted to stay out a little longer next time that she wouldn't be bothered by that at all."

"Nettie, we need to talk." He pointed toward the chair in front of his desk, then got up and came around his desk.

Sitting down, Nettie asked, "Is something wrong, Landon?"

Leaning against his desk, he hesitated, trying to think of the best way to break this to her. His mind was still fresh with the memory of the tears Nettie had shed in his office, the day she told him that she was in love with him. But as much as he didn't want a replay of Nettie's tears, he also didn't want Nettie wasting her love on a man who, at best, liked her a lot. "I think I may have been a little too hasty in my response to you a couple of weeks ago." Ringing his hands, not looking her in the eye, he continued, "You see, Nettie, I have so much respect for you. And your loyalty to our cause brings my heart great joy. But . . . "

She put her hand over his. "Whatever is troubling you, just spit it out. You can tell me anything."

Beads of sweat danced around his forehead as he looked into Nettie's adoring eyes. He had to push on. He couldn't allow Nettie to grow anymore infatuated with him than she already was. His heart was still aching from the devastating way Shar had discarded him. Landon wouldn't string Nettie along . . . he wouldn't let her hope for a future that would never be. "Here's the thing, Nettie." He used his handkerchief to wipe the sweat from his forehead. "I admire you a great deal, but I'm not in love with you. And I don't think my feelings are going to change anytime soon."

"B-but, I thought we had a lovely time at dinner."

"We did," he agreed. But then his mind drifted to Nettie singing that song, and all he could think of was how much his heart still longed for Shar. He closed his eyes, trying to block out the pain. When he opened them again, he confessed, "I'm not ready to date just yet. I enjoy your company, but I don't want to lead you to believe that anything more will ever happen between us. You're a lovely woman, and I want you to keep your eyes open for that special man who wants to steal your heart away. Okay?"

She stood up, smoothed out the creases in her skirt. "Landon, you don't have to tell me how wonderful I am while you're brushing me off." She threw her hands up in the air and then said, "I get it. You don't want me. Well fine, but you need to know that there ain't no other woman who'll love you like I do."

"I don't want to upset you, Nettie. I do so enjoy our friendship. I just don't want to lead you on, that's all."

Calming down a bit, Nettie said, "I didn't mean to get so upset, Landon. I just don't think you're giving me a fair chance.

I know that we could be good together if you'd just let loose with me."

He shook his head. "I don't think it's going to work." He held out a hand to her. "Can we just work on being friends?"

She looked at his hand without responding and then asked, "Do you go out to lunch or dinner with your friends from time to time?"

Nettie was a good dinner companion. As long as she understood that they were just friends, he didn't see any harm in enjoying a meal or two together from time to time. "That sounds lovely."

With that said, Nettie shook his hand and then walked out of his office.

✿

"Shar, oh my God, we were all so worried about you."

Trying to bring her eyes into focus, Shar looked around the room. Her head was pounding, and she was disoriented and dizzy. She heard Sallie talking to her, but her voice seemed as if it was a mile away. She tried to lift her head, but an explosion went off inside of it, and she fell back onto a soft cushiony pillow. "Where am I?"

"Oh, Shar, girl, I'm so glad that you're alive. I swear I didn't know if you was gon' make it." Sallie leaned down and hugged her.

Still trying to focus, Shar asked, "What happened to me? Where am I?"

"What? Shar, are you trying to say something?"

Shar grabbed hold of her throat as it was hurting when she spoke. "Can't you hear me? I want to know where I'm at."

Sallie stepped back a bit and gave Shar a funny look. She then said, "Poor chile, your voice is so hoarse I can barely hear you. But don't you worry none. After lying on the ground in the rain, anybody would be straining to talk."

"Somebody hit me?" Shar said the words as if she were asking, not telling.

Sallie strained to hear her. "Did you ask if someone hit you?" Shar nodded.

"You have a big bruise on your head, so I'd say you got hit with something."

"How'd you find me?"

Sallie sat down next to Shar's bed. "That ol' scallywag brought you back. Claims he found you lying in the street after you left him at some singing gig."

"I don't remember seeing Nicoli."

"You were in and out of consciousness for a little while, but we kept nursing you back to health, and thank God you opened your eyes again today."

Shar's mind began to turn as memories came flooding in. It had been raining, and a man was running up on her from behind. She remembered struggling with him over her handbag and then a lightning-quick pain in her head. Tears rolled down Shar's face as she tried to make sense of why anyone would beat her over the head and then leave her to die on the street. "Why, why?" Shar cried as she struggled with the hoarseness of her voice. She could do no more than whisper, a far cry from the way she used to belt out her vocals.

Shar's eyes widened in terror as the implication of losing her voice dawned on her. How could she sing if she couldn't even talk? Suddenly, she began grabbing at her throat, clawing and scratching as she screamed. Trying to hear the sound of her voice, but it didn't change anything.

"Shar, chile, calm down. Your voice will come back. You just have to give it time to heal." Sallie grabbed Shar's hands and moved them from her throat.

Grandma Gracey's voice had been beaten out of her, and it never returned. What if Shar's voice did the same to her. She remembered telling Mahalia that she didn't know what good singing did for anyone. But to have her voice taken away from her as if someone had stolen it, just like her handbag, was far more than Shar could bear.

"What's going on in here," Mammi, the mulatto woman who ran the boardinghouse they were staying in, asked as she stomped into the room.

"She's upset about her voice," Sallie said to the woman. "She can hardly speak."

Mammi tried to get Shar to calm down. But Shar was too far gone in her hysterics. She ran out of the room and came back with a pill bottle. "Take this. It will calm you down." Shar took the medicine and within a few minutes drifted back to sleep.

She slept comfortably the rest of the day. During the night as the sedative wore off, Shar began seeing shadows and hearing things. She screamed when the shadows came too close and the night noise set her on edge. Mammi came into her room and gave her another sedative; Shar took it again because she just wanted to get some sleep so she could rest her mind. As she drifted off, she was no longer seeing shadows, but a face appeared to her in her dreams that caused her heart to ache.

Waking in the morning, she stretched and yawned, turned on her side, and opened her eyes. Sallie was there again, sitting in a chair next to her bed. "How long have I been lying in this bed?" Shar asked as Sallie looked at her.

"This morning makes day three."

"Three days? Good Lord," Shar said, her voice was still hoarse, but it wasn't hurting her to talk anymore.

Sallie smiled. "You're pulling through pretty good, though. And I just can't tell you how glad I am that you're still among the living."

"Thank you," Shar whispered. Then she asked, "Has Landon been here?"

"Landon who? Are you talking about that preacher you left back home?"

Shar shook her head. "I saw his face in my dream last night. It seemed so real, I thought he had been here to see about me."

"Ain't nobody been here but that good-for-nothing, Nicoli James. And I was only too glad to see the back of him, when he left."

"Why, what did he say?"

Sallie put her hand to her forehead, rubbed it, blew out a long-suffering breath and then said, "I don't want to upset you, but Nicoli told me he was leaving town."

"What do you mean? How could he leave town without saying good-bye to me?"

Rolling her eyes, Sallie blurted, "From what I heard, he ran out of town with some nightclub floozy while dodging bullets from a gangster that he owed gambling money."

Shar figured the gangster was Mr. Marson and that Nicoli probably still owed him, since he kept on gambling. Shar knew that with the irresponsible way Nicoli would gamble away money and drink like a fish, she was better off without him. But her heart still ached for the man who had won her heart simply by smiling at her. Now he was gone, and she would be forced to get through these days without her voice and her man. "I've got nothing and nobody, and I just don't know what I'm supposed to do anymore," Shar whispered, trying not to strain her voice.

"What do you mean, what are you supposed to do?" Sallie stood up and boldly strutted over to Shar's bed. "You are going to do what we women been doing since the beginning of time—get up from this sick bed, dust yourself off, and keep on moving."

Turning onto her side and pulling the covers up over her shoulder, Shar said, "How can I keep moving, Sallie? You hear how my voice sounds. If I can't sing, what on earth am I supposed to do?"

Sallie leaned closer to Shar as she said, "Now, gal, I done told you that we don't do no pity parties around here. That beautiful voice of yours ain't gone nowhere. Let it rest, and God will bring it back."

Shar wished she could believe that, but Sallie didn't know what she had been doing with the voice God gave her just before she got herself knocked over the head. And Shar was too embarrassed to tell how she'd laid her morals down and stood on a stage dressed like a lady of the night and sang to a bunch of liquor-filled men.

God must be punishing me, Shar thought as she brought her hands to her face and poured out tears of regret . . . tears of sorrow . . . tears that wished she had never laid eyes on Nicoli James and all his big dreams and sinful ways.

Sallie put her hand on Shar's arm and lightly rubbed her arm. "Hush, chile, it will be all right."

She kept crying, even as she wiped the tears from her face, trying to dry her eyes and turn a stiff upper lip to her troubles. She wished she could just take Sallie at her word. But so much had gone wrong in her life that Shar didn't know what to believe anymore. "How, Sallie? How can anything ever be right again?"

Still rubbing Shar's arm, Sallie had this faraway look in her eyes as she said, "Life has a way of beating up on us so bad that we ain't never gon' find a way around them invisible fists. But if you trust God, I know you'll find a way."

Sallie sounded as if she knew exactly how Shar was feeling, as if she'd had her dreams and her heart ripped out a time or two and was still there to tell about it. But the problem Shar had was that she just didn't know if she truly trusted God anymore.

But she was grateful for Sallie, so she wiped her face again, gave a weak smile and said, "Thanks for being here for me, Sallie. I'm so glad I have you in my life. My mama's not here with me, but you have filled her shoes. I'll never forget your kindness to me."

Removing her hand from Shar's arm and getting tough again, Sallie wagged a finger at Shar. "Girl, can't nobody replace your mama. That's why I'm taking you home."

Did she hear right? Could it possibly be true? Was this nightmare truly coming to an end for her? "How can I go home? Don't we have a few more cities to go to?"

Sallie shook her head. "I already talked to the choir members. They are packing their belongings now. We're just waiting on you to get well enough for the journey."

When Shar first started working with Sallie, she had been terrified of the woman, thinking that she was just mean and surly. Although Sallie had some rough outer edges, she was plenty soft on the inside. Shar smiled for the first time in days. "I'm going home."

20

Home Again
1937–1940

Coming home didn't make all of Shar's troubles go away. Her mama was still in the hospital while Shar and her daddy was trying to come up with the money for her needs. She hadn't been able to find any day work when she arrived home, so Shar was singing in a club that Rosetta recommended her for. Sallie had been mostly right about Shar's voice coming back. She could sing, she experienced cracking every so often, but the folks in the nightclub were too drunk to know the difference. And Shar didn't care enough to work the imperfections out of her voice. She was no longer singing for the Lord, so all the joy she'd gotten from singing was now far from her.

She was at the hospital visiting her mama, so she tried to take her mind off of her troubles. The nurse had just wheeled her mother's bed outside so that she could get some fresh air. Shar had no understanding of how fresh air could cure tuberculosis, but she guessed it was the poor man's cure.

"Girl, why are you standing around gawking at me? Don't you have some songs to sing somewhere?" Marlene said with a hint of a devilish grin on her face.

Shar hadn't told her mama where she was singing at these days, and she didn't plan on having that conversation until her mother was good and well. But Shar was happy that her mother was in a joking mood. She'd been so fearful when she'd first seen her laying in that hospital bed, looking thin as a rail and coughing up her lungs. She smiled back at her mother. "Seems like you're feeling better this morning."

"I'll be better when these doctors stop poking and prodding on me."

"Stop giving them a hard time, Mama. I need you to get better. I've been terribly worried about you."

Marlene's body racked with coughing, as she tried to lift herself from her bed.

Shar jumped to action and helped her mother lift herself. She put a cup in front of Marlene as her mother spit out the gunk she'd coughed up. Breathing heavily, Marlene stretched back out on her bed. A colored nursing assistant rushed toward them. She looked over Marlene and then said, "I think you've had enough air today, don't you?"

Marlene nodded.

The woman turned to Shar and said, "You might want to let her rest. You can come back later on, okay?"

Her mother looked so frail and so ill all of a sudden, that Shar wanted to object to leaving her for even a moment. But her daddy had made her promise not to tire her mother out when she spent time with her at the hospital. He wanted his wife to get as much rest as possible while she could; they had no idea when the hospital would throw her out because of the cost of her treatment.

Grabbing hold of her mother's hand, she squeezed it. "I'll be back later on, Mama. You go get some sleep."

Marlene tried to squeeze her hand back, but the pressure was a little weak. "Go home and practice your singing. You need to get back on the road instead of sitting around here worrying about me."

Shar averted her eyes. "I'm not going anywhere until you get better," was all she said about that.

The nurse rolled Marlene's bed back into the hospital, and as Shar stood watching her go, a tear trickled down her cheek. So many colored people were denied access to hospitals when this epidemic first hit Chicago. But thanks to Provident Hospital and the visiting Nurse Association that had been trained at this colored hospital, her mother was receiving care. The hospital wasn't free. Provident relied on fees paid by patients, donations, and welfare reimbursements from the government. Shar might not be willing to tell her mama how she was making a living these days, but she was thankful that the earnings helped pay down the hospital bill they would now have to contend with.

As she left the hospital, she slowly walked home, kicking around street rocks as she thought about how life had taken her on so many twists and turns that she hadn't expected so early in life. She turned twenty-one that day, October the eleventh, and her mother hadn't even remembered to wish her a happy birthday. But Shar wasn't upset with her mama, not with all she was going through. She knew that if her mama had been in better health she would have baked Shar a yellow cake with white icing and her father would have sang happy birthday to her in his soft baritone voice.

But the world wouldn't stop rocking just because it happened to be Shar Gracey's birthday. No sir, that wasn't the way things worked for her family. No, even on sunshiny days, the Graceys still seemed to find the rain.

"What you moping around like that for on such a beautiful day like this?"

Shar lifted her head as she stepped on the porch of the poor excuse of a home she shared with her parents. Her father was in the doorway holding a slice of pound cake with a matchstick in it. "What's this?"

"You thought I forgot, didn't you?" Johnny Gracey asked as Shar walked into the house. "Now just sit down at the table and let me light this match so you can make a wish."

Shar was practically giddy as she sat down. "Mama didn't remember that it was my birthday, so I thought for sure you had forgotten because she has to remind you about everything."

"Girl, hush, your mama ain't the only one around here with a good memory." Johnny set the cake in front of her. He then sang, "Happy birthday to you, happy birthday to you. Happy birthday to you, my sweet little girl, happy birthday to you."

Shar smiled. "Thank you, Daddy."

"How old are you? How old are you?" he continued singing in that soft baritone, looking to her with expectation in his eyes.

Shar knew her father wanted her to sing-song, "I'm twenty-one years old." But she couldn't bring herself to try even such a small riff. If her voice cracked while she tried to sing, her father would immediately want to know what happened to her. It was enough that he knew she was singing in saloons. He didn't have to know of the other hardships that had befallen her while on tour. "I'm twenty-one, Dad, you know that," she said in her regular voice.

Johnny gave her a puzzled look, but he didn't question her. He just pulled the match out of the cake and scratched it against the wood table leg. As the match lit, he put it back down in the center of her slice of cake. "Now, blow that out and make your wish."

Shar closed her eyes, quickly trying to come up with a wish. She wanted to beg God to get her out of these nightclubs and to fully restore her voice, but with her mama being in the hospital and needing a healing, Shar felt selfish requesting anything for herself. So as she blew out the makeshift candle, she wished for health, strength, and long life for her mama. "There, I blew it out." She then kissed her father on the cheek, "Now let me eat my birthday cake and then I'll help you with the house."

Johnny grabbed his tool belt and hammer. "It's your birthday. You stay right in here and rest and I'll get the house done."

Shar shook her head as she watched her dad grab some wood blocks and head out to the porch. He was a hardworking man, taking odd jobs wherever he could and then still coming home and working on their raggedy old house, trying to get the draft out so that his wife wouldn't get sicker just by simply coming home to a drafty home.

Shar was so thankful that her daddy remembered her birthday, but she wasn't going to dally long. She would eat her piece of cake and then go help so he could get to bed on time tonight. Her father had been so happy for her to go off with Thomas Dorsey and sing in a group the way he had wanted to do, but he had never been able to. So, he'd let her to go off and live his dream. While Shar had been excited to go, leaving had caused her daddy to become the sole supporter and caregiver for her mother. He was worn out from the weight that had been placed on his shoulders, and Shar planned to do everything in her power to ease some of his load.

After eating her cake, she changed into a pair of old work pants that she used to wear while helping her mother with the wash. By the time she came out of her room, her daddy had finished boarding up the porch. He then walked back into the house with a bunch of plastic under his arms. "What are you going to do with that?" Shar asked.

"Got to close up some of the draft that's coming through these useless windows." Johnny threw all the sheets of plastic on the floor except one. He pulled out his hammer and a few nails and began tacking the plastic to the window pane.

"What do you need me to do?" Shar wasn't about to stand around twiddling her thumbs while her dad did all the work.

Johnny pointed toward the back of the house. "Bring those rugs that I laid on the back porch in here and start putting them against the walls in the kitchen."

"Aye-aye, sir." Shar got to work, helping her daddy in his quest to decrease the drafty feel of the old house. The rugs were all tattered, worn, and torn. Shar imagined that her father had been scouring trash bins all over town in order to get his hands on enough rugs to lay around the house.

She got down on her hands and knees and placed half of the rugs against the wall and the other half of them on the floor next to the wall to block the draft blowing into the house from outside. The draft wasn't so bad right then, in mid-October; however, within the next few weeks it would become unbearable. So she moved along the floor, placing one rug after the next against the wall.

"I like the sound of that," Johnny said as he turned away from the window he was tacking plastic to.

"Huh? You like the sound of what?" Shar asked with furrowed brows.

"You're humming. You and your mama used to do that all the time while you worked. Well, your mama used to do the humming while you sang. But it has always sounded good to my ears."

Shaking her head, Shar told him, "Daddy, everything I do sounds good to your ears."

"You better believe it. You're my baby girl, and I'm right proud of you."

"Thanks, Daddy," Shar said with a big ol' grin on her face. She liked knowing that her father was proud of her. As she started to turn back to her job, she caught a glimpse of her dad's face as it contorted a bit and he grabbed hold of his chest.

Shar jumped up and ran over to her father and just reached him as he began to stumble and fall. Grabbing hold of him just before he hit the floor, Shar started screaming, "Daddy, Daddy, what's wrong?"

His eyes bulged as if trying to burst out of his head. He tried to speak as he clutched at his chest, but then his eyes closed and his body went limp.

"Oh God, no, no, no. Don't let this happen." She grabbed hold of her daddy as tears blurred her vision. "Daddy, please don't leave us here without you. Please wake up."

Shar realized that she couldn't just sit there begging her father to wake up. She had to do something . . . had to get some help. She gently placed her father on the ground and ran out of the house looking for somebody, anybody who could lend them a hand.

21

*W*e did it," Nettie said with excitement oozing out of her as she closed the door behind the young educated couple who'd just walked out of Landon's office.

"Yeah, we got the ten people we need for our housing program, but we still don't have enough money." Landon stood and paced the floor, a look of concern etched across his face.

"Calm down, you're acting like more of a nervous Nellie than I do. The money will come. God wouldn't let you get this far without making a way to see you to the finish line. Isn't that what you preach to us all the time?"

Landon stopped pacing and stared at Nettie. She was right and he knew it. He preached faith and nothing less to his congregation, so he needed to maybe sit down and reread the notes of one of his sermons so he could calm himself. "You're right," he finally said. "Trust God and the money will follow. That's how we've been able to keep the doors of the church open, and that will be the way we get our people good quality housing."

Nettie gave Landon an atta-boy shove to the shoulder. "Now you're sounding like the confident pastor that I know."

"I guess I just needed someone to remind me that I'm not in this alone."

"You are never alone, Pastor Landon. God is with you, and I will always be here fighting this good fight right by your side." Nettie's eyes glowed with longing as she said those last words.

Landon was beginning to feel uncomfortable. His office was small, so they had no choice but to be standing in close proximity of each other. He gave her comment a curt nod and then retreated behind his desk. "Thank you for your kindness, Sister Nettie."

"Not at all," Nettie said as she sat down in the chair in front of his desk. "But my mama don't seem to think I'm being kind to you. She says you're just falling away . . . just skin and bones. And that it's my responsibility to see that you get a good meal every now and then."

Landon caught the playful lilt in Nettie's voice and played along. "I think your mama is on to something. I just might be adding a line about feeding the pastor to your job description."

They both laughed.

Then Nettie said, "No need to add it to my job description, Pastor. My parents would consider it an honor if you would eat dinner with us a few times a week. And you know that my mom's fried chicken is the best thing this side of heaven."

Patting his stomach, Landon agreed. "Of this I am well aware."

"Well then, you need to come and get yourself a plate. Tonight she's making meatloaf and mashed potatoes. And I know how much you love meatloaf."

Landon's stomach picked that moment to growl.

Nettie arched an eyebrow.

Landon said, "Let me finish working on my sermon and then I'll walk you home so I can sample Mrs. Johnson's famous meatloaf."

Grinning from ear to ear, Nettie stood and walked toward the door. "Let me get out of your way so you can get your sermon done. I have some typing to do anyway." As she put her hand on the doorknob the door jerked open, and Nettie jumped back.

"Pastor, pastor, I'm sorry to bother you, but we need you down at the hospital quick and fast," Deacon Monroe said as he rushed into the office, hat in hand.

Deacon Monroe and Landon took turns visiting the sick and shut-in. This was Monroe's week. "What seems to be the trouble, Deacon?" Landon asked as he stood and grabbed his hat and overcoat.

"It's Shar Gracey."

Landon heard the name, and it nearly knocked him over. He grabbed hold of the edge of his desk as he tried to stop his world from rocking. He'd tried desperately to get her out of his heart and mind, but truth be told, he thought about Shar all the time . . . heard the sweet sound of her voice even when he wanted to block out the sound and drown it in the laughter of another woman. "What's happened to Shar?"

"Johnny done had a heart attack. They got him to Provident Hospital. It don't look good. But then to top it off, the people down there told Shar that they were going to release Marlene to go home today and it was as if she lost her mind." Deacon Monroe fidgeted with his hat as if the whole event had turned him into a nervous wreck. "The nurses don't know whether to admit Shar or to call the police on her."

"Let's get down there and see what we can do to help." Landon put on his coat and rushed out of his office without a backward glance. He hurriedly made his way down the street.

"Wait a second, Pastor. Don't leave without me," Monroe said as he caught up with Landon. "I ran all the way here from the hospital and wouldn't mind some company on my way back."

"I wasn't thinking. I should have realized that you would be going back to the hospital. One of these days we'll be able to get us a car. It'll sure make visiting the sick and shut-in a lot easier."

"Haven't been driving nothing but these two feet all my life. Me and the missus gave up thoughts of a car and such for luxuries like food and shelter," Deacon Monroe joked.

Even with worrying about Shar, Landon smiled at Monroe's comment. The man was always in such good spirits. It didn't matter to him that he and his family didn't have much. It blessed him to just be able to serve God. The Black Belt needed more families like the Monroes. But then again, there were too many families like the Monroes when it came to poverty in their community. Landon didn't believe that colored folk were meant to stay poor and broke, taking whatever they could get all their lives.

He believed in progress and upward mobility. He also believed that God was just and that He saw the suffering of colored folk and would bring about a change. He just didn't know how much longer the people in that neighborhood could wait for that change to come.

Getting his mind back on the situation at hand, Landon asked Monroe. "When did Shar get back in town?"

"From what I heard, she been home about two weeks."

Landon nodded. "And Shar has been at the hospital trying to take care of both of them, I bet."

"You know how Ms. Shar is. Her ma and pa mean the world to her. They couldn't have asked for a better child if they had begged the Lord God Himself for her."

Once they reached the hospital, Landon and Monroe rushed in. Landon's eyes darted around the entry of the hospital. When he didn't see Shar, he turned to Deacon Monroe and asked, "Where is she?"

"When I left she was in Marlene's room arguing with the nurses. I hope she hasn't already been thrown out of here," Deacon Monroe said.

Since both men had visited Marlene previously, they knew right away where to go. As they headed down the corridor where Marlene's room was, there was no doubt that Shar was indeed still in the hospital. She could be heard shouting all the way down the hall.

"No, Mama, don't put that on. You are not going anywhere." Shar hollered.

As Landon and Monroe walked into the room, Shar turned to the nurse and said, "Leave us alone. She has every right to stay here a few more days."

Landon was caught off guard by the wild-eyed look Shar was flashing at the nurse and now he understood why Monroe thought the hospital personnel might have to admit her. Shar's hair was unkempt and going every which way as she pointed her finger in the nurse's face and looked as if she was about to lose her mind.

Landon had never seen Shar look like that. He instantly felt her pain, and his heart went out to her. Putting his arms around her he said, "Calm down. Don't upset yourself like this."

Shar fell into Landon's arms, tears gushing out. "Please, Landon, please don't let them throw my mama out of this hospital."

"Hush. You've caused enough commotion in here. Just hand me my clothes so I can get dressed and go home." Marlene started coughing even as she reached out her hands for her clothes.

With her head lying on Landon's shoulder, Shar continued to protest. "You can't go back to that house, Mama. I haven't had a chance to get it ready for you."

The nurse shook her head. "I wish I could help you with this. But we have tons of sick people out there who need rooms." She pointed toward the door. "Your mother has been here for weeks. We've done all we can for her."

"But my dad said that the house isn't safe for her. If I let her go home before I can get it ready, he might have another heart attack from worrying so much."

"All I can tell you is that my boss has decided to call the police. So you've got five minutes to clear out or risk being charged with trespassing." She started walking toward the door, but just before she walked out, she turned slightly and said, "I'm sorry about this. And I hope your mom continues to improve."

As the nurse left the room, Marlene said, "Shar, baby, just hand me my clothes so I can get out of here and stop causing trouble."

Shar folded over as she broke down in tears and began wailing out sorrows from way down deep, from somewhere Landon couldn't fathom. As Landon held Shar, it seemed to him that the pain she was fighting against was an immovable thing. And he wondered what had happened to her to cause such pain?

Marlene got out of bed, took her clothes out of her daughter's hand, and went into the bathroom to change. She walked a little slow and was still coughing, but Marlene didn't appear to be on death's door. So, again, Landon was puzzled by Shar's response. He sat her down in the chair next to the bed and said, "Your mom is going to be all right. You've got to believe that. Everyone at the church has been praying for her, and it looks to me like she's getting better."

"But the house is too drafty. Daddy said that she'll get sicker if we don't get the draft out of that old rundown house."

"Okay, calm down, child," Deacon Monroe said. "We'll figure out something."

"I'm sorry," Shar said as she wiped the tears from her face. "I don't mean to be so hysterical, but I know my dad had that heart attack because of how worried he's been over my mom's illness. If she goes back to that house, it just might kill him."

Landon sat down next to Shar and put her hand in his. "We have enough men at the church who can do the work on your parents' house. I promise you, we will get the house in tip-top shape."

Shar raised her head and stared into Landon's eyes. He saw her need to believe in something, but he also could tell that something was hindering her. And he found himself wondering again at the pain in her eyes.

"Thank you for being so kind, Pastor Landon. But even if you all helped us fix up the house, I still don't have anywhere for her to go while the work is being done. Winter will be here before we know it. And there's no way that she'll be able to endure the strong winds."

The bathroom door opened, and Marlene stood there holding onto the doorknob, looking as if the blood had drained from her face. "Deacon Monroe, can you please help me over to the bed?"

"Sure thing, Mrs. Marlene," he said as he hurried to grab her arm and escort her over to the bed. "You look all tuckered out."

"Putting on my clothes zapped all the energy out of me. Lying around in this old bed has just made me lazy," Marlene complained as she sat on the bed and took a few deep breaths.

"You don't have a lazy bone in your body, Mama. You're just tired from being ill. That's why I don't want you going back to that house. You don't have the strength to fight against the cold Chicago winds."

Marlene turned toward her daughter, and for a moment there was sadness in her eyes. Then as if willing herself, the look instantly changed to mischief as she said, "Don't you worry, Shar, I'll be around to do the two-step at your wedding and to listen to one of them gospel records you plan on recording."

At her mother's comment, Shar lowered her eyes and bit on her lower lip. Landon wondered why Shar didn't seem excited by her mother's proclamation. But in truth, he was more concerned about Mrs. Marlene dancing at Shar's wedding . . . a wedding that would not include him. Landon could still see the smug look on Nicoli's face when he told him that he and Shar were engaged. So much for love conquering all.

Landon visibly shook himself as he made up his mind to focus on the situation at hand. He and Shar were not meant to be. That was it; that was all . . . end of story. "Did you hear your mama? She plans to get better so that she can witness all of the wonderful moments in your life that have yet to occur."

Shar lifted her face toward Landon. Her eyes were brimming with unshed tears and defeat as she said, "There's no guarantee that any of those things will happen. I just want her to live for today, tomorrow, and the next day."

Landon could take Shar's despair no longer. He asked Deacon Monroe, "Do you and your wife still have that spare room for rent?"

"Well, sure we do, Pastor Landon. But as much as I'd like to help. My wife would skin me alive if I brought Mrs. Marlene into the house. She wouldn't want to take the chance of catching this tuberculosis."

"She's not even contagious anymore," Shar stood and proclaimed. "We need help. She can't go back to that house. Please help us, Deacon Monroe."

"Settle down," Landon said. "I wasn't asking for the room for Mrs. Marlene. I'm going to let you and your mom stay at my house while I rustle up some of the folks at the church to help me fix the house." Landon turned back to Deacon Monroe. "I'll be needing that room at your house, if you think Mrs. Lily will approve."

Deacon Monroe laughed. "Are you kidding? Lily would be honored to tell all the townsfolk that the high and mighty Pastor Landon Norstrom was a guest in our boardinghouse."

"Well, then it's settled," Landon said while clasping his hands together.

Marlene held up a hand. "Not so fast, Pastor Norstrom. Now my husband is a very proud man. He don't like taking charity from nobody." Before she could finish her statement, her body was racked with another coughing spell.

"Mama, be reasonable. Daddy don't want you in that house until we can get the draft out of it."

Marlene held up a hand silencing her daughter as the coughing subsided. "I know you mean well, Pastor, but I need to speak with my husband about this before I can accept your kindness." She pointed toward the wheelchair that the nurse had brought into the room for her departure. "Now if someone can wheel me down to his room, I'll just see what Mr. Johnny Gracey has to say about this, because heart attack or not, that man is still the head of this family."

22

Shar's father was still too ill to have visitors, so Landon and Deacon Monroe stayed behind in the waiting area while Shar wheeled her mother in to see him. Shar wasn't prepared for how hard it would be to see her father lying there connected to tubes and machines, and for how pale and thin he looked. Her father was her rock. He'd always seemed like the strongest man in the world to her . . . like John Henry, wielding his hammer down the railroad line, matching that big old machine, nail for nail, until he won the competition and then died with that hammer in his hand.

Johnny Gracey had always been big and powerful and could do anything but fail. That's the way Shar had seen him since she was a little girl, beaming up at her hard-working daddy. But that day, no matter how she tried, she couldn't compare Johnny Gracey to John Henry by any stretch of the imagination. That heart attack had severely weakened her father. But if she were to measure the depths of his fall, it was probably the constant worry and care for her mother that had taken its toll and robbed him of his vigor.

His eyes lifted slightly as Shar rolled her mother's wheelchair next to his bed and Marlene reached out to put her hand on his arm.

"Hey, you two," Johnny said with a groggy and tired sounding voice.

"Hey yourself." Marlene smiled at her husband then added, "I don't take kindly to you scaring me like this."

"Daddy, I was so worried about you. All I could do was thank God that you are still here with us."

His voice was low and lackluster as he told Shar, "You know I wasn't gon' leave you and your mom." He then turned to Marlene and added, "Baby, I didn't mean no harm. I want you to concentrate on getting better. So, don't you dare start worrying about me."

Marlene gently patted her husband's arm. "I know you didn't. I'll try not to worry too much about you, if you stop worrying so much about me."

Shar stood behind her mother's chair, watching her parents. They had weathered many storms during their twenty-five-year marriage. But one thing remained constant and that was the love they felt for each another. Watching her mother and father interact, Shar thought about how harsh Nicoli had been with her. It was at that moment that she realized she had fallen for a man who was nothing like her father.

Nicoli wasn't interested in working hard in order to take care of his family. He was always chasing sky-high dreams but was too busy drinking and gambling to fullfil any of 'em. She knew as sure as rain comes in the spring that she would have been miserable married to a man like Nicoli. How she wished she had waited for Landon. But why hadn't Landon taken the time to write back to her when she was pouring her heart out to him?

He said that he'd written back to her, that he had responded to her letters. But why hadn't she received any of his letters? Why didn't she know that he still cared for her before she got herself mixed up with Nicoli? None of those questions mattered now. Shar was positive that Landon had moved on with his life and wasn't in the least bit worried about her. She had to pick up the shards of her broken life and focus on helping her parents get well. Because as God was her witness, she was not about to let the only love she had left in this world leave her.

"Pastor Landon has invited me and Shar to stay at his house while he and some of the menfolk at the church work on our house," Marlene said.

"Mighty nice of him," was all Johnny said before he closed his eyes and drifted back to sleep.

"Well, you heard him, Mama. Daddy don't have a problem with us accepting help from Pastor Landon. So let's get on out of here and let Daddy get some rest."

Marlene gave her sleeping husband a lingering smile. She then looked up at her daughter. "All right, let's go."

Shar leaned over and kissed her father on the forehead. "I'll come back to see you tomorrow," she whispered in his ear and then grabbed hold of the handles on her mother's wheelchair and headed out of his room.

Landon stood as Shar guided her mother's chair back to the waiting room. "How is he doing?"

"He's tired, but I think he's going to make it. At least he promised as much," Shar said, while putting a brave smile on her face.

"Good." Landon clasped his hands together. "Well, let's get your mom to my house."

When Landon put his hands over hers, Shar felt an emotional tidal wave run through her very being. She glanced up at him. His eyes were so loving and caring that she wanted to reach out to him. But she quickly reminded herself that Landon was not her husband, and after the mistakes she'd made, he probably never would be. So she removed her hands from the wheelchair and stepped aside. "Thank you."

"No thanks needed. Just move out of the way so I can get Mrs. Marlene situated."

Shar did as he requested, all the while thinking as she watched Landon handle her mother with such care and concern that this was a good man. Someone who would stick and stay even through the hard times. A man like her daddy. "But I have to thank you, Landon. There's not a lot of men who would do what you're doing for my mama." Her voice broke as she continued. "I just want you to know that I'm mighty thankful and indebted to you."

"You being back in town long enough to sing in our choir is thanks enough, as far as I'm concerned. The whole church has missed the sweet sound of your voice."

Shar didn't respond to that, but there was no way on God's green earth that she was getting back in that choir, not after singing in nightclubs. She wasn't Rosetta and could never pretend to be.

✑

Once they were at the house, Marlene sat down on the bed and stretched out her hand to Shar. "Hand me my bag so I can change back into my nightgown."

"I can help you, Mama. You don't have to do this on your own."

Marlene waved Shar away. "Hush, girl, I might be sick, but I can still dress and undress myself."

"Okay," Shar relented and handed her mother the bag. She then walked out of the room with Landon and Deacon Monroe.

Landon pointed to the room next door to Marlene's. "You can sleep in there."

Shar shook her head. "I can sleep with my mama. I don't need my own room."

"I have two bedrooms in this house, Shar. You can take my bedroom. I won't be here anyway. I'm going to pack a few of my clothes and then head out of here."

She nodded. Then said, "Take your time getting your stuff. I'm going to walk over to our house to get some of our things."

Landon held out his hand. "If you give me the keys, I'll pick up some things for you and your mom and bring them back tonight."

She shook her head. "I can't let you do all of that. You have already done so much for us. Don't worry about doing this tonight, Pastor Landon. Just go on to Deacon Monroe's house and get some rest. I'll find a way to our house tomorrow and bring back the things that we need." How could she run him all around town when she had treated him so shamelessly?

"No such thing, Sister Shar," Monroe said. "Now you were out of sorts today at that hospital. And we know that you're dealing with a mountain load right now with your ma and pa taking ill. So go on in there and sit with your mama while we go get your things."

Sighing heavily, Shar's shoulders slumped as she admitted what everyone else could already see. "I am awfully tired."

Landon held out his hand again. "Give me the keys and I'll go to the house and get your stuff."

She had mixed feelings about leaning any further on Pastor Landon's kindness, but she didn't continue to argue with him at that time. She handed over the keys with a grateful heart and then went back to the bedroom and sat with her mother.

Marlene was already in her nightgown and just pulling up the covers over her shoulder as Shar sat down in the wooden chair next to her bed. "Deacon Monroe and Pastor left already?"

"Yeah, Pastor Landon and Deacon Monroe are going to the house to bring back some of our things."

"That's mighty nice of them."

Nodding, Shar said, "I tried to talk them out of it . . . told them that I could just go over there tomorrow. But they wouldn't hear of it."

"Pastor Landon is a gentleman. He wouldn't have you lugging all of our stuff over here by yourself." Marlene was overtaken by another coughing fit. Shar ran and grabbed a glass of water. When the coughing subsided, she sipped the water and then smiled as she said, "Remember how I used to have you taking cakes and pies to Pastor Landon?"

"I remember, Mama."

Getting comfortable as she laid her head on the soft pillow, Marlene said, "Why don't you bake a lemon cake for Pastor. You know, to show him how much we appreciate him letting us stay in this warm, draft-free house of his."

Her mama wasn't fooling her one bit. She knew that the cake wasn't just for no appreciation. Marlene Gracey wanted to showcase her daughter's cooking skills to the most eligible bachelor in the Black Belt. They tried it once before, and Landon had come calling, even asking for her hand in marriage. But after what she'd done to him, Shar didn't think a lemon cake would get him sweet on her again. To appease her mama, she said, "I'll get down to the store in a couple of days to get the items needed for the cake."

"Mmmh," was all Marlene said as her eyelids began to close.

Shar watched her mama sink into the mattress. Her mama appeared to be at peace, so she decided it was time for her to find some peace with the situation also. Yes, she had lost the affection of the only man who truly cared for her and both of her parents had taken ill, but they were still alive. Shar decided to find hope in that. For now it was enough.

"Shar," Marlene whispered her daughter's name.

"Yes, Mama, do you need me to get something for you?"

"No, baby, I'm tired right now and just want to sleep. You go get yourself settled in the other room."

"Okay, but I'll leave my door open. So just holler if you need anything."

Marlene smiled.

Standing, Shar prepared to leave, but Marlene reached out for her hand. The two women clasped hands, and Shar waited to see what her mother needed.

"I don't want you fretting over me and your daddy. Let God's will be done and then move on with your life. Whatever the outcome, promise me."

What could she say to that? Would God's will be what she wanted? Or would she be devastated by some outcome that she couldn't even bring herself to think about? She was weak in these matters, but her mother was waiting for a response, so she simply nodded and left the room.

23

$\mathscr{L}$andon wanted to call in sick. After a late night of packing at the Gracey's house and then packing his own items to take with him over to Deacon Monroe's house, not to mention the time he spent going from house to house trying to find able-bodied men willing to help over at the Gracey house . . . he was plum worn out.

But he had no time to lie in bed and nurse his aching back. He had to pick up Joe Peterson, Mike Johnson, and Paul Benson. These men were out of work at the moment, so they had time on their hands to work on the Gracey house. He picked them up and dropped them off. He then dragged himself into church because it was Friday and he still had a sermon to write. He'd gotten sidetracked yesterday after Deacon Monroe scared the life out of him when he said that Shar was in the hospital.

Landon had immediately assumed that Shar had been hurt. And in truth, she had. When they arrived at the hospital, Shar was in such a state that he feared for her health. He certainly hadn't planned to give his house to Shar and her mother when he and Deacon Monroe first walked into the hospital. But after seeing her and hearing what her concerns were, Landon knew that he couldn't allow Marlene to go back to that drafty house, not when he knew that his home was comfy and warm.

Shar may have ripped out his heart with the engagement, but he would never turn his back on her. But Landon couldn't help wondering where her fiancé was, and why, other than the vague comment about doing a two-step at Shar's wedding, Mrs. Marlene and Shar never said a word about plans for Shar's upcoming wedding. But he wasn't going to fret over things that weren't his to fret over.

Landon sat down behind his desk, opened his Bible, and began reading, trying to pinpoint which scriptures he wanted to build his Sunday sermon on. Twenty minutes into his studies there was a knock on his office door.

Rubbing his eyes, Landon looked up. "Come in."

The door opened, and Nettie swept into the room carrying a plate with aluminum foil over it. "What happened to you?"

With furrowed eyebrows, Landon said, "Huh?"

"My mom slaved over the stove yesterday, fixing the meatloaf that you love so much." She put the plate down on his desk. "She told me to bring you some of the leftovers, but she wants to know why you didn't show up to eat it in person."

Landon hit his forehead with the palm of his hand. "Things got crazy after Deacon and I went off to the hospital yesterday, but I am so sorry that I forgot about dinner."

"I'm not the one you should be apologizing to. Maybe you should come by the house after Sunday service and give Mama your apologies in person."

Landon nodded. "I'll do that. But can you please tell her that I had an emergency with a few of our members last night and got so involved with helping them, that I didn't eat at all last night." He pulled the foil off the plate. "Matter of fact, I didn't eat anything, but a piece of toast for breakfast. So if you don't mind, I think I'll eat this scrumptious meal right now."

Nettie smiled, "Let me grab you a fork out of my desk drawer." She left the room in search of her fork.

As Landon looked at the mashed potatoes, green beans, yams, and meatloaf, his mouth began watering. He pinched off a piece of the meatloaf and popped it into his mouth. It was so good, he just about moaned.

Nettie came back into the room holding the fork. "Here you go."

"Thanks," he said as he took the fork and dug in. His belly was enjoying every bite. As a bachelor he didn't get those kinds of meals every day and sure appreciated when he did.

Sitting down in front of Landon's desk, Nettie asked, "You like?"

"Mmmh." His mouth was full so he couldn't respond with words.

Nettie laughed. "That good, huh?"

Landon nodded. Kept eating.

Nettie sat in the chair just watching him, saying nothing.

It took Landon a moment to realize that she was staring at him. He took his last bite and then looked up. Nettie smiled at him. The smile was sweet and endearing, but Landon had the feeling he was missing something. "What? Do I have some food on my chin or something?"

"No, I was just watching you enjoy a good meal."

"That it was. Please thank your mother for me."

Nettie shook her head. "You need to thank her yourself this time. Her feelings are going to get hurt pretty soon if you don't stop by the house sometime soon."

He took on an ah-shucks look. "You are so right. I will come over after church on Sunday to show my appreciation to your blessed mother."

Nettie pointed a finger at him as she stood. "I'm going to hold you to that."

Lifting his hands as if he'd been cornered by the law, he said, "I promise. I'll be there. Nothing could keep me away."

Before leaving his office, Nettie asked, "How is Mrs. Marlene?"

"She's still a little weak, but I'd say she's on the mend."

"Good, and does Shar need help watching out for her mama on the nights she sings down at Ray's?"

That caught him offguard. "Since when has Shar been singing at that nightclub?"

Nettie hunched her shoulders. "I wouldn't know. I just overheard a friend of my dad's saying that he saw her there last week."

Landon leaned back in his seat as Nettie left his office. He would have never thought that Shar would use her Godgiven gift for singing in saloons. But he was discovering that there were a lot of things he didn't know about Shar Gracey. Landon wished he could will his heart to fall for Nettie. She obviously was still interested in him, and it seemed to Landon that she would look after him. If she could cook anything like her mother, then Landon knew for sure that he would enjoy his meals. He also enjoyed spending time with Nettie. She was easy to get along with. The only problem he had was that he didn't feel that spark for Nettie that he needed to feel for a woman he wanted to spend the rest of his life with.

He'd had that spark for Shar. He used to stand outside the church, pretending to be excited about greeting everyone as they entered the building. But in truth, he had been there because his heart did a flip every time he saw Shar walking or running toward the church. He would chat with her about nothing much at all for a moment or two. But in those moments, Landon had felt alive.

Chastising himself for allowing the image of Shar to sneak into his mind and heart again, Landon stood up and grabbed his hat. As he opened the door to his office and entered the reception area, he told Nettie, "I'm going to visit some of our sick and shut-in."

He waved as he left the building. Mother Barnett had fallen and hurt her arm and her back. Her doctor had told her to take it easy, so she hadn't been able to attend church for two Sundays in a row. Mother Barnett lived alone, since her husband ran off, so Landon wanted to make sure she was all right.

When he arrived at the house, her niece answered the door and showed him to the back room where Mother Barnett was lying with her arm propped on a pillow. "It does my heart good to see that you are following doctor's orders, Mother Barnett."

"As old as I am, can't do nothing but obey doctor's orders." With a sly smile she added, "My back hurts too bad to move it."

"I'm sorry to hear that, Mother."

"Charlotte," Mother Barnett shouted.

"Yes, Ma'am?" The girl made her way into the room.

"Get Pastor Landon a chair so he can sit down for a while."

Charlotte grabbed a folding chair from the living room and then brought it back to Landon. "Here you go, Pastor. Sorry it's not something more comfortable."

"It's just fine. Thank you." Landon sat down and proceeded to tell Mother Barnett about the goings-on at the church. "The Mothers' Board sold chicken dinners last Sunday and raised forty dollars."

"You kidding. The last time I helped with the fish fry, we only raised thirty dollars. I guess church folk like chicken better than fish these days."

"I wouldn't kid you, Mother Barnett. We made a whopping forty dollars." Landon was grinning as he told the story. But even though he thought the Mothers' Board did an awesome job with the fund-raiser, he still knew that earning forty dollars a week on chicken dinners would not get them where they needed to be in order to help people with their home situations in enough time.

"Well now, I bet that was something to see . . . sure wish I had been there." Mother Barnett rubbed her arm as a look of agony crossed her face. "But this old arm been hurting me something powerful."

In a joking mood, Landon asked, "How's that knee?"

Mother Barnett smiled. "Surprisingly, it's about the only thing that doesn't hurt on me today. So you know what that means, don't you?"

"This must be a good-news day."

"That's right."

Landon guessed that there would be a light in her front window tonight. After they chatted for a while, he told her that either he or Deacon Monroe would be around to check on her next week.

He left Mother Barnett's house and headed for Provident Hospital. Three of their members were in the hospital; Deacon Monroe had managed to visit with two of them before he found Shar in disarray. Landon was going to visit with the last one on their list and then he would add Johnny Gracey to the list and check on him that day also.

Landon was in the hospital about an hour before he had a chance to see Johnny. Normally only family was allowed to visit with the seriously ill patient. But since Landon was clergy and the hospital staff knew him well, they allowed him to go in.

Johnny's eyes were closed as Landon entered his room. He sat down in the chair next to the bed and very quietly began praying for the man who, if things had gone the way Landon had planned, would have been his father-in-law. But things never go as planned, as Mother Barnett's life had shown.

When he finished praying, Landon lifted his head to see that Johnny's eyes were slightly opened. He was having a hard time breathing but still wanted to talk. "Th-thank you . . . for . . . coming by . . . Reverend."

Landon put a smile on his face, trying to cover up the concern he felt for this man. "How are you feeling today, Mr. Gracey?"

Clearing his throat, he managed, "I've been better. That's for sure."

"Well, I'm praying for you. And I'll be adding your name to the sick and shut-in list so that the Mothers' Board can begin praying for you, as well. And you know those women got some powerful prayers. Must be living right, is all I can say," Landon added.

"You done more than enough for me when you allowed Marlene and Shar to stay at your home." Johnny shook his head. "I don't cotton much to charity. Like to do things on my own, but what you done for my family—" Fresh tears glistened in his eyes as he added, "I could die a happy man, just knowing that Marlene don't have to go back to that drafty house."

"Hey, there will be no talk about dying. Not anytime soon anyway." Landon wagged a finger in Johnny's face. "Your wife and daughter would be devastated, so you have no choice but to get well. You got me?"

Johnny held up a hand in surrender. "I promise. I will not die . . . yet."

"That's better. Now I have some positive news to report back to your family."

Johnny half-heartedly laughed at that comment, then he turned serious as he looked Landon straight in the eye and said, "I didn't do right by you and Shar. I sent her away from you, and now I've ruined both of your lives."

"I'll get over it, Mr. Gracey. Don't you worry about me. And I'm sure that Shar doesn't concern herself about what could have been either."

Johnny shook his head. "Shar's changed since she's been back. She don't have that same fire in her eyes. Something happened to her back on them roads. And I have only myself to blame for it."

This revelation mystified and angered Landon. What could have happened to take the fire out of Shar's eyes? Had someone done something to her? Was it Nicoli? Landon was determined that he would get to the bottom of the matter. "Do you think her fiancé did something to her while they were on the road?"

A puzzled look was on Johnny's face. "What fiancé?"

Had Shar not told her family about the man she planned to marry? "His name is Nicoli James. I met him when the choir came to Chicago a few months back."

"Well, I sure never met him. Shar didn't bring him around me and her mama when she was in town that week."

"I met him, sir. He seemed smitten with Shar. Even told me that they were engaged."

Johnny closed his eyes and took a few deep breaths. "I wonder if this Nicoli is the reason that Shar's been singing in that saloon."

"So you know about that?"

Johnny shook his head. "Told me that a friend set her up in that club so she could make some money. But Shar never would have dreamed of making money that way before she went out on the road. And I'll tell you something else. She might be performing and earning money for it, but she don't have that same love of singing that she used to have."

Landon remembered mentioning the choir to her the night before. He also remembered that Shar hadn't given him an answer. But Landon hadn't thought anything of it at the time. "Why do you think Shar has lost her love for singing?"

Johnny shook his head as though it was painful to even think about. "That girl has been singing around the house since she was two years old. But ever since she came back home, the most she has done is hum . . . and that didn't even go on for long before she stopped herself from doing that."

"You don't say," was all Landon was able to get out of his mouth. He truly had become perplexed by the news Mr. Gracey had laid on him. Shar loved to sing. If that had somehow been stolen from her, then Landon had found the answer to his questions about her actions the day before. He had known that something other than her parents' illnesses was stressing her.

The curtain was pulled back, and Shar walked in. "I see that you're awake," she said to her father as she walked into the room.

"Sure am. I knew you'd be around to see me today." Johnny hadn't lifted his head from his pillow, but his eyes were a bit brighter as he watched Shar walk toward him.

Landon stood up. "I don't think the nurses will want you to have too many visitors at one time, so I'll just get back to the church."

"It seems like I'm following you around today. I just left Mother Barnett's house, and she said you were there," Shar told Landon.

"Yeah, I stopped by to see how she was doing."

"Well I hope that Deacon Monroe's house is to your liking and that you're at least getting enough rest so that you can do all this running around during the day," Shar asked.

"I am very comfortable there, thank you for your concern."

"I'm glad. I would hate for you to be miserable after extending such kindness to us."

He'd been miserable, but it had nothing to do with the Monroe's boardinghouse. He put on his top hat and left father and daughter alone, all the while thinking about Shar and the reasons that she might not want to sing anymore. He had no idea how to help her, but this was certainly going on his prayer list.

24

$\mathcal{R}$unning into Landon at the hospital that day almost caused her to come unglued. Shar had been doing nothing but thinking about the mistakes she'd made in the past year. She'd done a few things that she wasn't so proud of, but the costliest mistake she'd ever made was the day she allowed Nicoli James into her life and subsequently allowed Landon to walk out of it.

Now here she was with the evidence of just how much Landon really did care for her. She was living in the man's house while helping her ailing mother to get well. He was visiting her father in the hospital and even shopping for groceries. Landon was doing all of these things for her family, but she no longer saw that look in his eyes. When he looked at her now, she didn't feel special. She felt as if his kindness for her was something he would do for any of his parishioners.

Shar had almost lost her voice and her self-worth in cities far from home. But while all of that was going on she hadn't realized that what would hurt more was the knowledge that she had also lost the love of a good man. Before she'd left home to tour the country and become some great gospel star, all she had ever dreamed of was becoming Landon's wife and moving into this two-bedroom home with him. Now lying in his bed, all she could do was weep.

"Shar, Shar, girl, what's going on over there."

Shar let go of her pillow and bolted upright in bed. Had she been crying so loudly that her mother heard her? Wiping the tears from her face, she got out of bed, threw on her house-coat, and went into her mother's room. Sniffling, she said as she leaned against the doorjamb, "I didn't know you were up. You were sleeping so soundly the last time I checked on you, I thought you'd sleep through the night."

"I heard you crying." Marlene lifted up a bit in bed as a coughing spell overtook her. When it was finished it left her weak, and she flopped back on her pillow.

Shar rushed to her side. "Are you okay, Mama?"

Marlene waved off the concern. "Don't worry yourself about me, Shar. I want to know what's got you so upset."

Looking away from her mother's prying eyes, Shar grabbed the covers and pulled them up to her mother's chest. "It's warm in here now, but sometimes it gets a little cold through the night, so keep this cover up to your chin. Okay?"

Marlene grabbed her hand before she could move away. "Tell me what's going on, Shar. Why are you so unhappy?"

Shar flopped down in the chair next to her mother's bed. She didn't know how to explain the things she was feeling and didn't know if her mother would understand. "I've just been worried about a few things."

"I hope you're not spending your time fretting over me and your daddy. Because we are both too stubborn to die before we see you settled."

"I've been praying like never before that you and Daddy get better. But I'm just so confused about so much these days, I don't even know if God is listening to me anymore."

"Hush all that foolish talk, girl. Of course God hears your prayers. Why wouldn't He?"

Sighing, Shar's chest heaved up and down as she confessed, "I've made some mistakes, Mama. And the worst part about it is that I have no idea how to turn things around."

"Have you prayed about it?"

Shaking her head, Shar admitted, "I've only thought to pray about you and daddy's health. I may be miserable right now, but I'd be ten times more miserable if I didn't have you or Daddy."

Marlene pursed her lips together as she thought for a moment. "I can't be talking to the same girl who used to sing 'What a Friend We Have in Jesus'? Have you forgotten how much of a friend Jesus wants to be to you?"

Shar didn't respond, but a tear did escape from its hiding place.

"Well," Marlene said, "since you're busy praying for me and your daddy, then I guess I need to get busy praying for you."

"Mama, you don't need to do nothing but rest and get better. I'll figure this out and find a way to turn things around."

"Does the thing that's troubling you have anything to do with Pastor Landon keeping his distance from you."

Shar's eyes bucked. "You noticed, too?"

"What, girl, do you think I'm blind?" Marlene rolled her eyes. "He has been nice enough . . . offering us the use of his house and all, but he doesn't look you in the eye, and he doesn't seem to want to sit anywhere near you."

Shar lowered her head, but didn't respond to her mother's words. What could she say? That she had also noticed that the man who claimed to love her no longer wanted anything to do with her. And anyway, she didn't want to talk with her mother about this or she'd end up confessing about the relationship she had with Nicoli James. Shar had never written a word to her parents about him. She hadn't even brought him over to the house the time the choir sang in Chicago.

At the time she had told herself that she didn't want her parents worried about her respectability, since she was traveling from town to town with a man she wasn't married to. But in truth, Shar had known that Marlene Gracey would never approve of a man like Nicoli. Maybe that had been part of her attraction to him.

"What you thinkin' 'bout now?" Marlene questioned.

Shar tried shaking the memory of Nicoli and all that he had cost her out of her mind as she focused back on her mother. "I was thinking that you need to get some sleep. We can talk some more tomorrow about my nonexistent love life." Shar stood, pressed a kiss to her mother's forehead, and then went back to her bedroom.

This time when Shar laid down she knew that she couldn't cry. But she couldn't get herself to fall asleep either. Whenever she had insomnia before, she would sing herself to sleep. But she certainly didn't want to hear any of the songs she'd been singing lately.

Her mama reminded her of a song she had once loved to sing. Maybe if she sang it again, she could get back to where she used to be when she had believed that Jesus was her friend. She opened her mouth and began to sing.

What a friend we have in Jesus,
All our sins and griefs to bear!
What a privilege to carry
Everything to God in prayer!

Oh, what peace we often forfeit,
Oh, what needless pain we bear,
All because we do not carry,
Everything to God in prayer!

Shar's eyes closed as pain etched across her face. She had betrayed God and didn't feel worthy to sing this song anymore. Mahalia had told her that a gospel singer shouldn't seek to do anything but sing for the Lord. But Shar had thought that she could do both because Rossetta Tharpe had done it.

But Rosetta ended up apologizing to her church quite often, just so she'd be allowed to sing in the choir again. If Rosetta was so happy with her choices, why did she keep coming back to the house of God?

Shar would apologize to God a thousand times if she thought it would do any good. "Is that what You want, Lord? If I apologize for going astray and following Nicoli into that den of evil, will You give me the peace I so desperately crave?"

She waited, hoping that she would hear an audible answer from God. But when none came she said, "Lord, please forgive me. I am so sorry for using the voice You gave me for anything other than to glorify You. I've been plum miserable ever since I made that awful decision. I'm asking . . . begging and pleading with You to please take away my shame and restore me to fellowship with you."

Her eyes began to water, but then Shar reminded herself that she was done crying. If she wanted to express herself, she was going to sing. She opened her mouth to belt out the lyrics to the second half of that song . . .

Have we trials and temptations?
Is there trouble anywhere?
We should never be discouraged—
Take it to the Lord in prayer.
Can we find a friend so faithful,
who will all our sorrows share?
Jesus knows our every weakness;
Take it to the Lord in prayer.

"That's what I'm doing tonight, Lord. I'm bringing You my problems. I'm confessing to You that I've been weak, discouraged, and tempted away from Your will. But I don't want to live like that no more. I want to know that if I can't count on nobody else, I can still count on You. I'm hoping and praying that You still want to be my friend, Lord, because I want to be Yours again. Please show me the way."

On Sunday right after church, Landon kept his word and went to Nettie's house for supper. Loraine and Raymond Johnson had one of the finest homes in the area. They had a huge wood dining room table that seated up to eight people at one time. The Johnsons entertained frequently because Raymond was running for State Representative. So you could get a meal and a full political conversation at the same table.

Landon wasn't much into the politics that many in Chicago wallowed in. He much preferred to leave politics to those more suited for the job, because Landon knew that he was not only called, but committed to preaching and teaching his congregation concerning the things of God. However, he did see the poor housing that his parishioners were forced to live with as a real moral issue. In order to help the people in the Black Belt, Landon had to do a bit of wheeling and dealing with political types. So he was happy to be at the Johnsons' table, not just because the food was good, but because Raymond Johnson could snap a finger and make things happen in that part of town.

"It's about time you showed up for dinner with us, Pastor," Raymond said as he slapped Landon on the back.

"I hear there's some smothered pork chops being served up today, so you know I wasn't going to miss this," Landon said.

"Well you came to the right place. My Loraine is the best cook this side of Georgia."

"Nettie helped with dinner," Loraine said as she and Nettie walked out of the kitchen carrying bowls full of scrumptious-smelling food that they placed on the table.

Raymond gave a big belly laugh. "Loraine is always bragging on our Nettie. And she has good reason because Nettie is getting to be as good a cook as my sweet wife."

Loraine smiled. "Thank you for your high praise, Raymond. Now bring Pastor Landon on over here and y'all have a seat while Nettie and I get the rest of the food."

Raymond turned to Landon, "You heard her. Let's have a seat at the table while the ladies finish setting the table."

Raymond took the seat at the head of the table and directed Landon to a seat to the right of him. When Loraine and Nettie came back out of the kitchen, Raymond instructed his wife to sit next to him on the left and Nettie to sit next to Landon.

They filled their plates, and Landon said grace over the meal. As they began to eat, Raymond said to Landon, "Nettie tells me that this housing project that you've been working on is going well."

"Yes, sir, I now have all of the families I need to get this thing rolling with the NAACP, but we're lacking some of the financing that's also needed."

"Ain't that the way it always is with our people . . . big on dreams but can't find a way to save a dollar to make things happen," Raymond said as he leaned back in his high-back chair.

"It's not like that, Daddy," Nettie protested. "These are hard-working colored folk, who just don't have any extra to put in savings after paying the high rents in this area of town."

"And all the repairs that need to be done on those houses are another reason they can't save any money," Landon added. "A few of the men from my church are working on the Graceys' house right now, trying to plug up holes in the floor boards and find a way to close out the draft that's coming from those windows."

Reaching for the green beans, Loraine chimed in. "And it was mighty fine of you to allow Marlene to stay at your home. I took some soup over to her a few days ago, and it seems like she is getting better."

"To God be the glory," Landon said with a hand raised to heaven. Then he said, "I'm just thankful that Deacon Monroe had a room available in his boardinghouse for me."

"You're a good man, Pastor Landon. With a good heart. Someday you'll make a lucky woman a wonderful husband, I have no doubt about that," Loraine said while pointedly looking at her daughter.

Nettie clasped her hands together. "The food is getting cold. Let's eat and then we can talk about these things later."

"I second that," Landon said as he began cutting his pork chop. He put a piece in his mouth and savored the flavor of the pork chop smothered in a rich gravy sauce that was just about the best gravy he'd ever tasted. Smacking his lips, Landon declared, "Mrs. Loraine, you sure know how to put your foot in a meal. This is delicious."

She blushed and then said, "Thank you kindly for saying that, Pastor."

Raymond rubbed his big belly and added, "I didn't get this way by accident."

Before anyone could respond to that, the doorbell rang. Nettie popped up. "You all keep eating. I'll get the door." She rushed over to the front door, which was just about twelve steps away from the dining room table. She flung the door open and, before addressing the person at the door, turned back to the group and said, "Look who we just talked up."

Shar stepped in and waved at everyone. She then turned back to Nettie and asked with a curious look on her face, "Didn't you remember that I was coming? You told me that your mother would need this pot back after Sunday service."

Nettie waved the assumption away. "She used other pots, so you could have kept it. Did your mama like the soup?"

"Yes, she certainly did."

"Well come on in. You can thank Mother properly and then stay for dinner if you have time."

Shar glanced at Landon and then back at Nettie. Shyly, she said, "With my mama and daddy being ill, I don't have much time for socializing."

Nettie took the pot away from Shar and walked her into the dining room. "I understand. Well, you can come and say hi to everyone, before you run off." Nettie left Shar standing in front of the dining room table as she rushed the pot into the kitchen.

Shar nodded at everyone. "Mr. Johnson, Mrs. Johnson, thank you so much for the soup." She then turned to Landon who was looking at her, but not really. "Nice seeing you also, Pastor Landon."

"You as well, Shar. How's your mother doing today?" Landon asked as Nettie came back to the table and sat down next to Landon.

"She's doing better and believing God for her total healing," Shar remarked.

"Sit down, child," Loraine said. "Have something to eat before you go back home."

Shaking her head, Shar told the group, "Thanks for your kindness, Mrs. Johnson, but I must get back and check on my mama." She turned sharply and quickly made her way to the front door. Waving to everyone as she opened the door, she said, "Bye all. Have a nice day." She exited and then closed the door.

"Well, she certainly raced out of here. I wonder what was wrong?" Loraine said to no one in particular.

Landon stared at the door for a moment, feeling as if something was odd in the way Shar rushed out of the Johnson home, as well. But she was dealing with two sick parents, so no one could expect her to spend much time socializing just as she said. But in the past few days, Landon had found himself wanting to stop by his house for simple little reasons, like picking up a tie he forgot or checking on the mail. Each time he arrived at the house, he pretended that he didn't have the slightest bit of interest in Shar or anything else going on there. But the truth was far from that. Landon prayed daily for God to release him from the hold Shar had on his heart. He waited patiently for the day that his heart would be free again. He wanted desperately to love someone who could love him back.

Raymond swallowed the food that was in his mouth and then snapped his finger. "I think I just came up with an answer to your dilemma."

Landon put his fork down, hoping that Nettie's father hadn't figured out what he had been thinking about. "What dilemma, sir?"

"The money that you need," Raymond said excitedly. "That church of yours has some pretty good singers. And if you could convince Shar Gracey to help you put on a production, I know I could help sell the tickets for you."

"I've never charged anyone to come to church in my life," Landon said.

"The charge won't be for coming to church. You can hold your singing program after church. Let the people know that you are raising funds for housing and they will turn out to support the fund-raiser . . . especially if you have Shar Gracey singing."

Landon leaned back in his seat as he recalled Shar's father telling him that his daughter had lost her love for singing. Maybe something like this could help Shar as well as the people he wanted to provide housing for. "You know something, Mr. Johnson, that idea of yours just might work."

25

$\mathscr{S}$har couldn't believe that she ran out of the Johnson house like that, just barely saying good-bye. If she was younger and her mama had found out about her rudeness, Marlene would be outside looking for a switch. She hadn't wanted to be rude, but she had a terrible need to escape. Seeing Landon seated with Nettie was more than she could bear. He was supposed to be her love and she was supposed to be his, but now it looked as if Landon was Nettie's and there wasn't one thing she could do about it.

Shar started walking toward home, which was really not home at all. They would be leaving as soon as their home was finished. But Shar had no idea when that would be since the men were having a hard time blocking the cold wind. It seemed as if there were just too many spaces through which the wind could seep in, and not enough lumber and plastic to cover it.

"Hey, Shar, wait up." Rodney Oldham ran up behind.

Shar kept walking.

"It's like that, huh? You're not even going to speak to me after I put a quarter in your tip jar a couple weeks ago?"

"I didn't ask you to do that."

"You didn't stop me either. I bet you spent it quick and fast enough."

"Okay, well, why don't you stop following me and go on back to whatever you were doing."

Rodney grabbed her arm and stopped her from walking. "I know you're not still looking down your nose at me. Little Miss Holier-than-thou, singing in a nightclub."

"Don't touch me." She yanked away from him. "You don't know anything about me. So, stay away."

"I'll stay away all right," he yelled at her as she walked down the street. "But you just remember that you ain't no better'n nobody else. So stop pretending to be all high and mighty."

Running into Rodney just made Shar feel worse than she'd already been feeling. She kept her head down as she walked the street, hoping not to run into anyone else who'd heard her sing at Ray's place. She turned on the next block over, with her head still down, so it took her a few seconds to notice the commotion that was going on around her. People were standing on the side of the road pointing toward a house that was engulfed in flames. As Shar looked toward the house, her heart sank as she realized Mother Barnett's house was on fire. "Oh my God!" she screamed as she attempted to run toward the house.

Two women grabbed her arms. "You can't go over there. The house is about to collapse."

"What do you mean, it's about to collapse? Where are the firemen?" Shar was turning every which way trying to escape the hold the women had on her, but nothing was working.

"Listen to us," the heavy-set, dark-skinned woman said, "The firemen never showed up. A couple of the menfolks have been running from house to house grabbing buckets of water to put out the fire, but nothing has worked."

"But we can't just let Mother Barnett die in there."

"Nothing we can do. Now, we're going to let you go, but I don't want you running toward that house or we're going to grab you again," the other woman said.

When they let Shar go she was tempted to make a run for it toward the house, but the fire had begun to rage higher than it was moments earlier. Shar didn't know what to do, but she knew that Mother Barnett didn't deserve to die like that. Then she thought of Landon. He was, after all, Mother Barnett's pastor. He would want to know about this. So she took off running back up the street and around the corner, back to the Johnsons' house.

She made it to the house in less than five minutes and started pounding on the door as if she was trying to get her man out of a den of sin and ill repute.

Raymond Johnson swung the door open and demanded, "What in the world has gotten into you, young lady?"

Shar was bent over, trying to catch her breath. She lifted her head and told him, "It's Mother Barnett. Her house is on fire."

Landon came to the door, brushing past Raymond Johnson. "What happened, Shar? What's got you in such a state?"

"Come quickly, Pastor. Mother Barnett's house is burning down. I don't know what to do, but I figured you'd be able to help her."

"My Lord," was all Landon said as he stepped outside the house and started running down the street.

Shar couldn't keep up with him. As she began her trek back down the street she heard Mr. Johnson tell his wife that he would be right back.

Nettie hollered, "I'm coming with you, Daddy."

"Grab your coat," he said, and then they were beside her, walking with her all the way back to Mother Barnett's house.

When they rounded the corner Shar saw Landon helping the other men pass buckets of water to one another. The man in the front of the line flung the water onto the house and then passed the bucket back for a refilling. They were utilizing several buckets at once, but it still was not enough to get the job done. Just as the woman had warned earlier, the two-story house became one story, and then no stories at all as the whole house folded in on itself.

"No, no!" Shar screamed as she took off running again. "Mother Barnett, Mother Barnett," she was yelling as she made her way to the house. She had to find the woman who had so much faith and believed so fervently that her husband would return to her that she set a light in the window to help him see his way home.

Someone grabbed her from behind. "Let me go. I have to get Mother Barnett out of that house."

"You can't, Shar. It's not safe."

"Please, just let me go," she begged as she clawed at the hands holding her around the waist.

Landon pulled her closer, holding her tighter. "I can't let you hurt yourself. I don't know what I'd do if anything happened to you." Pulling her away from the flames, Landon continued to hold her close to his side. "I'm going to take you home. You shouldn't be here right now."

"But I can't leave Mother Barnett like this. She's been waiting so long for her husband. How will he ever find the house now that it's burned down?" Shar's mind was running a mile a minute, trying to figure out what was going on.

Landon didn't answer, just kept walking down the street with Shar close to his side.

Nettie and her father ran over to Landon. "What's going on, Reverend?" Raymond asked.

"Shar has been overcome by the fire. I'm taking her home. I'll be back once I get her settled, so I can help the men with the cleanup and recovery." He didn't say what they would be recovering, but it was understood.

At Landon's words Shar let out a yelp that sounded like a wounded animal. She began crying and leaning her head on Landon's shoulder.

Raymond eyed Shar suspiciously as he suggested, "Maybe Nettie should take her home. You wouldn't want people to assume anything unseemly was going on. I mean, you have already moved the girl into your house. A house that's paid for by the church, might I add."

Nettie rushed around Landon, until she was standing next to Shar. She put her hand on Shar's. "Come on, Shar. I'll walk you home. Pastor Landon has his hands full with everything that's going on with Mother Barnett's house."

Shar lifted her head from Landon's shoulder. She didn't want to walk back to the house with Nettie. She needed Landon like she needed to breathe, but she wouldn't burden him with her frailties. She let go of Landon and allowed Nettie to take her arm. "I've got to get home to check on Mama." When she said that, Shar's eyes widened as the thought hit her. "What if Mama is on fire?"

"Your mama isn't on fire, Shar." Landon pulled Shar back toward him. "Thanks for your willingness to help out, Nettie. But Shar is in a terrible state right now. I'll see her safely to her mother."

As Landon and Shar walked away, he saw the way Raymond's mouth twisted, as though he was tasting something foul. But

Landon didn't have the slightest interest in whatever Raymond's mind was leading him to think.

Shar clung to him as she asked, "Why does God let all these bad things happen to us? Why doesn't He protect us? I keep praying to Him, but bad things keep happening anyhow."

As a preacher, it was Landon's job to have a ready answer concerning the things of God. But for the life of him, he couldn't find the words to explain why Mother Barnett had to burn up in her house while on her sickbed. Mother Barnett was one of the sweetest women he'd ever had the pleasure of knowing. His heart would ache with this loss for a long, long time. "I don't know, Shar. I just don't know," was all he could say.

"And why do we call Him the good Lord, when we don't never see nothing but bad and more bad?" She stopped walking and dropped down onto the ground, brought her knees up to her chest, and bawled like a baby.

Seeing Shar like that was further confirmation to Landon that he needed to walk her home, rather than let Nettie do it. The Bible said that it was God's loving kindness that draws mankind to Him. So Landon didn't want to chastise Shar for her anger at God. He wanted to show her God's love so that she could grow from this horrible experience and come out on the other side, while retaining her sanity and love for God. He sat down next to her, put his arm around her shoulder, and admitted, "It's not fair, you're right about that. I see so much each and every day that I can't explain. I also don't believe that colored folk need to endure this much pain and sorrow just to learn how to be humble."

She was still crying and her nose was running as she said, "I thought I felt terrible being on the road watching white men beat on some of the men in our choir, but this is ten times worse. Mother Barnett never done nothing to nobody."

Landon took his handkerchief out of his pocket. He wanted to use it to wipe his own eyes, as they had begun to blur, but Shar needed it more, so he handed it to her. "I believe in a bright new tomorrow, Shar. Things may be awful for us now, but God hasn't forgotten us. It's hard to see that with all that has happened," Landon nodded, encouraging himself, "but we've got to keep the faith."

Wiping her face and her nose with the handkerchief, Shar asked, "What if it never gets better? What if misery is all we will ever know?"

"I don't believe that. I believe God is looking down on us, and He is working things out in ways that we can't see right now."

Shar shook her head, clearly having trouble believing anything Landon said.

This wasn't the time; Landon could tell that he needed to let Shar stew for a while and then discuss this on another day . . . on a day when they hadn't just lost the most beloved Mother of their church. He stood and pulled Shar up with him. "Let me get you home so you can take comfort in being with your mama." When they reached his house, he knocked on Mrs. Marlene's bedroom door.

"Come in," Marlene said from inside.

"Mrs. Marlene, it's me, Landon." He opened the door and walked in with Shar still clinging to him as if he was her life support unit. "I just wanted you to know that I brought Shar home. She's very upset, so I don't know if she should be alone right now."

"What happened, chile?" Marlene swung back the covers and tried to sit up.

"Don't get up, Mrs. Marlene. I'm going to sit Shar down in the chair next to you and then I'm going to get the roll-away bed that's been kept in the back of the house and set it up in here with you."

As Landon helped Shar into the seat next to her mother, Shar said, "You're okay, aren't you, Mama?"

"Yeah, baby. I'm just lying here resting."

"I'm thankful that God didn't take you away from me," Shar said as she laid her head on her mother's bed and began to cry.

"Tell me what's troubling you," Marlene said, the pain in Marlene's voice was a clear indicator that what bothered Shar, bothered her.

"It was awful, Mama. Just awful," Shar cried out.

Landon rushed out of the room so he could get the bed as fast as possible. His one thought was to make Shar comfortable so she could get some sleep and spend a few hours not thinking about the horrific events of the day.

When Landon came back into the room, rolling the bed along with him, Marlene was still trying to get answers out of Shar. He opened the bed and set it up, whipped off the cob-webs, because it had been some time since the roll-away had been put to use. He grabbed the linen and brought it back to the room. He put a sheet on the bed and then grabbed the pillows off of Shar's bed in the other guest room. The room was cramped with the two beds, but Landon figured that Shar didn't need to be alone. "Come on, Shar. I want you to lie down and try to get some sleep."

Once Shar had climbed into the bed, Landon took the seat next to Marlene.

"What done happened to my baby?" she asked him.

"Mother Barnett's house burned down. We weren't able to get her out of it before it caved in on itself," he whispered.

Marlene shook her head in sadness. "I warned Mother Barnett about them candles she kept putting in the window. I don't know why she wouldn't listen to nobody . . . just kept believing that good-for-nothing husband of hers would find his way back home."

"Mother Barnett had more faith than anyone else I've ever known. Got to be a special place in heaven for faith like that."

"I hope you're right about that, Pastor. I'd sure hate to think that she died like that and wouldn't be receiving no reward for keeping the faith all these years."

Landon stood. "I've got to get back over there to help out in whatever way I can. But I'll get some dinner brought here for you and Shar. I doubt that she'll be in any mood for cooking."

Marlene put her hand over Landon's and said, "You've been mighty good to us. And I especially want to thank you for how good you've been to Shar."

Landon looked over at Shar. She was curled up in the bed with the covers pulled up to her chin. Her eyes were closed, but he noticed that tears were seeping out. Shar had so much pain that even her sleep couldn't hold it back. He turned back to Marlene and said, "You don't owe me any thanks. I would do anything for Shar . . . just wish I could bring her some comfort to ease some of the pain she's carrying around."

"I appreciate your saying that," Marlene said. "But Shar is going to need to find a way to ease the pain she's feeling all on her own. I'm just hoping that you'll still be here for her once she's found her way back to us."

He nodded and then left the room. It broke his heart to leave the house without being able to do more to ease the pain Shar was feeling. But Landon was convinced that Shar's pain was coming from so many different directions that he doubted if she even knew how to get out of its way.

26

Shar's daddy had been released from the hospital and they were now back at the house she grew up in. The only draft that was coming into the house now was from the windows. They were old and in need of replacing, but there was never enough money for repairs like that. Yet, her mama was coughing less and up on her feet a lot more. Marlene and Johnny had switched places.

Before Marlene went into the hospital, Johnny had been taking care of her and trying to do everything possible to make her comfortable. But even though the hospital released him, Johnny was still frail and weak. Every time Shar looked at her father, she thought, John Henry done dropped his hammer.

Shar was thankful to help around the house as much as she could. It took her mind off of other things like Mother Barnett dying in that fire two weeks ago. The fire department had arrived on the scene a week late. When the rubble of the house was finally inspected, they determined that the fire had not been caused by a candle left burning in the window, but by faulty wiring.

It was strange how that knowledge felt bad in one way but good in another. She felt bad that Mother Barnett lived in a home that was so shabby it eventually became a death trap for her. But Shar was glad that Mother Barnett hadn't died while keeping a light burning for a man who wasn't thinking about coming back home.

At one point in Shar's life, she had romanticized what Mother Barnett had been doing, but not anymore. She now realized that dying old and alone after spending all your days waiting for some no-account to come back to a home he never should have left in the first place was no way to live or die.

Shar had left the nightclub and was now working in a neighborhood beauty salon. It wasn't much, but it helped her parents make ends meet, and she hadn't so much as thought about Nicoli James in weeks. Landon Norstrom was a different story. She couldn't stop thinking about him and how wonderful he had been to her family in their time of need. Even though Landon was far from being a no-account or good-for-nothing kind of man, Shar still wished she didn't have him on her mind morning, noon, and night. What good would all this thinking on Landon do anyway? Any love he might have felt for her was long gone. And she wasn't worthy of it anyway.

"Shar, can you shampoo Lisa for me?"

"Sure thing," Shar said to Dolly Peterson, the owner of the salon. She then brought Dolly's client to the shampoo bowl and proceeded to do her job. "How are you doing today?"

Lisa smiled. "I'm doing good. Just happy to get out of the house and have something done to this nappy head of mine."

Shar smiled back, but even as she did so, she found herself thinking back to those days of singing her heart out in Mr. Dorsey's choir. She was thankful for the job, but Shar still felt the sting of dried-up dreams. She tried her best not to let it get her down. This was where life had taken her, and she was just blessed to be able to help her parents in any way she could. So, she kept coming to work, doing her job, collecting her tips, and then going home and helping her parents around the house.

She was also doing the weekly washings to help her mama, and then once the clothes was dry and taken off the clothes-line, Marlene did the ironing. She would then see to it that the clothes were taken back to her mama's customers during her daily walk to work. By the end of the week, Shar was worn and tired. Her one day off was on Sunday. She skipped Sunday school so she could get an extra hour of sleep. She then got up and made her way back to United Worship Center.

When Shar arrived, the choir was still singing. Nettie stood before the church and took lead vocals on "Precious Lord, Take My Hand." Shar closed her eyes and pictured herself singing that same song while on tour. The congregation had given her a standing ovation when she'd finished. But with the way she'd trampled on her faith in order to make a little money in them nightclubs, she'd probably be stoned to death if she tried to sing that song today.

When the choir sat down, Pastor Landon took the podium and began preaching like a man with a cause. Today it felt like his message was for her and her alone, as he preached about God's spirit departing from King Saul because of Saul's dis-obedience. From the time she belted out her first song of praise, Shar knew that her voice was only meant for gospel music, and now that she had ignored the call on her life, she too felt as though God's spirit had departed from her. Even though Pastor Landon had cut too close to home, Shar was still grateful that she was able to hear Landon preach. He inspired her in so many ways.

When the service ended, Shar stayed behind so she could thank him for the words he'd delivered straight to her heart. So she stayed in her seat waiting for him to shake hands and provide well wishes to all of the parishioners who stopped by to talk to him before leaving the church.

Once most of the church members had filed out of the building, Shar was about to make her way over to Landon, but that's when Nettie grabbed hold of his arm and whispered in his ear. Landon leaned his head back, looked at Nettie, and the two of them shared a great big old belly laugh.

Shar wanted to know what Nettie had said to cause Landon to laugh so. And why was she the one to put that smile on his face? Shar could hardly stand to watch the two of them. She got out of her seat and made her way to the door without saying anything to Landon. She would have to thank him for the beautiful sermon on another occasion. Because she truly felt as if she would break down and cry right in front of him and Nettie if she stayed there one second longer.

As she reached the door, Shar heard Landon call after her. "Hey, Shar, don't go yet. I wanted to talk to you."

She turned and watched him walk away from Nettie as he headed in her direction. Shar's heart began to race, just as it had in times past while in Landon's presence. He just had that kind of affect on her. She wished he didn't, but she hadn't figured out yet how to tell her heart what to do and who to love. "I was waiting on you because I wanted to tell you how wonderful your sermon was," Shar said as she glanced in Nettie's direction. Catching the irritated look on the woman's face, she continued, "But I didn't know how long you would be, so I figured I would just get on home."

"How are your patients doing?"

"Daddy is still pretty frail and weak. But Mama seems to be getting better day by day."

"That's good." Landon stood there, looking as if he didn't know what to say next.

Shar said, "You wanted to speak with me about something?"

"Oh yeah." He touched her arm, guiding her back toward the sanctuary chairs. "Can you sit down with me for a few minutes? I'd like to talk to you about something."

With each step she took, Shar dreamed that Landon wanted to tell her that he was still in love with her and couldn't live without her one second longer. As they sat down on the front bench, Shar leaned forward, a look of expectation on her face.

Landon cleared his throat. He appeared to hesitate as if choosing his words carefully. The sanctuary was cleared out, and the only person remaining was Nettie. She was in the choir stand busying herself with a bunch of nothing.

Go on, Landon. Tell me that you still love me.

"You know about the project we've been working on at this church for the last few years, right?"

Well, his words didn't sound anything like, "I love you and I want you back." But maybe he was doing a little small talk before letting her know what was in his heart. "Of course, yes, I remember. You've been trying to get decent housing for people in our community."

"Here's the thing," Landon began. "The NAACP has agreed to help us with a lawsuit against the city, but first we need to have at least ten qualified candidates for home ownership . . . we've got that. But we also need to have the money available for each of those families to be able to purchase their homes. We don't have enough money yet."

Shar's hand went to her heart, truly feeling pain for Landon's dilemma. "But you've worked so hard on this. Isn't there some way you can come up with the money needed to get those people into a nice home." Shar understood firsthand the benefits of not just having a place to lay your head, but also having a nice and decent place. The people in this community work hard night and day. Wasn't it time for some of those better days to come their way?

Clasping his hands together, like a man with a plan, Landon said, "That's why I wanted to talk to you." Landon looked to the choir stand and began waving Nettie over to where they were seated. "Could you come over here for a moment, Sister Johnson?"

Why was he inviting Nettie into their conversation? Did Landon not have anything special he wanted to say to her? She knew that Nettie was now working as his office assistant or something, but did that mean he couldn't carry on a conversation without her? Exactly how close were Landon and Nettie these days? All these musings went through her head, but no answers were forthcoming as she watched Nettie trot over to them.

Landon smiled at Nettie again, as if he was just so pleased to be in her company. He then turned back to Shar. "Nettie's father has agreed to help us with promotions and tickets sales for a fund-raiser that he suggested. And I wanted to talk to you about it because we would be mighty grateful if you helped us with it."

She could fry chicken with the best of 'em. Bring on the fund-raiser. Maybe helping someone else would take her mind off of her own troubles. "I'd love to help with a fund-raiser. I think what you're doing to help our people is commendable. And if I can help in some small way, then I'm thankful to God for that."

"I'm glad you feel that way, Shar. The choir is going to begin rehearsing for the fund-raiser next week, so that will give you a little more time to get things settled at home before worrying about any obligations to the church."

Shar lifted up her hands, trying to back the conversation up. "Wait a minute, I might of missed something. The choir is doing the fund-raiser?"

"Of course the choir is doing the fund-raiser, silly. Why else do you think we need your help?" Nettie said as if Shar was good for nothing else.

"I thought we might be doing chicken dinners or a fish fry. I've helped Mother Barnett with those kind of fund-raisers at the church," Shar said.

"The Mothers' Board has always been willing to do fund-raisers when we've needed them. But unfortunately, the most we've raised with one of our dinners has been forty dollars," Landon told her.

"We've made more than that," Shar declared. She wanted to do anything but get back in the choir and have everyone see that she couldn't sing the way she used to. "We raised nearly seventy dollars with one of the fund-raisers I helped out with."

Nettie had no patience for Shar. She rolled her eyes heavenward and then told her, "The food cost money, the plates cost money . . . forks and spoons aren't free."

Landon's head whipped around to face Nettie. "What's gotten into you? This is no way to talk to someone we need help from."

Nettie's head dropped low. "Sorry, Pastor."

Landon turned back to Shar. "What Nettie was trying to say is that there is a cost associated with those kind of fund-raisers. And to be honest, they just don't make the kind of money that we need right now."

"How much money do you need, Pastor Landon," Shar asked as if she could write him a check on the spot.

"In order to qualify all ten people, we need several thousands of dollars. That's why we were hoping that if we spread the word that Shar Gracey would be singing at a United Worship Center fund-raiser, we'd be able to at least get a bit closer to what we need." The look on Landon's face was hopeful.

But Shar didn't have much hope in her heart concerning her abilities. "Nobody's gon' pay good money to come hear me sing."

Landon's eyes lit up as he encouraged her, "Are you kidding, Shar? Word has been spreading around town about you. People who heard you sing in other towns have now moved right here in Chicago, and they always have good things to say about Shar Gracey's singing."

"And the people who've heard you sing at the nightclubs will most likely buy a ticket also," Nettie added.

Shar's eyes grew wide as she looked from Nettie to Landon. "You know about that?"

Landon nodded. "I've been praying for you."

Oh God, he knows, he knows what I've done.

"We're all praying for you, Shar. None of us ever imagined that you would lose your religion. But I guess being on that tour without your mama to guide you caused you to do all sorts of ungodly things." Nettie was smirking as she cut Shar with each unkind word.

Landon gave Nettie the eye. "That's enough. No one is accusing Shar of being ungodly."

Shar popped out of her seat. "I got to go."

"I'll walk you home," Landon told her. "But can we talk about the choir event first?"

Shaking her head as tears formed in her eyes, Shar told him, "I don't need you to walk me home, and I'm sorry but I won't be able to help with the fund-raiser." She rushed out of the church before the tears rolled down her face. Because she now knew why Landon didn't look at her the same anymore. He was too holy and righteous to ever want a woman who could turn her back on the gospel music she claimed to love to go sing blues and jazz songs. Shar was full of shame and guilt for what she'd done. She wanted to change, wanted to turn back to God, but it seemed like God just kept pushing her away.

When she arrived home, she sat on the porch trying to get herself together. Wiping the tears from her face, she lifted her face to the heavens and decided to have a little talk with Jesus, because she needed some answers. "When will Your punishments end? I never should've gone off on my own and done the things that I did. But why won't You just let me repent and come back to You?" Wrapping her arms around herself, she then asked, "Will I ever feel or know the love You have for me ever again?"

27

he nerve of that Shar Gracey," Nettie said to no one in particular as she walked into her house and threw her purse on the sofa.

Her mother came out of the kitchen carrying a bowl of mashed potatoes. "What's got you in an uproar now?"

"That Shar Gracey," Nettie yelled through the house again.

"Come on in here and help me get the dinner on the table and you can tell me and your daddy all about it," Nettie's mama said.

Nettie followed her mother into the kitchen, put the green beans in a bowl, and took them to the table, while her mother brought the roast and bread rolls. They all sat down at the dining room table, and then Raymond said, "I heard you screaming about Shar Gracey when you came in the house. What's got you so upset with that young lady?"

"I don't mean to be uncharitable, Daddy. It's just that Landon and I have worked so hard on this home ownership project, with very little help from anyone else."

Her father interrupted her, "I offered to help Pastor Landon with a fund-raiser. I know you think we have endless money and

I should just write Pastor Landon a check. But the truth of the matter is, I've had to spend almost all of our savings on my latest election. My opponent has acquired financial backing from a few of my enemies who want to see me out of public office."

"I'm not blaming you, Daddy." Nettie patted her father's hand as it lay on top of the table. "But I thought you came up with an awfully good idea about the fund-raiser. And Landon asked Shar if she would help us raise money for our housing project, and she flatly refused to help."

"Isn't that something," Loraine said while fixing her husband's plate and sitting it down in front of him.

"Sounds like little miss Shar done traveled the world and got too big for her britches," Raymond said.

Loraine handed Nettie her plate and then sat down with her own. Nettie said, "Well anyway, now we're going to have to come up with another fund-raiser, even after Pastor Landon told that girl that chicken dinners ain't making us no money."

Loraine pointed a finger at her daughter. "Nettie Johnson, what have I told you about using 'ain't' in this house?"

"I'm sorry, Mama. I'm just so mad about the whole situation that I can barely think straight. But oh well, I guess we'll just keep on selling dinners and hope for the best."

Raymond said grace over the food, and then while they were eating, he said, "I think you had it right the first time. Chicken dinners ain't making no money. And they won't help your daddy with this upcoming election."

"How would the choir fund-raiser help you win the State Representative seat?" Loraine asked her husband.

"Well," Raymond rested his back against the high-backed chair and used a toothpick to get a piece of roast beef that lodged between his teeth. "The way I see it is if I'm the one printing the flyers and helping promote this event, my name ought to go on those flyers somewhere. That way the good people in our district will be able to see that I'm a man of the people, willing to lend a hand when needed."

"That would be wonderful, Daddy, except for one thing. Without Shar we won't be putting on that fund-raiser. I'm sure we have singers in our choir who are just as good as Shar, but none of us have toured with Thomas Dorsey," Nettie said.

"And that's exactly why Shar Gracey is going to rejoin the choir at United Worship Center whether she likes it or not."

Nettie put her fork down and stared at her father. She had a lot of respect for him, but if Landon—the same man Shar had been trading letter with—couldn't get her to do it, she seriously doubted that her father would have much luck. "She ran out of church, all fired mad because I mentioned her nightclub singing. I'm sorry if what I said to her ruined your plans."

"You didn't ruin nothing. I will get Shar back in that choir, I can promise you that."

"And just how do you plan to do that?"

"Don't you worry about it Baby-Girl. Your daddy has a few tricks up his sleeve."

Shar didn't work at the beauty salon on Mondays, so she got up bright and early, fixed oatmeal for her parents, and then started on the washing. Once she had that under control, Shar went back in to check on her parents.

"So how are my patients doing this afternoon? Are you two ready for some lunch?"

"Girl, you just fixed us breakfast a couple of hours ago. Hold your horses and let me do some work today," Marlene said as she sat on the side of the bed, feet planted on the floor, but she hadn't pushed herself off the bed yet.

Her father was lying on the right side of the bed, his head propped on a pillow as he eyed Marlene. "Your mama's been hacking all night. She wants me to believe that she's all right, but I'm not so sure."

Marlene waved away his concern. "Stop all this fussing over me, Johnny. I told you that I'm going to keep my heavy housecoat on when I'm walking through this house."

"No, no," Johnny said while hitting the mattress with his fist. That single act seemed to drain him so much that he took several deep breaths before speaking again. "Shar, I want you to go down to that church and tell Pastor Landon that we are mighty grateful for the work them church folks did on the house. But if he could send a few more men here to put the plastic on the windows I'd make sure to pay each one of them something as soon as I can get out of this bed."

"Oh, Daddy, please don't make me do that." Shar hated denying her father his simple request. Johnny Gracey didn't like asking nobody to do nothing for him that he couldn't do for himself. So, for him to ask Shar to get help for the windows, she knew that her father was still feeling poorly. And his concern for her mama's health was outweighing his never-ask-nobody-for-nothing attitude.

"What's wrong with you, girl? You belong to that church don't you . . . been putting money in the collection plate?" Johnny stopped talking, took a deep breath as if something was hurting him, and then continued, "Pastor Landon won't mind providing us the help we need."

"Look at you, speaking good about a preacher," Marlene joked, because her husband didn't trust too many people outside of his own family.

"He's a good man," Johnny fired back.

"How would you know, Johnny Gracey? You don't even go down to that church when you've got Sundays off and just sitting around the house waiting on me to feed you."

Her parents fussed about one thing or another at least two or three times a week, but the love bond between them was unbreakable so Shar mostly ignored the fussing. Johnny turned back to Shar. "I want to know why you can't do as I ask."

With shoulders slumped, Shar sat down on the edge of the bed to be closer to her parents. She confessed, "The truth is that Landon just asked me to help out with a musical fundraiser at the church by singing in the choir. But I told him that I was too busy helping out at home to sing in the choir." She didn't look her parents in the eye as she finished her confession. Her eyes were on her hands as they rested in her lap.

"What has gotten into you that you suddenly don't want anything to do with singing?" Marlene questioned.

"With you and Daddy under the weather, I've got a lot that needs to be done right here, Mama. I can't be concerning myself with no choir."

"But you love singing in that choir," Johnny added.

Without looking up, Shar said, "Maybe I just don't love it the same way I used to." Shrugging her shoulders as she stood back up, she added, "I'm a grown woman now, and I think it's high time for me to start thinking about getting married and raising a family, like Mama always talks about, rather than chasing a dream that ain't never gon' come true."

"Now, Shar," Marlene began, "You know that it is my fondest wish that I would live to see you married off and having babies. But after you left home and I read some of your letters about how so many people became overjoyed after you led one of them songs, I came to believe in your father's dream for you. Things might not have turned out so good on the tour, but I feel it," Marlene gripped her stomach, "way down deep in my soul. God's got something good in store for you, chile. So, don't be so quick to give up on your dreams. Them dreams of yours and your daddy's is the only thing we got worth holding onto in this world."

Tears sprang up and seeped down Shar's face. Her mother's words meant everything to her. As long as Shar could remember her mother had been trying to stifle any and all thoughts of singing because she wanted Shar to focus on becoming a good wife to a man who'd be able to provide her with a good living. But now her mother believed in her dream. The irony of the situation was that Shar no longer believed in it. "The songs just don't feel the same to me no more."

"What this world done to you, Shar? When you gon' be ready to tell your mama so I can help you?"

Shar would never tell her mama what she did to earn the money for her care. Her mama would blame herself, and Shar couldn't have that. She turned, heading out of her parent's bedroom. "Let me see if I can rustle up some plastic so I can get started with putting it on the windows."

"Shar Gracey, if you get on that ladder, I swear to God, I'm gon' come out there and skin you alive," Johnny said, his voice gaining strength.

"But Daddy, how you gon' get out of that bed and chase me around this house when you can barely lift your head as it is?"

"I'll do it. I swear I will. Even if it kills me, I promise that I'll get you down off that ladder before you wind up killing yourself." Johnny harrumphed.

Shar knew her daddy was stubborn enough to do just what he said. She would not be responsible for killing him. She threw up her hands. "All I'm trying to do is help around this house. If you won't let me help with the windows then what do you want me to do?"

"I want you to go to that church and talk to Pastor Landon."

"Daddy, I already told you why I can't do that."

"And another thing," Johnny began as his eyes filled with tears. "I want you to sing in that choir. And if you do, I'll be sitting in the front row cheering you on."

Marlene's mouth hung open. She swiveled around to face her husband. "I don't believe it. In all the years we've been married, you ain't never once stepped foot inside the church."

"If Shar agrees to sing in that choir, I promise you, Marlene, I'll go to that church for the rest of my days. I'm the reason she went on that tour, and I'm to blame for the reason she don't want to sing no more. I just pray that God forgives me for what I done to our child."

Everybody in the room was crying now. Shar knew how it pained her mother to go to church without her husband. So many of the saints would inquire about his whereabouts and her mama would just say, "The good Lord knows what he's doing with my husband. So, I'm not gon' get in the way." How could she deny them now? Shar opened her mouth to tell her mama about what she'd done. Her daddy already knew she had been singing down at Ray's place. But she'd made him swear he wouldn't tell her mama.

Her mama was so proud of her, and it was clear to see that she loved her more than life itself. She didn't want her mama thinking less of her. She also didn't want to defy her father just because she was embarrassed to face Landon. Maybe she could go down to the church and do just as her daddy suggested without even so much as bringing up the choir. Landon was a good man and if he knew that the drafty windows was stopping Marlene from healing as well as she should be, Shar had no doubt he would help.

She was about to tell her parents her decision, when there was a knock at the front door. "I'll get it," Shar said as she headed toward the living room.

Mr. Cordey Turner, the landlord, and Mr. Raymond Johnson, Nettie's daddy, was both standing on her porch at the same time. Shar was surprised to see the two men together because she had no clue that they even knew each other. She opened the door and stepped back so they could come into the house and get out of the windy cold of this late October day.

"Good day to you, gentlemen. To what do we owe for the privilege of having our state representative and our landlord come visit?"

Both men took their hats off, then Raymond said, "We're mighty sorry to trouble you, Miss Shar, especially since your parents are ailing."

"Who's at the door, Shar?" Marlene hollered from the bedroom.

"It's the landlord, Mama. And Mr. Johnson."

Marlene got out of bed and came into the living room. "How are you doing, Mr. Turner . . . Mr. Johnson?"

"Good day to you, Marlene," Cordey said. "We didn't mean to get you out of bed."

"Just tell me what you gentlemen are here for, so I can go back to resting."

Cordey fidgeted, looked at the floor, and then said, "I'm here about the rent. I haven't received full payment for this month, and I'm just hoping that I can collect today."

Marlene lifted her hands wide as she tried to explain. "We don't have it. Me and Johnny been in and out of the hospital this month, and we just barely keeping food in the house."

"You understand my situation though, don't you?" Cordey asked.

"I just started down at the beauty parlor last week. I'll be able to get the rent to you sometime next month if you can just be patient with us," Shar assured him.

"I appreciate that you would cover the payment for your parents, Shar. But I need the money today or I'll have to evict you all."

Shar couldn't believe what she was hearing. The house they were staying in was barely habitable. Her mother stayed sick in here, and Mr. Turner did nothing about the draft. Now that some of the church folks came and helped them with the house he wanted to throw them out. This just wasn't fair.

Raymond patted his chest and then cleared his throat before speaking. "The reason I came here with Mr. Turner is that I believe I can help you all out."

"And how is that?" Marlene asked, looking at Raymond Johnson as if he was a snake in the grass worse than the one standing next to him.

"I might be able to scrape up enough money to get your rent paid. But if I can, I'll need you all to do something for me."

"Nothing ain't never free when it comes to dealing with you, Raymond Johnson," Marlene said.

"Now come on, Mrs. Marlene. I've never done you a bad turn. I'm here to help." Raymond looked from Marlene to Shar. When neither woman said anything, he put his hat back on and said, "Well, don't say I didn't try to keep you out of the cold this winter." He began walking toward the door.

"What's going on in there?" Johnny asked.

"I'll tell you about it in a minute, Johnny. Now get some rest and let me handle things for a little while." Marlene turned back to Raymond and said, "Wait, don't go. Just tell us what you want."

Raymond turned back around, took his hat off again. "I just want Shar to sing in this fund-raiser that Pastor Landon and my daughter are putting together. That shouldn't be a problem, right?"

Marlene turned to Shar. Shar looked into her mother's eyes and saw the need in them. This house was old and rickety, but they still didn't want to be living on the streets in the coming winter. "Shouldn't be a problem at all, Mr. Johnson," Shar said out loud. Inwardly she was dreading the conversation that she would now need to have with Landon and her parents. It's just like they always say, what's done in the dark will come out in the light. Shar only prayed that there'd be some forgiveness in the light that was about to shine down on her.

28

Taking her normal path to church, Shar was weighed down with thoughts of obligations and deceit. She wanted so badly to help her parents, and she was tired of deceiving everyone around her. It was time for her to tell the truth and shame the devil.

When she reached the church, Nettie was seated at her desk looking at her with malice in her eyes. "So, my father spoke the truth I see."

Ignoring her, Shar said, "Can I speak with Pastor Landon please?"

"You don't have to admit it to me, but I know that you don't really want to help the people in this community. You're only here so that you can help your own family." Nettie was almost snarling as she finished her statement.

"I'll knock on the door to see if Pastor Landon has time for me," Shar said as she stepped away from Nettie's desk and headed toward Landon's office. Nettie was always so hateful to her. Shar never understood why Nettie acted as if the devil himself had jumped into her body whenever she was around. Nettie's parents had money and influence, and they could give her just about anything she wanted. Shar had nothing, so she saw no reason for Nettie to waste her time hating her.

Nettie jumped up from her seat and beat a path to Landon's door. She stood in front of it, barring Shar from coming any closer. "I will tell Pastor Landon that you are here. Just because you've traveled with some fancy choir, that doesn't give you the right to come in here and go against the office protocol that we have set in place."

Not wanting to be out of order in God's house, Shar stepped back and waited.

Nettie knocked on the door. When Landon invited her in, she opened his door, went in, and closed the door behind her. It took several minutes, but when Nettie finally opened the door, she told Shar, "Pastor Landon has a few minutes for you."

Shar wanted to thank Nettie for doing her job, but she didn't think anything charitable would come out of her mouth if she said something to her, so she walked past the woman.

Landon stood up and walked around his desk to greet Shar. "How are you doing, Shar? Is everything okay at home?"

"That's what I wanted to talk to you about among other things, but if you're busy, I can come back at another time," she said since Nettie was still hugging the door and watching them like a hawk.

"Thank you, Nettie. Can you close the door behind you?" Landon directed Shar to the small sofa in his office. "Have a seat," he told Shar as Nettie closed the door. Shar sat down, and then Landon asked, "Now, what's troubling you?"

Shar gathered the courage she needed to tell Landon every bit of truth as she knew it. She took a deep breath and began. "I wasn't actually telling the truth when I said I was too busy to help with the choir fund-raiser."

Landon was silent, listening and giving her the time she needed to say all that was in her heart.

"Truth is, singing for God just don't feel the same no more. After singing in them nightclubs I just don't feel worthy."

Landon shook his head to that. "God loves you, Shar. He hasn't left you. He'll always be there to lead you back home."

"Tell that to my voice. One night after singing in a night-club, someone hit me over the head and left me to drown in a puddle of rain. My voice hasn't held the same anointing since. Like maybe God has decided He don't want me in gospel choirs no more."

The look on his face said it all. Landon was just as devas-tated as Shar by the news. "I'm so sorry that something like that happened to you."

She came to tell it all, not just to receive sympathy and act like a victim that had done no wrong. "I can't rightly say that the only reason the anointing left my voice is because of some bandit on the street. I didn't do right by God while I was on the road, and now I'm paying for it by not being able to use my voice to glorify Him anymore."

Landon put his hand in Shar's as he said, "I don't believe that. Not in a million years would I ever believe that a voice as angelic as yours would lose it's anointing. I don't believe that God would take your anointing to sing His praises like no one I've ever heard, simply because of a few youthful indiscretions."

"But you don't know everything I've done," Shar blurted out.

"No, I don't, but I'm right here if you want to tell me," he said patiently.

Shar covered her face with her hands. "I'm just so ashamed of myself."

Compassion filled Landon's face as he watched Shar begin to fall apart before his very eyes. "You won't find any condem-nation in this office. The Bible tells us that all have sinned and come short of God's glory. So, whatever happened, I guarantee you that it already happened to others before you. And God done already figured out a way to forgive the doing of it."

When she dropped her hands, tears were streaming down her face. Landon wiped them away with the back of his hand. "You are so good to me," Shar said as more tears came. "And I surely don't deserve your kindness."

"You're too hard on yourself, Shar."

She shook her head. "No, I'm not hard enough on myself, or I would have never lied to you when you visited me at that church a while back."

"What are you talking about?"

"I was just so angry with you for never returning any of my letters. I had been going through so much while I was on the road, and crying out to you the whole while. But you stopped responding." Landon handed her some tissue, and she blew her nose and continued. "Anyway, Nicoli wasn't exactly telling the truth when he told you that we were engaged. I could have said something right then and there, but I was glad he'd said it because I wanted you to know that I wasn't waiting idly by for a letter from you anymore."

"Shar, I already told you that I sent you several letters. My heart was bleeding for your situation, but at the same time I was making progress on the housing project and couldn't leave town to come see you when I wanted to." Landon hesitated, appearing to be second-guessing himself. "I don't know . . . maybe I made the wrong decision. But you must believe me, Shar, my delayed response was not because I didn't care what was troubling you."

"I know that you said you wrote letters, but I stopped receiving them. Anyway, that wasn't what I came here to talk to you about." Shar gathered all of her strength and began to tell Landon the story of her ruining. "Once I allowed Nicoli to tell that lie, it seemed like everything just began to go wrong. We did become engaged. But Nicoli was a drinker and a gambler. He kept getting into trouble, so Mr. Dorsey ended up firing him.

"Then he got in trouble with this nightclub owner that he owed a boat load of money to. They beat him up real bad, and then they said that they'd forgive his debt if I would agree to sing in that nightclub."

"Oh, Shar, no." Landon closed his eyes, clearly pained by what he was hearing. "A voice like yours comes along once, maybe twice in a generation. It's a voice that has been culti-vated for the praises of God."

Nodding, Shar said, "I tried telling Nicoli that I wasn't meant to sing any of that old secular music that he wanted me to sing in order to make more money." She turned away from Landon, unable to watch his face as she told the rest. "Nicoli wouldn't listen, so he got himself into a jam that I had to get him out of."

Landon turned her back to face him. "It's okay, Shar. You obviously made it out of there because you're here with me now. And if you have asked for forgiveness for going astray, you just got to believe that God has forgiven you."

Looking like a woman without a friend in the world, Shar said, "I'm terrified that if I get back in the choir and try to sing, everyone will know that the spirit of God has left me, just like that message you preached about God's spirit leaving King Saul." She hung her head low as she closed her mouth and waited for the condemnation that was sure to come. She might as well have gone to Paris and flaunted herself all around like Josephine Baker. At least she would have earned enough money to get her mother and father into a decent house . . . one they could afford and one that wouldn't keep them sick.

"Shar, don't you know that God is married to the backslider. He is always willing and ready to lift us back into his arms."

"But I never wanted to be one of those singers who can sing gospel one minute and then turn around and sing the blues the next."

"Then from this moment on, don't be that kind of singer. If you truly believe that God has called you to sing gospel music, then it's time to forgive yourself and move forward." He stood up and paced the floor, searching for the exact words. When Landon turned back to her, he said, "Don't you see, Shar? This fund-raiser is your chance to use your God-given gift to help colored people gain some dignity. Now if the Lord don't place His anointing on that, then I just don't know why He wouldn't."

Hesitantly, Shar asked, "And you still want me to sing in the choir, even after everything I just told you?"

He rushed back over to the sofa and took her hands in his. "Of course I want you back in the choir. I can't wait for you to come back."

Shar had been holding her breath, waiting for Landon's answer. "I'm so glad you feel that way because Mr. Johnson said he'd stop the landlord from evicting us from our home if I changed my mind about singing for the fund-raiser. But I didn't want to join back up with the choir without letting you know what happened to me."

"Wait a minute, hold on." Landon waved his hands in front of his chest. "Are you telling me that somebody threatened you concerning this fund-raiser?"

Shar shook her head. "Mr. Johnson didn't threaten us. He came to the house with Mr. Cordey. When Mr. Johnson found out that we didn't have the money to make the rent for this month, he offered to pay it for us as long as I agree to sing."

Landon's fist balled as anger overtook him. "I should have known not to trust that man when he offered to help us raise the money we need. Raymond Johnson doesn't do anything unless it benefits him."

She stood and put her hand on Landon's shoulder. "Don't be angry. If Mr. Johnson hadn't offered to lend a helping hand I don't know what we would have done when Mr. Cordey came knocking on our door."

Landon didn't say anything, but Shar could tell that he was still fuming. He stalked around the room several times and then turned back to her.

"I thought you came here to talk to me about the choir because you had changed your mind. But if you're not ready to come back to the choir yet, if you still need a little more time to pray and seek the Lord, then you take all the time you need."

"But I have to do this for my parents."

"No, you don't," Lance said authoritatively. "I have a little money saved. I'll pay your parents' rent."

Shar loved how protective Landon was of her at times. She wanted to put her hand on his cheek and reassure him that she would be okay. But things were different between her and Landon these days, and she was confused about what she should and shouldn't be feeling, or what she could or couldn't do around him. He was an anointed man of God, and she had lost her anointing. She didn't deserve to be in the same room with this man, let alone presume to think of his offer of help as more than what it was. A pastor trying to lend a helping hand to one of his members.

She had no right to ask him for anything, but Landon loved helping others regain their dignity. Her mother and father deserved some dignity out of life. And if her singing could get them some of that, then she had finally found a reason for the voice God gave her.

"I truly want to sing, Landon. I'm just not so sure I'll be able to pull it off, but if I do I want you to promise me something."

"I'd do anything for you, Shar. Just tell me what you need."

Landon was already upset over Mr. Johnson taking liberties. So, she didn't want him to think poorly of her, but she had to speak up because if she didn't, her parents might never get out of the God-forsaken neighborhood they lived in. "You told me that you had ten families that were eligible for homeownership. I'm wondering and I'm hoping . . . that you wouldn't mind adding one more family to that list."

"You know of another family that qualifies?" Landon asked.

Nodding, Shar said, "I sure do. My parents don't have the money, but ain't nobody more in need than them." She lifted a hand. "Now, I'm not asking for them to take money that the other families need. But if there is enough left over after the fund-raiser, do you think it would be much trouble to add them to the list?"

She was holding her breath again. Hoping and praying that her parents would finally get the break, they need.

Landon pulled Shar into his arms and hugged her. "You don't have to carry this burden alone, Shar. I promise you that I won't forget about your parents. And if we earn enough money, we will be looking for a new house for Johnny and Marlene Gracey along with the rest of them."

29

Shar now had two things to look forward to: her father coming to church and her parent's getting blessed with a new house. They would still have to pay the mortgage on the house, so Shar kept praying that her parents would get better soon enough to get back to work. Landon was planning a week-long concert. Tickets were being sold for a dollar each for each night of the concert. Flyers were being passed around the city of Chicago announcing, "Shar Gracey is back! Come hear her anointed voice as she sings praises to the Lord."

Shar almost laughed out loud as she read that line on one of the flyers. It took months for her to be allowed to sing a solo in Thomas Dorsey's choir. And when the big named singers were on the tour, Shar had barely been needed, except to sell the sheet music. But her church was now billing her as some gospel-singing star.

The line right below the information about Shar read: "Lend a helping hand to break the Restrictive Covenants designed to keep colored folks in the Black Belt." So, even though Shar doubted that anyone seeing that flyer would willingly part with one of their hard-earned dollars just to hear her sing, she prayed that they would come to lend a helping hand to the people in this community.

So it was with that frame of mind that Shar showed up for her first rehearsal. Calvin, the choir director, was behind the piano, tuning it, while the guitar player fiddled with the strings on his guitar. It was all so familiar to Shar as she walked into the choir stand. She passed the chair that Mother Barnett normally sat in, and Shar had to control the emotions that threatened to explode right out of her body. Shar didn't know if her voice would have the same anointing that it once had when she sang in this church, but she would be dedicating her voice to Mother Barnett that week. Maybe the Good Lord would show her some grace for one of His saints that done gone on to glory.

The Mothers' Board had gotten in on the event too. They were dedicating their services to Mother Barnett. So while the choir practiced, the Mothers' Board made preparations to sell dinners after the concert.

"Okay, everyone, stand up so we can warm up those vocals," Calvin instructed.

As she stood up, Shar realized that she was glad to be home. Glad to be back where things were normal and predictable.

"Place your hand on either side of your mouth and use the tips of your fingers to hold up the weight of your cheeks," Calvin said as he looked around to ensure that everyone was following his instructions, then he continued, "Now keep your lips very loose and floppy and blow."

The members of the choir did as instructed.

"Now, hold that pose and make a dopey MMMMMM sound."

When they finished warming up, Calvin was ready to begin the worship. "Shar, come over here so I can work with you on this song."

Shar had hoped that she wouldn't be singled out so soon. She was still praying and seeking the Lord, trying to get her anointing back. Would Calvin recognize the difference in her voice? Would he call her out in front of the whole choir?

When she stood before him, trying not to show her nervousness, Calvin said, "I know that 'Amazing Grace' is a favorite around here. But since you've been touring with Mr. Dorsey, I want you to sing a few of his songs. Are there any of those songs that are special to you?"

Shar immediately thought of one that she would love to sing, but she wasn't sure if her voice was strong enough, so she struck it from her thoughts. "I've sung 'Old Ship of Zion' and 'Precious Lord.'"

"Okay, well then, let's start off practicing those." Calvin put his hands on the piano keys and was just about to signal Shar to sing, when Landon appeared in the back of the sanctuary.

"Calvin, can I speak with you," Landon called out so loud that everyone in the room turned in his direction.

Calvin popped up and jogged to the back of the sanctuary. "What's up, boss?"

Landon leaned closer to Calvin and whispered, "Shar has been under a lot of stress lately, with all that's been going on with her family."

"You want me to go easy, for the day?"

Landon shook his head. "I want you to let her sit out for a while. Let her listen and join in with the choir, but don't have her sing any solos right now. She needs to rest her vocals."

Calvin turned and glanced at Shar as she stood by his piano. Then he turned back to Landon with a quizzical expression on his long narrow face. "Are you sure? She didn't say anything to me."

"I don't think she wants anyone to know what kind of stress she's under. So, I don't want you repeating this conversation to anyone else."

Calvin nodded and then headed back down to rejoin his choir. "Change of plans," he told Shar. "Have a seat in the sanctuary and just listen to the songs that we'll be singing."

"But I thought you wanted me to practice those Thomas Dorsey songs?"

"I do, and we will practice them. We have one week before the concert. So, don't worry. We'll get to them." Calvin turned away from Shar and pointed into the choir stand. "Nettie, come here. I want to practice this Mahalia Jackson song with you."

As Nettie sprang to her feet, Shar headed to the back of the sanctuary where Landon was now sitting. She sat down on the bench in front of him. She put her hands on the top of the bench, turned to Landon and asked, "Did you say something to Calvin?"

"I only told him about the stress you've been under with your parents and asked that he allow you to rest your voice a few more days."

Landon was always thinking about her . . . always being kind to her and trying to make things better for her. He was nothing like Nicoli. That scoundrel would have made her sing until her voice dried all the way up if he could have gotten an extra nickel to gamble away. Her eyes were beaming at him as she said, "Thank you. I have to admit that I was a bit nervous when Calvin asked me to sing."

He put his hand over Shar's. "I just think you need your confidence back. Being home and around your original choir just might be the thing you need."

"I hope you're right. I just don't want to disappoint you."

Landon shook his head. "Nothing you do could ever disappoint me. Not as long as the doing of it made you happy."

Shar felt heat on the back of her neck as Landon patted her hand. She turned around in her seat as Landon let her hand go. Nettie was shooting daggers of fire at Shar even as she finished up singing one of Mahalia's most beautiful songs. Shar got the message. She needed to stay away from Landon. She didn't want to ruin whatever he had going on with Nettie, even if she thought Landon was making just as big a mistake as she had made with Nicoli.

Four days into rehearsal, and Nettie's daddy came storming into the church, looking like he'd caught a bull by the horns and was just about to go in for the kill. He marched over to Landon, who had been conferring with Calvin over by the piano. "Can I have a word with you, Preacher?"

Landon turned around, greeted Mr. Johnson, and then asked, "What can I do for you?"

"Can we go to your office and speak in private," Mr. Johnson asked, barely able to contain himself as his nostrils flared.

"Follow me." Landon walked out of the sanctuary without looking at any of the people standing around watching what was sure to be exploding fireworks. He closed his office door after Raymond Johnson set in, but his office was right outside of the sanctuary, and the door was so paper thin that the choir could hear everything being said because the two men wouldn't lower their voices once the argument got going.

"I thought you told me that you actually wanted to make money with this fund-raiser," Raymond demanded.

"It is not I who wants the money, Mr. Johnson. This community needs that money so that we can finally do away with these Restrictive Covenants that bar our people from acquiring decent affordable housing."

"Then whose cockamamy idea was it to let Shar Gracey sit out there all week and not open her mouth once to practice?"

"Why does what we are doing in choir practice concern you?" Landon demanded just as forcefully.

"I'm the one who put those flyers together for you, I'm the one out there trying to get those tickets sold. And all I keep hearing is skepticism from everybody about giving up their hard-earned dollar when Shar Gracey might not be singing anyway." Raymond's voice was booming with anger.

"You just go back and tell all of your skeptics that Shar Gracey will be giving the performance of a lifetime when this concert begins next week. And if they don't want to miss it, then they need to get their tickets now." Landon's words were filled with hope, faith, and a belief that passes human under-standing . . . like he'd come by his knowledge firsthand as he sat down in the throne room of heaven.

"Your word isn't enough for me. Not when it's my reputation on the line."

"What does your reputation have to do with anything? You're worried about that State Representative seat. That's it and that's all."

"I'm going to find out for myself," Raymond said as the door to Landon's office swung open. He marched over to where Shar sat, grabbed her arm, stood her up, and then demanded, "Sing."

"Get your hands off of her," Landon said as he rushed to Shar's aid.

Here she was again. Shar thought back to the night that the salon owner who Nicoli owned money to demanded that she get back on stage and sing. She had looked to Nicoli for help. As usual, he'd done nothing for her. But her knight in shining armor was always there for her. He would never let anything happen to her. She wanted to fall in Landon's arms and beg him to love her again. Because she now understood why her mama had been so concerned that she might miss out on the love of this good man.

Landon stepped in front of Shar and faced Raymond Johnson down. He pointed toward the front door of the church and said, "I have never thrown anyone out of this church. But I am two seconds away from making you the first."

The look on Nettie's face was horror-stricken. She'd never seen her father act in such a manner, but it was only going to get worse.

"After all the work I've done to help you and the people of the church, you dare to talk to me in such a manner." Raymond pointed to Shar. "I paid her daddy's rent so that she would come and sing with this choir."

"I never asked you to do that," Landon said.

"Yeah, but you were mighty grateful to have her back in such close proximity to you, huh?" Disappointment shone through as Raymond added, "And to think I let you keep company with my precious daughter, when all the while you were just biding your time until Shar Gracey came back to town."

There were collective gasps throughout the choir stand at Raymond's words. Nettie burst into tears and ran out of the room.

Landon watched her go and then turned back to Raymond Johnson. "Nettie and I are friends . . . good friends at that. But you had no reason or need to besmirch the good name of Sister Gracey. I have done nothing unseemly. It is just your dirty mind working on overtime."

Landon continued, "Now I'm getting ready to go find Nettie to make sure that she is all right. I suggest you come with me, and then I want you to leave us all alone until the event next week." Landon didn't wait for a response. He walked out of the sanctuary in search of Nettie.

Raymond eyed Shar but then looked as if he thought better of what he was about to say. He then turned and followed Landon out of the sanctuary.

All eyes were on Shar, and she felt as if she owed everyone an explanation. She walked over to the choir stand, gave a small weak smile, and then said, "I know that you all have been wondering why I haven't been singing with the choir while we practiced this week." She turned to Calvin and added, "And I know that Landon told you about the stress I've been under with my parents, but I want to tell you all what really happened."

"Speak the truth, and shame the devil," one of the choir members hollered from the second row.

"That's what I aim to do," Shar said as she closed her eyes and said a silent prayer. She really needed unconditional love right now. If the choir turned on her and began judging her, she didn't know what she would do. She took a deep breath and said, "My voice has been cracking."

"Oh my Lord, no," one of the women said. "A voice as beautiful as yours don't have no business cracking."

Shar couldn't bring herself to tell every detail, so she simply said, "I was out later than I should have been one night. I was by myself, it was raining, and someone hit me over the head in order to steal my purse, which had less than ten dollars in it."

They were all quiet, listening, waiting for the rest of the story.

"I was knocked out and laying in a pool of rainwater. When I woke up, I couldn't barely speak. Once my voice came back, I was able to sing once again, but it just doesn't have the same anointing as my voice once held. Now, I'm not saying that to be vain. But I do believe that God had anointed my voice," she shrugged, "once upon a time.

"Pastor Landon has done nothing more than encourage me to believe that the problems with my voice are only temporary."

She looked at each member of the choir, imploring them to understand her plight. "I go home each night and practice the songs, and I've been on my knees praying to the good Lord that I'll be able to live up to the faith that Pastor Landon has in my singing abilities."

"He's not the only one with faith in your abilities, Shar Gracey." Calvin stood up and directed his choir to stand as well. "I've been your choir director for some years now. I know your voice better than you know it, and I'm telling you that I believe that with you singing lead next week, this choir will see the best performance we've ever had." He looked to his choir, "Are y'all with me?"

They all either nodded or said, "Yes," with loud boisterous voices.

As Landon walked back into the room and down to where the choir stood cheering Shar on, he asked everyone to come down from the choir stand. "Let's all join hands and pray, not just for this event, but for Shar as well. She has a gift that the enemy tried to steal. But we need to pray that God restore the sweet sound of her voice so that she will be able to do what she was meant to do before the foundation of the world. Amen."

30

The choir's loving response to her gave Shar the courage she needed to sit down and tell her parents about what had happened to her while on the road. Her daddy took the news harder than her mama. But Shar reassured him that she didn't blame nobody but herself, because she didn't have the strength to stand on her convictions. But she told them, "I'm standing now. I'm thankful for the experiences I had out there on the road, because it opened my eyes to the dangers that can come to us when we let our guard down."

"Well, I guess my baby is all growed up now," was all Marlene said as she dabbed at her eye with a cloth.

Shar felt better than she had in a long, long time. It was as if she was walking on a cloud instead of the raggedy old streets in the Black Belt. She made it to the church an hour before the concert was to begin. Shar wanted to have a little time to work on warming up her vocals with Calvin. He had been so good about letting her rest her voice all week long, that Shar wanted to surprise him with how hard she had been working on each of the songs while at home. But Calvin had a surprise for her when she arrived at the church.

Standing around the piano, singing as if they were also getting ready for the concert were Sallie Martin, Mahalia Jackson, and Rosetta Tharpe. Shar ran over to the women and gave them a big hug. She was so surprised to see them that she could hardly contain herself. "What are you all doing here?"

"You didn't think we was gon' let you do this concert by yourself, so you could feel like a big shot, now did ya!" Sallie Martin harassed Shar.

Shar hugged the woman again as she laughed. "I can always trust you to bring me down a peg or two."

"Or three or four," Mahalia added with a smile on her face.

Shar turned to the woman she had admired for so many years. She put her hand on Mahalia's shoulder. "I missed you so much when you left the tour."

"I know you did. But God took care of you. You're home safe and sound, and we are going to do this concert so we can raise this money and get our people some better housing."

"So, are you all really going to sing for the concert tonight?"

Calvin sprang up from the piano. "They sure are. We've already picked out the songs."

Shar turned back to the women who had become more than her rivals while on the road. Today, they were showing themselves to be friends. "What are you all going to sing?"

Sallie had a smirk on her face as she said, "I'm going to take 'Old Ship of Zion.'"

Mahalia said, "Oh, and there's no need for you to sing 'Precious Lord,' because I'm going to take that one."

Yep, this was like old times. Next she was going to be told that all she was needed for was to sell Mr. Dorsey's sheet music after the concert. Shar put her hand on her hip and turned to Rosetta.

"Don't look at me. I'm singing one of my own songs."

"Calvin?" Shar questioned. "How could you let them come in here and take both of the songs that I'm supposed to sing? I've been practicing those songs at home and been praying that I'd get them right."

"Don't you worry about it none, Shar Gracey." Sallie told her. "We picked out another song for you to sing. Something real special."

"What is it? I came early so I could practice with Calvin. Did you give him the sheet music?" Shar was looking from Sallie to Calvin, waiting on a response.

Finally Calvin said, "I have the sheet music."

Sallie chimed in, "But we don't want you to practice it right now. You just continue resting your voice until it's time to perform it."

That was outrageous. Sallie always made sure that she had practiced the song before going before a crowd of people to sing it. "But I need to practice before the concert."

Rosetta stepped forward. She held onto Shar's hands. "We all know what happened to you out there on the road. I know better'n anybody else what you're going through. But trust us on this one. You'll know the song and you'll sing it better'n it's ever been sung if you wait on it and allow yourself to just feel it." Rosetta squeezed her hands before letting go. "Just trust us. Okay?"

Shar nodded. She then sat down on the front pew. "I'll just sit here and listen why the three of you make sweet, sweet music."

❦

In his office, Landon scrambled around looking for the note paper he'd jotted some notes down on. He could hardly believe that they'd sold five hundred tickets to tonight's concert. Nettie's daddy might be a pain to deal with, but the man certainly knew how to promote an event. If the rest of the week went as well as tonight, then they would certainly have the money needed to help some of the families on the list. Landon wasn't going to give up though. He wouldn't stop until everyone who wanted a decent affordable house could get it.

A knock on his door stopped his search. He turned away from his desk and said, "Come in."

Nettie slowly walked in as if she were marching toward that old rugged cross and wanted the journey to last as long as possible.

"Nettie, just the person that I need. Have you seen my note paper?"

She walked over to his desk, opened the top drawer and pulled out the note paper he'd been working on, and handed it to him.

Smiling, Landon said, "What would I do without you?"

"You don't need me, Landon."

Landon shook his head. "This place wouldn't run as smoothly as it does without you. The best thing that happened to United Worship Center was Nettie Johnson."

Nettie should have been overjoyed at Landon's comment, but her face was overcome with sadness. "You might mean that as far as your office goes. But when it comes to the sanctuary and anything else, you'd pick Shar over me any day."

Landon leaned against his desk as he took Nettie's words and saw the hurt in her eyes. He didn't want to lie to Nettie or make her believe in something that would never happen between them, so he simply said, "I'm sorry, Nettie. I've tried to be as honest with you as possible."

She held up a hand. "Stop, Landon. I feel terrible enough as it is."

He lowered his head and again said, "I'm sorry."

"And stop saying you're sorry. I'm the one who owes you an apology."

Landon was confused by that comment. He lifted his head to look at her and saw that Nettie was in tears. He wanted to go to her and put his arm around her. But his feet wouldn't move forward. He was so afraid of further damaging their relationship that he didn't know what to do right now . . . should he be her pastor or her friend? Then Nettie began talking, and his heart sank with the knowledge of what she had done to him and to Shar.

"Do you remember those letters you asked me to mail for you?"

"Yes, of course. You always mail my letters when I don't have time."

Her voice caught as she admitted, "I didn't send them."

Landon's brow was up as he asked, "Which letters didn't you send?"

"The ones you asked me to mail to Shar." She opened her purse and pulled out several envelopes. "I kept them."

Landon's hands went to his mouth. "Oh my Lord," was all he could say. So much damage had been done to him and to Shar because of those missing letters. Landon was convinced that she wouldn't have fallen for Nicoli if she had believed that he still loved and cared about what had been concerning her. Now he and Shar just seemed to be two misguided people, holding onto a love they didn't know what to do with. He took the letters from Nettie.

Now she was the one saying, "I'm sorry," as she left his office.

Landon sat down behind his desk and cried like a little lost sheep who'd gotten all tangled up in weeds until his Shepherd came and found him and helped him break free. So that he could finally be free to love the only woman who'd ever claimed his heart.

The people were filing into the church in droves. Some came to worship, some came to fellowship with other saints, and some came to see if Shar Gracey had gone out into the world only to lose that beautiful singing voice that the good Lord gave her.

Surrounded by the women who had helped her hone her craft, Shar wasn't as nervous as she had been throughout the week of rehearsals. She could do this, she could do this, she just kept telling herself. And even if she flopped, no one would complain about the concert, not with Sallie, Mahalia, and Rosetta in the house.

To kick off the event, Landon stood behind the podium, looking as fine as any preacher had ever deemed to look. Shar was so proud of him. He had kept the faith and kept fighting for what he believed in, and now all of these people had turned out. Shar wondered if Landon knew that he was a dreamer just like her. But his dreams were coming true, and Shar couldn't be happier.

She now knew that Landon and Nettie were only friends, but she didn't know what that meant for them. She still wondered about those letters and why he hadn't come to her when she'd needed him most, but she was trying to put that behind her and press on.

Looking down at his notes, Landon began, "I thank each and every one of you who listened and heard our hearts and decided to join this cause by purchasing a ticket to tonight's gospel concert." He looked down at the front row and said, "And I see that we have a few special guests." He asked Sallie, Mahalia, and Rosetta to stand so they could be acknowledged by the crowd. Everyone began clapping and hootin' and hollerin'.

"Okay, okay, settle down," Landon told them as the singers took their seats. He then said, "We also have a special treat for everyone because United Worship Center's own Shar Gracey is back home where she belongs." Landon asked Shar to stand from where she was seated in the choir stand. She quickly stood, waved to everyone, and then sat back down.

"Before I turn the microphone over to the choir, I just want to let you all know that this week will not be the end for us, but only the beginning. The Restrictive Covenants will one day be a thing of the past, and our people will be able to live anywhere they choose." The crowd exploded with applause at those words.

Shar looked around the room. Many people were on their feet, some were crying, others yelling. It seemed that so many people were tired of being forced to live as second-class citizens. Hope sprang up in her heart as she watched her mother and father walk into the church. She'd known that they would most likely be late, if they showed up at all, so she'd asked the usher to save them two seats. As she watched the usher seat her father, she was thankful that she'd agreed to sing and that her father had kept his word.

"Now let the singing begin," Landon said as he turned the microphone over to Calvin.

Nettie was the first singer up. She sang "Amazing Grace" as tears streamed down her face. Shar lowered her head and prayed for the girl. Nettie had never had a kind word for her, but Shar felt led to pray for her. If others hadn't prayed for her, who knows where she would be right now.

Sallie was up next. She took the microphone and in normal fashion began telling a story as she sang.

I was standing by the banks of a river
Looking out over life's troubled seas

When I saw an old ship that was sailing
Is that the old ship of Zion I see

Sallie turned and looked up in the choir stand and said, "Now, Shar, you might have had a little trouble, might have even felt like giving up, but we came here today to let you know that the old ship of Zion is not hardly about to sail without you. You were born to sing God's praises, and you will soon know it way down deep in your soul."

Shar's eyes misted over. She hadn't known how to take Sallie when they first met, but Shar now could see that the woman's heart was as big as an ocean. Sallie turned back to the audience, hunched over, and kept on singing.

It's hull was bent and battered
From the storms of life I could see
Waves were rough but that old ship kept sailing
Is that the old ship of Zion I see

The crowd was on their feet, waving and singing along. Nobody sang "Old Ship of Zion" like Sallie Martin. Shar was grateful that Sallie was here to give that song the extra flair it needed.

Things were moving right along. Rosetta sang, then the choir delivered two selections. After that the deacons passed the collection plate. The people seemed genuinely excited to put their coins and dollar bills into the offering. If things kept going like this throughout the week, Shar was confident that Landon would have the money he needed for the homeownership program.

After the collection plate had been passed, Mahalia stood up and wowed everybody with her rendition of "Precious Lord," and Shar was once again glad that she hadn't sung that song tonight. "Precious Lord" would forever belong to Thomas Dorsey and Mahalia Jackson, him for writing it, and her for singing it like nobody else could.

She still didn't know what song she was supposed to sing. So when it was her turn at the microphone, she stood there, with her eyes closed, praying that she wouldn't mess up whatever song she was required to sing tonight. "Help me, Lord."

Calvin struck a few cords on his piano and then began playing the music to "Never Turn Back." Shar's eyes sprung open, and she searched until she found Sallie sitting on the front row grinning at her like she'd just been offered a record deal. Shar was confused. She had once begged Sallie for the chance to sing this song. But Sallie had told her that she hadn't experienced enough of life to even think about such a song. Said there wasn't enough heartache in her to deliver the song in the way that could touch an audience

As Shar looked at her now, Sallie mouthed the words, "It's time for you to sing it."

Shar thought back to the things she'd endured over the last few years, and tears streamed down her face as she realized that although this song wasn't written for her, it had always been her destiny to sing it . . . to encourage a world of hurting people that they needed to always look to Jesus and never turn back, no matter what. She opened her mouth and began:

I started out for heaven such a long time ago
For the world of temptation made my journey hard and slow

Shar wanted to start talking to the audience like Sallie normally did. But Sallie was the storyteller. She was just a singer, but she was a singer whose voice hadn't cracked on one note of the song so far. So, she kept on singing, hoping that the words of the song would encourage anyone that might be feeling as low as she had been feeling.

I turned to worldly pleasures, but I only found pain and woe
I'm back on the road to the city, and I'll never turn back no more
No, no, no more, no more, no, no more . . .

Back when Shar had first practiced "Never Turn Back," it had only been a song to her and nothing more. But now, every word she sang became her testimony. The spirit overtook Shar as she began strutting around the church, singing that song like it belonged to her. She put her hand on her hip, let her head swing back, and kept going to town.

Wind may blow, storm may rise
Wind may blow me, Lord, side to side
I'll never turn back to the city

Shar meant every word she sang. She didn't care what happened or which way the wind blew, she wasn't never turning her back on God and His sweet promises ever again.

When the song was finished, the anointing fell over the church while Calvin banged on the piano keys and the guitar player played. The audience from Mahalia, Sallie, Shar's parents, and all the way in the back of the sanctuary got to shouting. The people were no ways tired and weren't about to give up on their God or their dreams. Shar could see a change sweeping over the people . . . like the song had helped them believe that them better days Landon preached about were on the horizon. She was believing it herself as she grabbed the microphone and did an encore without even being asked. God was being glorified, and Shar couldn't stop singing His praises if she wanted to.

⚘

Thirty minutes after the church erupted in praise, Landon grabbed the mic and said, "Now let the church say Amen." He dismissed them.

As the people began filing out, Landon walked over to Marlene and Johnny and asked, "How are you feeling?"

"After that performance, I'm feeling like I'm going to live for a very long time . . . at least long enough to see that little girl of mine sing for the Lord about a hundred more times," Johnny said.

That declaration from her husband made Marlene smile. "I guess we gon' carry on then."

Landon turned and caught a glimpse of Shar. People were coming up to her, shaking her hand and giving her hugs. He was so proud of her . . . and so in love with her. He asked Johnny, "Do you mind if I have a private word with Shar before you all leave?"

Johnny sat back down and pulled Marlene next to him. "I'm done interfering. You go on and talk to that girl. We'll wait right here."

Landon walked over to where Shar was standing. He waited for her to finish speaking to a woman who appeared to be just bursting to talk to Shar. When they were finished, he tapped her on the shoulder. Shar turned toward him, and his heart almost stopped at that very moment. She was the most beautiful woman in the world to him. Nothing had changed his mind since that first day he saw her on that stage in the Miss Bronze America pageant. "Can I speak with you in my office? I won't take up too much of your time."

"Of course," Shar said as she followed Landon out of the sanctuary and into his office.

After telling her how much he enjoyed her song, Landon asked Shar to sit down behind his desk.

"But that's where you sit."

"I know. But just this one time, I'd like you to sit there."

"Okay," Shar said as she walked around the desk and then sat down. She looked up at him, waiting for further instructions.

"I left a few things on my desk that belong to you. I thought it was past time that you received them."

Shar looked down. She scanned the desk and then put her hands on several envelopes that had her name on them. She saw the addresses of the different towns she'd been in with Thomas Dorsey's choir. When she looked back up at him, she asked, "You never mailed them?"

"I thought they had been. That's why when you accused me of not writing to you, I was so confused about the entire matter. But Nettie confessed to me today that she never mailed the letters."

Anger began rising up in Shar. "Why would she do such a thing?"

"It doesn't matter, Shar. All that matters to me now is that you read those letters. Would you mind doing that for me?"

In answer, Shar opened one of the letters and began reading. As she read the second and then the third, her eyes began to water. Landon handed her a tissue, and she continued. "I thought you forgot all about me," Shar said as she picked up the last letter.

"Never, Shar. Never in a million years could I forget about you."

She read the last letter and then turned to him with love in her eyes. "Nettie actually did me a favor by not giving you these letters until today. For so long now I've been feeling unworthy of your love. I wouldn't have been able to receive the message of your letters if I hadn't felt God's sweet forgiveness while I was singing 'Never Turn Back.'"

"But have you forgiven yourself?"

Shar nodded. "Yes, I think I have. This event was just what I needed."

"Good." Landon got down on his knee in front of her and said, "Shar Gracey, I asked you once before to marry me. It didn't turn out so well for me back then. But I'm on bended knee, ready to ask you again."

Her hands went to her mouth. Her eyes were flickering with so many emotions all at once.

"I don't care about what happened in the past. I only care about our future."

She put her hand on his cheek, loving the feel of his soft skin in her hand. "What about my singing, Landon? Is it too much for me to ask to have two dreams in one lifetime?"

"Not as long as one of those dreams is me," Landon said lightheartedly.

"You have always been my dream, Landon Norstrom. But after singing here tonight, the fire has been lit in me again. So, I'm admiting to you right here and now that I want to sing also. Can you handle having a wife who wants a recording deal?"

"Are you kidding? I'll build you a studio and we'll record the records ourselves."

With that they kissed, hugged, and laughed. Holding onto her man as if he was made of pure gold Shar said, "Yes, Landon, I will marry you."

Epilogue

Landon and Shar were married a month after they finally declared their undying love for each other. Although Shar never went on the road again, she managed to record ten records and give birth to three baby girls in her lifetime.

With the money Landon raised, two families were able to purchase houses outside of the Black Belt. However, it was not until 1948 that Restrictive Covenants began to be toppled.

Actually the issue began in 1945, in neighboring St. Louis, Missouri. The Shelleys purchased a house in which a Restrictive Covenant barring Negroes from occupying property had been placed. The Shelleys weren't aware of the Restrictive Covenant. However, Louis Kraemer, a white man who lived ten blocks away from the property, sued to restrain the Shelleys from living in the home they had purchased. The case went all the way to the Supreme Court. And then finally, in 1948, the Supreme Court ruled that the Fourteenth Amendment prohibits a state from enforcing restrictive covenants that would prohibit a person from owning or occupying property simply based on race or color.

Even though the case took place in St. Louis rather than in Chicago, Landon and the entire Black Belt community shouted the victory because what they believed was finally coming to pass. Landon stood before his congregation the Sunday after the Supreme Court rulings and said, "Brothers and sisters, the day is coming . . . we will soon live in a world where a man is free to buy property wherever he can afford. Now, how sweet does that sound?"

We hope you enjoyed this book by Vanessa Miller. She is one of our bestselling authors, and we hope you'll enjoy this sample from her first book with us, *Long Time Coming*. Her next book with Abingdon, *Blessed Assurance*, will be available in May 2015.

Prologue

The double doors opened, and the guests stood as Deidre Clark came into view. She was a vision in white. Small clusters of sparkling beads accented the front and back of the bodice and traveled down the wrap of the skirt. Her veil was covered with the same sparkling beads that accented her gown. The princess-style headpiece was pinned to her hair and the veil flowed down her back. Her mother had asked that she not cover her face with the veil. Loretta Clark's pastor had taught them that the veiled bride held secrets that the husband would have to uncover. But Deidre's mother didn't believe that a husband and wife should have secrets.

The musicians began to play, and the soloist stood.

"Are you ready?" Deidre's uncle asked.

She looked at her uncle, standing in for her beloved father, who had died way before his time. She pondered her uncle's question for a moment. Was anyone ever ready for such a thing as matrimony? She looked down the aisle at her groom, Private Johnson Morris. He'd told her when they met that he was career military. His dream was to one day wear general's stripes like his hero, Colin Powell. Johnson had lots of dreams, and Deidre wanted to help him achieve them all. She nodded. "I'm ready."

Still behind the double doors and not quite in the sanctuary yet, Deidre took a step as the soloist sang, *"At last, my love has come along."*

Although some might say that this particular song wasn't appropriate for a church wedding, Deidre requested it anyway. She had been terrified that no one would ever want to marry her. But Johnson had come into her life and swept her off her feet at last. She took another step and then her wedding coordinator stopped her.

The woman lifted the veil and put it over Deidre's face. "There . . . simply beautiful," she said as she gently pushed Deidre toward the sanctuary.

"My lonely days are over," the soloist continued.

Deidre kept walking once the veil had been placed over her face. But as she neared her groom, Deidre's thoughts turned to a conversation she had had with her mother earlier that day.

Loretta had walked into her dressing room, kissed her on the cheek, and then asked, "Did you tell him?"

Deidre turned toward the full-length mirror and smiled at her image.

"Did you tell him?" Loretta asked again.

"Not yet," Deidre said. She could see her mother's eyes fill with worry as she glanced at her. She turned back to the mirror, choosing to ignore her mother. This was her day—her never-supposed-to-be day—and she wasn't going to let anything spoil it, not even reality.

She was standing next to Johnson now. They recited their vows, and the preacher pronounced them husband and wife. Deidre let out a sigh of relief as Johnson lifted her veil of secrets and kissed her.

1

$\mathcal{T}$wenty-three and played out. Like the words of a tired old blues song, Kenisha Smalls had been strung and rung out.

"Too young to give up," she chided as she pulled herself out of bed. But when her feet hit the floor and her knees buckled from unexplained pain, she reminded herself that she had actually lived a hundred dog years, lapping at the crumbs from underneath other folks' tables, and being kicked around by more good-for-nothings than she could count. A few years back, Kenisha thought some good would have to come into her life to even out the bad. But when James, her first baby's daddy, got arrested for armed robbery, and then Terrell, her second baby's daddy, got himself shot and killed trying to be a kingpin, she'd stopped praying for the sun to shine through her drab days and resigned herself to embrace the rain.

Guess that's how she'd hooked up with Chico. Kenisha had been dazzled by his olive skin, wavy hair, and bulky arms. Dazzled by his corporate job and technical school education.

Of course, all that dazzling occurred before her responsible boyfriend started hanging around her crackhead brother, Kevin Carson. By the time she had given birth to her third child,

Chico had quit his good-paying job so he could give crack his undivided attention.

Now the only time Kennedy saw her crackhead father was when he made his first-of-the-month visit. Begging for a loan that he knew his broke behind couldn't pay back. She remembered the first time she refused to give Chico her rent money. He'd punched her in the face so hard her teeth clickety-clacked. Grabbing the iron skillet that she'd been frying chicken in, she'd chased him out of her house. When she walked back in and saw Jamal, her oldest child, standing in the kitchen holding a butcher knife, his eyes blazing with fury, she swore right then that she would have nothing more to do with Chico and his crack demon.

Shaking her head to ward away bad memories, Kenisha grabbed a washcloth and towel from the hall closet. Jumping in the shower, she allowed the hot water to assault her weary bones. As the steam filled the small bathroom, she wallowed in the horror story her life had become. What next? How much can happen to a person before the Almighty decides it's time to pick on someone else?

"Ah, dawg." She knew she'd forgotten something. Bumping her head against the tiled wall of the shower, she turned the water off and stepped out. She had an appointment that might make her late picking up Jamal from school. Not wanting to leave it to chance, she decided to call her sister Aisha Davis to see if she could pick up her son.

Before she could get her clothes on and make it to the telephone, Chico knocked on her back door. She was familiar with his knock. It was the first-of-the-month, "baby, can I please get a loan" kind of banging that rolled through her head twelve times a year. "Don't I have enough to deal with?" She picked up the pink frilly robe James had bought her on her fifteenth birthday. It had been soft and pretty, but the drudge of life had worn on it. Thought she would have replaced it long ago. But the kids kept coming, and the men kept leaving.

She picked up Jamal's leather belt, secured her tattered robe, stalked downstairs and flung open the back door. "What do you want, Chico?"

"Ah, girl, quit tripping. You know you're happy to see me. Them hazel eyes of yours sparkle every time I come over here."

She ran her hands through her short layered hair as the skeleton strolled up to her and puckered his lips. The five-day stench and sunken cheeks made Kenisha back up and give him the hand. "If it's money you want, my welfare check hasn't even arrived yet."

Crossed eyes and a deep sigh accused Kenisha of misjudging him. "How you know I didn't come over here to see my beautiful little girl?"

"Did you happen to get a job and bring your beautiful little girl some child support? 'Cause Kennedy likes to eat."

"Why you got to be like that?" He leaned against the kitchen sink. "See, that's why I don't come by more often. You always trippin'."

Kenisha opened the back door. "Boy, who do you think you're fooling? You don't come by more 'cause the first only comes once a month." A strong wind blew her robe open, exposing two bony thighs.

"Girl, you need to quit selling them food stamps. You know I like a woman with meat on her bones."

Kenisha rolled her eyes and waved him toward the coolness of the outdoor wind.

"Oh, so it's like that?" Pushing himself off the sink, he told her, "Just get Kennedy down here. Let me see my baby girl, and I'll be on my way."

"She ain't here. They spent the night over at Aisha's."

Walking toward her, he got loud. "How many times have I told you not to have my daughter over at your sorry sister's house?"

"When the telling comes with a check, that's when I'll start listening." Still holding the door open, she motioned him outdoors again.

He poked his index finger into the middle of her forehead.

"Make sure my daughter is home the next time I come to see her."

He walked out. But before Kenisha slammed the door, she told him, "Yeah, right. We'll see you in thirty days, Chico."

She sat on the couch as her body shook with rage. Her rage was directed not only at Chico, but at all the men who'd promised her sweetness, then made her swallow dung. She was tired. Wished she'd never met any of them. She sure wouldn't be in the fix she was in now if she'd waited until marriage to have sex. Maybe she should have signed up for karate classes when she was six or seven. That way she could have broken her mother's boyfriend's neck that night he took all her choices away.

Clicking on the TV, she hoped to find enjoyment in somebody else's drama. Dr. Phil was putting a smile on the face of a woman whose house had been robbed and ransacked. "Ain't that 'bout nothing? My life is raggedy, but I don't see nobody offering me so much as a needle and thread to stitch it up." She turned off the TV and stood. Might as well just deal with it. She picked up the phone and dialed Aisha.

The phone rang three times before Aisha's angry voice protruded through the line. "What have I told you about calling my house so early?"

Caller ID wasn't meant for everybody. It was 10:45 in the morning. And Aisha's lazy behind was still in bed, screening calls. "You need to get up and fix breakfast. My kids have a hot meal every morning."

Aisha yawned. "Your kids ain't no better than mine. They can walk downstairs and fix a bowl of cereal just like the rest of them monsters."

Rolling her eyes, Kenisha wondered why she'd agreed to let Diamond and Kennedy spend the night over at her sister's house. But she had been too tired to get on the number 8 bus and pick them up. Blinking away unwanted tears, she allowed her fist to smash against her living room wall.

Ever since her doctor had told her about the cancer eating away at her body, her walls had gotten punched. When her doctor told her that having sex at an early age was one of the factors for cervical cancer, she'd wanted to kill the men who had paraded through her life, taken what they wanted, then left her diseased. "I need you to pick Jamal up from school today."

"Oh, no. I've already got two of your kids over here. Dawg, Kenisha, I've got four kids of my own. What makes you think I want to babysit another?"

Grabbing some tissue, and wiping the moisture from around her eyes, she said, "Look Aisha, I've got an appointment." Kenisha's third radiation treatment was scheduled for today.

She'd missed her second appointment when Aisha promised to pick up her kids, but never showed. "It's important or I wouldn't ask."

Kenisha heard the rustling of the sheets as her sister sat up in bed.

"What's so special that you can't pick up your own son?"

"Nothing special. Just another rainy day."

✑

Deidre Clark-Morris sat behind her oak desk trying to decide whether to respond to her emails. At last count, she had seventy unopened messages. She just couldn't make herself read another parent complaint about the athletic programs she was forced to cut. And she didn't have the patience to deal with teachers complaining about old textbooks. The superintendent had already given her his sorry-about-your-luck look the last time she told him that she needed to replace the textbooks.

Today, she didn't have the energy to fight. Deidre had other things on her mind. Consuming things. Things between her, Johnson, and God. *Please God, don't let it come.*

It was her monthly cycle. Due yesterday, but thankfully absent. If *it* didn't show up today, maybe she'd finally have some good news to report to Johnson.

Another email appeared in her inbox. This one was from Johnson. The header read, "How are you doing?" On an ordinary day, a simple message like that from her husband would have put a smile on her face. Would have made her think of the "When a Man Loves a Woman" song.

But today was not ordinary. This was the day she would either get her period or be pregnant. So she knew that her wonderful, loving husband's email really meant "After seven long years of wishing and waiting, are you finally pregnant?"

Leave me alone. Those were the words she wanted to shout back across the email line. But salvation in the name of Jesus, and a couple deep breaths stopped her tirade. Consigning Johnson's email to the same devil the other seventy could go to, Deidre signed off her computer. It was 3:30; the students had been gone since 2:50.

"It's time to go."

A knock at her door stopped her from packing up. "Come in."

Mrs. Wilson, the stern-faced second-grade teacher, walked in with little Jamal Moore in tow. Deidre knew Jamal. Had greeted him several times in the hallway. He was always well groomed. One of the first things she noticed about Jamal, after his signature zigzag cornrows, was that his pants fit. Either he or his mom didn't buy into that sloppy, hanging-off-yourbackside fad that most kids were wearing.

"What's up?" Deidre asked.

Pointing at Jamal, Mrs. Wilson told her, "His mother didn't pick him up. I need to leave him with you."

"I was just getting ready to leave, Mrs. Wilson. I can't stay with him today."

Mrs. Wilson gave Deidre a piercing glare. "Now, I understand that you are the principal of this school, and therefore more important than the rest of us, but you are also the one who closed down the after-care program—"

Deidre held up her hand. "The superintendent closed down our after-care program, Mrs. Wilson. Not me."

With hands on healthy hips, Mrs. Wilson told her, "I don't care if it was you or the superintendent. You didn't stop him. And you promised to take turns watching these errant children. Well, it's your turn."

Deidre looked toward Jamal. With the exchange going on in front of him, he couldn't be feeling very wanted or cared about. For goodness sake, his mother had left him to fend for himself. Abandoned him. He didn't need to listen to this babysitting tug-of-war. "Go home, Mrs. Wilson. Jamal and I will be just fine."

"What's your number?" Dismissing Mrs. Wilson as she harrumphed out of the office, Deidre smiled at Jamal. "We'll get your mom on the phone. She'll be here in no time, you'll see."

She opened her desk drawer, grabbed the Reese's peanut butter cup she'd been saving for a special occasion, and tossed it to Jamal. She stood and picked up the telephone. Her smile disappeared. The oozing warmth between her legs screamed, "Failure." With as much composure as she could muster, she put down the phone. "I'll be right back."

Picking up her purse, she ran down the hall to the teacher's restroom. In the stall, sitting on the toilet, her worst nightmare was confirmed. "Oh, God. Oh, God, no." She had done everything right. She'd used that chart religiously. She and Johnson had waited until her body temperature was at the right level. How could she not be pregnant? Banging her fist against the restroom stall, she declared, "It's my turn, God." But, no matter how much she wanted it to be, it was not her turn. Would probably never be her turn.

She put her elbows on her thighs and her hands over her face, and cried as if she'd carried a baby to full term, watched him play in the backyard, watched him grow into a young man, then held him as he slowly died in her arms.

Twenty minutes later, Jamal found her still crying. He tapped on the stall door. "Mrs. Morris, what's wrong?"

"I-I g-got my period," she blurted between gasps. She clamped her hand over her mouth as her eyes widened. The superintendent had been itching to fire her. He'd certainly do it now. How could she blurt such a thing out to a seven-year-old child?

Jamal smirked. "My mama always screams, 'Thank You, Jesus' when she gets her period. The only time I heard her cry was when Mr. Friendly—that's what Mama calls it—came late one month."

Although she hated to admit it, Jamal's statement caused her to be upset with God. Women who didn't want children seemed to spit them out, while she and Johnson remained childless.

She closed her eyes, blinking away the remnants of tears as she thought of her husband. The day they met, he'd overwhelmed her with his deep, dimpled smile. Scared her when he declared that he believed in destiny and she would be his wife. But the following week she was hooked, so into him that when he told her how many children he wanted, she couldn't bring herself to tell him that two doctors had pronounced her infertile.

She should have told him. But he was all she'd ever wanted. Their love was so new, she'd been terrified of losing him. After the Lord saved her soul, she'd thought that if she charted her fertile periods and prayed . . .

"Mrs. Morris?"

Sniffling, Deidre wiped the tears from her face. "I-I'm sorry, Jamal. I'll be out in a second." She blew her nose, took the pad out of her purse, and lined her underwear with it. Flushing the toilet, she adjusted her clothes before opening the stall.

As if he were talking a lunatic down from a ledge, he asked, "Do you need me to get you anything?"

Washing and drying her hands, Deidre shook her head.

"When I'm sad, Mama holds my hand. That always makes me feel better." He stretched out his hand. "Do you want to try it?"

Deidre's heart swelled with love for this little boy who reached out to her when she needed it most. She grabbed his hand as they walked back to her office.

He squeezed her hand. "Feel better?"

A tear trickled down her cheek. "Much. Thank you, Jamal."

Back in her office, Deidre put her files in her briefcase. "If you don't mind, Jamal, I'd like to go home. I'll call your mom and give her my telephone number and address."

"That's fine with me. Just as long as you let her know where I'll be. I wouldn't want her to worry."

Deidre almost told him that she was sure his mother wasn't all that concerned. If she were, she wouldn't have forgotten to pick him up. That was the other beef she had with God.

She and Johnson would be great parents. They'd never leave their children to fend for themselves. But alas, the babies were gifted to the unfit, while she, Deidre Clark-Morris, babysat.

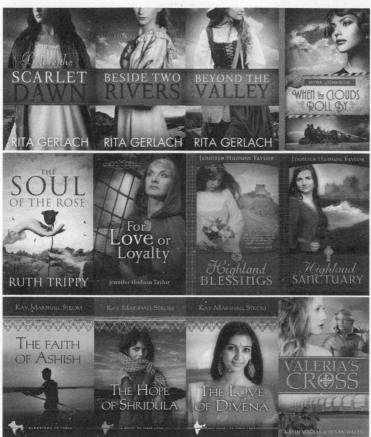